ABOUT THE AUTHOR

George Violet Parker (A. G. Parker, they/them) is a non-binary, pansexual and disabled writer, performer, editor, disability consultant, and workshop facilitator. In 2022, they were crowned Disabled and Queer Artist of the Year, and co-founded *Queer Stage Revolution*, a co-operative organisation promoting queer and disabled artists. They host *A. G. Parker's Cabinet of Curiosities* podcast, are an editor for *Angeprangert! Spoken Word*, and co-host of *Rebel Riot Poetry*. Their performance history includes *Edinburgh Fringe, Manchester Pride, Pride in London, London Fashion Week, Sapphic Manchester, Bar Wotever,* and *IDAHOBIT*. They were a featured artist at *16 Days of Activism to End Violence Against Women and Girls*, and *H&T Hackney*'s June 2021 slam winner, placing third at regionals. They are producer and host of *Cabaret of Curiosities*.

Their work appears in *Mslexia, The F-Word, Financial Times Weekend, Human/Kind Press, Arachne Press, Women in Jazz Media, Aeva Magazine, Elevator Stories, Poethead, The Daily Drunk, The Feminist Library, Prismatica, Mooky Chick, SpoonKnife, Sufi Journal, Sage Cigarettes, Tales from the Moonlit Path, Earth Pathways,* and more. They've secured Arts Council-funded mentoring with The Literary Consultancy in order to complete their second novel.

TWISTED ROOTS

Twisted Roots

A. G. PARKER

Reconnecting Rainbows Press

Published in the UK by Reconnecting Rainbows Press CIC

ISBN 978-1-915893-03-1

Second edition, 2023

First published in e-book format by Wild Wolf Publishing, 2022

Reconnecting Rainbows Press CIC (14570208) is a community interest company registered in the United Kingdom. All of our profits go back into helping marginalised communities publish their works and tell their stories.

www.reconnectingrainbows.co.uk

For my injured Wild Self,
I hope I have written you a path back home.

Content Warnings:
violence, self-harm, alcohol, suicide, assault

~ I ~

CHAPTER ONE

Something stirred in the moonless night.

It wriggled and crept and devoured. The feeble breeze bore no tender scent of the dying summer; only the stench of death, wrought rank in mist, pervaded the lungs of the earth. The stagnant air trembled, disturbed by the beat of the blackest of hearts. From your bed, on the edge of dreams, you heard the Tree screaming your name.

And you waited.

High above parched ravines of sun-baked earth, in the shadowed recesses of the oak, Laela watched. The carnival had arrived only moments before, yet already the fields heaved with red-striped canvases and great, ageing lorries – lumbering behemoths stained with curling paint. Laela steadied herself in her perch in the oak's upper limbs, pressing her back and bare toes into the gnarled crevices of the bark as she licked and smoothed

1

the cigarette paper, and cast her eye past long-fingered branches to the movement on the outskirts of the village. She flicked her Zippo and let the cigarette burn, savouring the harshness of the smoke as she drew it in.

'Fire stick, please, Lady Lae.'

She passed the lighter silently to Jacob, stretching slightly downward to meet his hand, and scanned the scene for exotic strangers doused in magic, for mystery revealed between the flaking paint, but the carnival folk stayed hidden behind their trucks and equipment, showing themselves only as bobbing scaffolding and the rickety frames of rides.

'Looking out for the triple-tittied women?'

'Fuck off, Jacob.'

'True though, isn't it?' he cackled below.

'Well, I already know where the World's Ugliest Dog Boy is.' She smirked at Jacob, poking his cheek with one of her toes.

'You asked the lovely Mira to come tomorrow?'

'I've asked Sam.' She winked.

Jacob's eyes narrowed and his brows knitted under his auburn curls. 'You're not gonna drop this, are you?'

'Ha! Nope. Not until you two drive off into the sunset, your head on his skinny shoulder.'

Jacob growled beneath her, but Laela saw the burning red in his cheeks. In the distance, church bells struck six. Jacob pitched his cigarette dangerously close to a dried-out tangle of black-berries and sighed. 'Speaking of which, I better get going. Dad'll be home soon, my favourite time of day. See you tomorrow.'

'Wear something pretty.'

Jacob flipped a solitary finger in return. 'See ya.'

Laela stayed where she was, alone amongst the barely-moving boughs clad with sunlit leaves, feeling the weight of the evening take hold of the sky. She watched out of narrowed eyes as Jacob shimmied over the stone wall that separated their gardens, knowing he'd be lucky to get the smell of smoke out of his fingers and hair before his dad came home, knowing that he'd do the same thing tomorrow and the next day, repercussions aside. As the village lulled into the quieter hours, the carnival kept its steady progression. Only when she could hear the steady rumble of her own father's van, she allowed herself one last drag and a lingering glance at the cherry-swirled tarpaulins, then clambered groundward.

She did not see the distant eyes watching intently back.

* * *

Sleep took Laela far from the safety of her bed in her father's house. Just as she had the night before every birthday, she dreamed of the Tree. Now, on the eve of her fifteenth birthday, it rose above her, its pale twisted trunk a pained monument on the dead black earth; a body writhing in agony, spine bent and arched toward a bleak and cloud-shrouded sky. There were no leaves on its limbs. The air around it didn't stir; nothing breathed and Laela's lungs ached as she tried to keep her fear silent.

Each year the Tree grew, until now it towered above her, humming with a deadly intensity that, when she'd tried to describe it, even to Jacob, she found she could not. Her father, so distracted in recent years, seemed increasingly to struggle to reset his face into that of a man celebrating her birthday and not one marking the anniversary of a painful death, and so the dream and its horror were bound to her in secrecy.

The Tree's voice – its non-voice – remained the same. It emanated from somewhere within the twisted limbs, channeled through roots or earth or air, Laela didn't know, but this year, as every year before, it struck the same point inside her skull, scratching at her brain; a half-numb painful pleading that she couldn't shut out.

Help, it trembled.

Each year it begged, and each year Laela was too afraid to answer.

Help. Help me.

This time, for a moment, she stood, transfixed; and then summoning the courage not to run, not to fight, but to stand and face her terror, she turned to the skeletal tree.

'How?' Her voice shook but she forced the words into the air. 'How can I help?'

The reply, thrumming inside her head like insidious machinery, came low and dreadful.

Let.
Me.
Eat you up.

Great roiling bursts of mist amassed at the roots of the tree, creeping out across the earth toward her, the Tree's voice buzzing inside her head. Laela ran, dream-slow and stumbling. She fled the woods, scrambling through undergrowth and brambles until she found a familiar path. Tangled knots of brambles clawed her skin, branches and ditches threatened to trip her, but then she was through the trees, out into a pale pre-dawn.

Her house was ahead, but changed somehow – the thatching sturdier, fresher. She darted to the kitchen door, hoping to find her father, for him to hold her, protect her, but the door stayed firm against her banging fists and the mist rolled onward from the treeline, swallowing vast chunks of land in its ever-churning grey.

She left the boundary of their land, running to the village on paths where walls should have been and across greens that didn't exist. There were no cars, no sign of the world she knew, save for the vague shapes of the landscape she'd grown up with.

And then it was daybreak. Laela stole a glance behind her. Nothing. She scrutinised the cracks and corners of the fields around her, but the mist was gone. No evil pursued her. She wandered, dazed, into the village. There was no church spire that watched over the abandoned green, no cars parked up on the streets, no teenagers swigging cider from cans behind the newsagents, no circus tents lining the fields, but it was her village, she knew, and she knew she'd been there, at that moment in time – *before.*

Fog hung low over the ground, though it was different from the clouds that had hounded her. As the sun rose, it cleared. As it lifted, it exposed piles of dead, their features contorted, their final stories carved in the lines of their broken bones and torn skin. Laela flinched but didn't look away, and she found herself joining those tending to the dead.

The Elders.

The thought rose from nowhere.

She watched her fingers as they stirred in strange yet familiar movements, drawing sigils on the air; echoed rituals from a previous life. She felt as though she were retracing history with her hands, that with every motion she were casting herself back into this other version of her, her body bound to a set of previously-ordained movements. And then, obedient to the past, she followed the others as they left the dead and sought vengeance.

They'd tracked the Witch across continents, following trails of blood and fear, and so it was with ease they stalked her final path through the woods. They found her wrapped in the skin of the village guardian, swathed in the bloody hide as though it were the furs of an animal. The Witch grinned out from beneath its ragged edges, her pointed teeth shining white among the angled peaks and hollows of her blood-smeared face.

The Witch did not try to run.

She was compliant as they cut out her tongue.

The Elders dragged her deeper into the woods and knotted her to a yew's twisted trunk.

When they were done, the Elders returned to the village and lit the funeral pyres to put their dead to rest. Laela listened to the steady crackle and spit of the blaze as it seared up into the indigo sky, filling the air until there was nothing left but ashes.

Her dream – the vision of a moment long behind her – died with the fires, and on the edge of reality, in the house that stood between the village and its guardian's secrets, Laela felt something deeply interred slip from the earth and bleed into the night. She shuddered under the covers, tightening the sweat-soaked fabric around her, and tried to laugh at her irrational fear that the Tree, the Witch, was somehow making their way from her dream into the waking world.

Instinctively, she reached for her tobacco pouch, blowing smoke from her window into the night and not caring about the bollocking she'd get in the morning; who could care about the future when the past seemed to clutch at her skin? She rolled over, and under the dim starlight, her fumbling fingers retrieved a photograph from the bedside table. As she comforted herself with each drag, she studied its time-dulled lines, and at last, she fell asleep, her breath soft against the cheek of her mother's faded colours.

* * *

Sam was practically vibrating. 'I can't wait for the dodgems!'

'Shut up, Sam. Laela gets to pick; it's *her* birthday.'

Jacob elbowed Sam in his ribs, and the boys made a show of throwing punches at each other; but the fight, as ever, resulted in a headlock sort of move that was more embrace than grapple. This time it was Sam's turn to come out on top, which he did, panting and pinning Jacob's head under his arm. Laela knew as well as anyone did – if it ever came to an actual fight, Sam wouldn't stand a chance. Luckily for him, Jacob had no interest in fighting him.

'What do you want to go on next, Lady Lae?'

The carnival looked different from this angle. They'd wandered past the ticket desk and under an archway of paint and chipboard, dodging chalk-white faces twisting balloons, and stilt-shod jugglers who leered down from under hats of crumpled velvet, then slipped out of the rush to observe their surroundings. The vast chaos and anonymity brought a sense of familiarity and peace; she felt at once lost and at home, as though she could wander untroubled through its throngs and madness, untouched in the eye of the storm.

It was as though a giant jack-in-the-box had sprung open and each component had leapt apart from its comrades. From there, they'd hit the stalls, Jacob winning a stuffed giraffe he'd subsequently pretended was *for kids* and thrown at Sam; Sam had clutched it tenderly. They'd hoarsened their voices on the rickety rollercoaster and spinning teacups and stumbled from the metal steps with the world shaking around them. Another year and perhaps it wouldn't hold this appeal.

Already, Laela felt it slipping, but it was this fading of interest that made it even more bewitching, as though her childhood were giving her one final blazing send-off. She looked around until her eye alighted on a ride across from where they stood.

'That,' she said.

Sam flinched as he spotted the giant silhouette of the ghost train looming behind him, the jaws of some undead monster opening and closing mechanically above his head. His sallow face blanched, his fear leeching further colour from his already pale cheeks so that his skin melted into his white-blond hair. He looked wraith-like in the sunlight. The only contrast was a raw, brown scar that ran from his left temple to his ear. Jacob laughed and prodded the accentuated mark.

'Scared?' he said.

'Only 'cause of what happened last time...' Sam mumbled, fingering his scar.

'Aww, Sam. We'll look after you.' Laela winked at Jacob.

'Fine. In the absence of any firm decision, how about a smoke while we decide?' Jacob said, eyebrow raised. Sam groaned.

Laela flashed a grin. 'Quick one. We've got to meet my dad soon.'

'Ah, Elliott'll be fine if we're a bit late.'

Laela shook her head. 'You know what he's like this time of year... better not stress him out.'

They slunk out of the crowd, sheltering themselves between caravans and scaffolding. Laela caught Jacob by the wrist and pulled his ear to her mouth. 'You and Sam are almost unbearably cute, y'know.'

Jacob's face transfigured as his head snapped from Laela to Sam, checking if they'd been overheard.

'Oh, as if he doesn't know,' she laughed.

He cleared his throat and glared at Laela. 'Fuck off,' he whispered, and loudly, 'Nicked them off my dad.'

Laela squatted next to the others. 'Aren't you worried he's going to figure out you've been pinching them?'

Jacob shook his head and snorted. 'Not likely. He was so drunk last night he could barely get up the stairs. He'll think he got so blind he lost them.' He shrugged and his face changed, shifting into the squinting eyes of a drunk. 'Ehhh, Lesley,' he drawled, staggering over to Laela with his finger prod-ready in her face. 'You been taking my smokes again, eh? Do you need a lesson from my belt?' He mimed removing his belt from his waist and then, as his drunk father, tripped over his own feet and spun into Sam. 'Oh, Jakey boy, looks like a lesson for you instead! Where's your manners, boy?'

Sam pushed him away, laughing weakly.

Laela readied herself to step in and defuse the situation – she knew Jacob couldn't help himself, that this was his way of dealing, but she wanted a day – one day – where he and Sam and her could just *relax*.

She paused mid-roll. The bottle-green roof of the fortune-teller's caravan had caught her attention. Atop the steps, the door's curtain fluttered. She licked and smoothed the paper and tucked it behind her ear. 'Anyone fancy hearing their fortune?'

Jacob followed her gaze and rolled his eyes. 'Oh god, Lae, no, that's so boring!'

'Yeah,' said Sam. He glanced sidelong at the caravan and shifted his weight toward it. 'Boring.'

Jacob sighed, and his face puckered into a grimace underneath his curls.

'You could, you know, come along? Just for a laugh?' Sam shifted from foot to foot, watching Jacob.

Jacob wavered, but something in him was immovable. He pinched the unfinished cigarette from Laela's fingers. 'Nah. You two go on. I'll see you in a bit.' He kicked his foot against the scaffolding, clanging loose metal against metal and flicked the lighter, his dark auburn catching hints of the flame.

Laela raised an eyebrow at Sam, who let her lead him through the ever-moving horde to the base of the crooked wooden steps, where his confidence faltered. 'Isn't it time to go and meet your dad?'

'Not yet!' she called, already making her way upward and waving for Sam to follow.

Sam looked around in desperation for Jacob, only to find him eaten up by the carnival, and Laela disappearing into a flurry of lace and pungent aromas. He sprinted up the steps behind her, just as a veined hand was pushing the door closed. Inside, the scents were stifling. Sickly sweet roared over undertones of acrid sweat and mouldering fabric. Sam had to fold himself almost double to avoid pendants and bundled herbs and lanterns that hung from the low ceiling.

'Lae, I'm not sure...'

Black eyes turned their glittering focus to Sam and a mirthless chuckle escaped the shadows. 'Knowing the script won't change the story, my love...' The black beads seemed to burn where they lingered, looking Sam up and down. The fortune-teller frowned. 'Much as you may wish for a different outcome.'

'Lae, I've changed my mind. I'm not into this anymore. I think we should go.'

The fortune-teller's eyes narrowed and she reached for Sam's hand. He drew back sharply, knocking something from the wall that broke with tinkling laughter.

'Sam, what's wrong?'

Sam stumbled backward, reaching for the door with hands it seemed he feared might betray him and reveal a future too short, too painful, too filled with horror.

Laela struggled to her feet. 'Sam, wait!'

'You'll have to pay, my love. We all do eventually.'

Laela pushed the old woman aside and followed Sam out into the too-bright sunlight, ushering him down the steps. She spoke calmly, deliberately. 'Come on, let's find Jacob.'

The fortune-teller grabbed Laela's hand. 'The fee, girl.'

Laela felt her face flush and yanked herself free from the fortune-teller's grasp. 'He didn't mean to break your... whatever. And if I remember rightly, you didn't read either of our fortunes. You just scared him, and I'm not paying you for that. Come on, Sam.'

Laela pulled him into the noise of the carnival, Sam stuttering a half-apology over his shoulder. 'Well that was a fucking waste of time. We should go meet–'

The fortune-teller's voice rang shrill across the field, calling for help, for Laela and Sam to be stopped.

'Oh, for Christ's sake.' Laela rolled her eyes, then turned to Sam and grinned. 'Guess we better leg it!'

'Lae, no, wait–'

But she'd gone, excitement burning through her as she ran. She kept running through the ache in her side. She sped past the blare and carnage of the carnival until the trimmed blades of the village green turned to tufts and tangles of wild grass. She ducked behind the ruins of the old bell tower, a lonely sentinel between the village and the wilds of the East. This was her playground. She knew the land here better than anyone, except perhaps Jacob, and so she knew she was safe; she could relax. She squatted in the long grass, breathing in its scent.

'Sam?' Laela panted, peering around one crumbling stone corner, but the meadow was empty.

Fuck. He'd have been caught; he'd never been much good at outrunning danger. She cursed having to eventually return, and hoped that by then those looking for her would have found other things to occupy their attention. Something besides Sam. Laela leant against the tower and pulled her tobacco from her pocket. Something flickered in the corner of her vision, and for a moment she turned to stare into the heights of the tower where once a bell had been but now only shadows hung.

The sun spun golden fingers around its edges and across the meadow, but the recesses behind the dilapidated stone remained cool and dark. Idly, she began to roll. Suddenly, a blotch of darkness broke from the belfry and swooped onto the grass. Laela scrambled back, ready to run again, but held still when she saw what had startled her. She would have laughed, but some instinct in her made her freeze instead.

The crow shuffled its wings. It stared silently. She'd grown up with the creatures of the woods and wilds, but now she felt irrational panic. This crow made her feel something. Dread, perhaps? And while it chilled her flesh to look at it, she couldn't drag her eyes away.

The crow cawed, a loud refrain that shocked the hazy day and seemed to Laela potent with urgency. Keeping her eyes on its ice-white gaze, she shuffled back to the cool stone. Her fingertips found the corner of the tower, and just as she began edging away, the crow blinked and launched itself toward her, screaming. It consumed her vision with its dark, roiling shadows and Laela shrank back from its shrieking beak, its hooked talons, and then its wings skimmed the hairs on her arms as it darted upward at the last moment. She stared after it, her legs unsteady beneath her as it wheeled beyond the tower and into the sky until only a brief sliver of violet glinted, and then the crow was gone.

Laela exhaled, leaning into the stone, heart hammering in her chest. She waited until her breathing calmed, then picked up the tobacco and turned to head back to her friends, to her father.

She didn't make it far before her skin prickled and panic returned. Bells, clear and baleful, sounded from the hollow tower above her. She looked up, knowing the bell tower was empty, wishing it wasn't so that the sound she was hearing would make sense. But there was nothing to see. An invisible hammer struck an unseen bell, the clang reverberating around the vacant belfry. There was no way the sound could be coming from elsewhere, and no way it could be coming from where Laela was staring.

Her mind reeled, trying to understand what was happening. Her thoughts skittered around, unable to fix on reality, and so she missed the shadow that bloomed on the meadow beside her, its appearance like a starless midnight.

It spilled across the grass, silent and rapid. Another crow? No. By the time she caught its slinking movement, it was too late. She saw the shadow take hold of her arm and felt a touch like winter. As she turned to watch, forcing her gaze along the frost-cold fingertips, up the shadowy arm, it became solid, flesh-coloured, person-shaped.

She knew the lines of those lips. She knew those eyes.

Her eyes.

Laela watched anguish flutter across the familiar face, and her heart thrashed against her rib cage. Her breath caught as she tried to speak.

'Mum?'

* * *

Elliott had gone to meet Laela and Jacob and Sam at the carnival, that much he knew. But then he felt as though he'd blacked out, and now it felt like nothing else had existed before that moment – the moment he'd found the body – that everything leading up to that point had been a dream and that now he was awake, jolted and hard-edged and staring death in the face as it kicked and jerked its way through the fragile figure in front of him.

This is what life is.

The limb of the tree from which she swung brought her feet within reach of Elliott's arms. *Who are you?* he wanted to say, and then a lever flipped inside him and he grabbed the woman's calves, trying to take her weight, trying to push her upward. He yelled, shouting in a guttural language that he hardly recognised.

Gravity seemed to conspire. He couldn't keep her upright. Her torso kept falling, her knees buckling. Her body flopped and bent in the middle, at the knees, waist. She became a twisting ornament; her juddered spin punctuated by Elliott's desperate fumbled grasp. He felt the muscles in his shoulders burn and cramp and fight him for control.

Someone, help.

The sun beat down on his neck. Sweat trickled. Birds sang. The tattooed back of a ride showed at brief intervals a swinging capsule filled with screaming fair-goers. Tinny music mixed with the sounds of summer and childish triumph. The quiet pocket of the world in which he and the lurching corpse danced seemed to exist to none but themselves. He wanted to ask her what he should do, would she mind if he let go?

Thudding feet ran to him. He felt the weight of the woman taken from him and his arms flopped to his sides. A dark figure shimmied up the tree with a knife clamped between their teeth while another, all ribbon and colours, held her legs as the rope that bound her neck was cut and she dropped like a rag doll into their arms.

A rough-face peered into his. The man from the carnival pulled at his arm and snapped nicotine-stained fingers in front of his eyes, but Elliott couldn't hear the sound, couldn't move. And then he was being led away, given sips of water, talked to in quiet tones.

'Laela...' he stammered. His eyes came back to him and he focused. He mumbled at the carnival man and left the blanket in a heap on the chair and went to find his daughter.

* * *

Laela's mother staggered forward, pressing her cold undead body against her. She was no longer shadow; she was real and trembling and clutching at Laela. Wide eyes. Desperate touch. Flesh against flesh. 'Laela, you have to stop her.'

'Mum?' That was all she could do. Repeat. *Mum? Mum?*

The voice wasn't as she'd imagined. Her mother's arms weren't the comfort for which she'd yearned. Mother and daughter crumpled against the tower. Laela wanted to cry, to scream, to be held. Nothing came out. She pushed the revenant away, stumbling as she tried to run, but one bitter-cold hand held her firm.

'There isn't time.' Her mother's eyes were locked on hers. Anxious. Insistent. 'I didn't want this for you, I tried to... but there's no other way. You have to stop her. You must find the ancient place, beyond the veil. Listen for the drums. Take the ash from our fire and cast it into the Hearth. Find me here under the next new moon.'

'Mum? I don't understand, I...'

From beyond the smattering of trees on the meadow's edge, the bells from the village church began to strike three. Their first toll loosened the flesh. Laela felt her mother's grip weaken and saw the panic in her eyes.

'Laela, I love you.'

'Mum, what's happening? Wait! Who do I have to stop?' Laela grappled at her mother's body, now no more than a wavering cloud.

The second toll let the sunlight burn through the shadow and Laela buried her face in her mother's hair, inhaling its swarm of jasmine and incense, desperate to keep her close even as she turned transparent.

'The Witch! You must stop the Witch!'

The third bell left Laela alone in the meadow, clinging to the ruins of the bell tower beneath the stark sun that allowed for no shadows, ghosts or comfort. Laela wasn't sure how much longer she stayed, swaying between the logic of reality and the truth she had seen.

The present seeped slowly back in. Tinny songs of rides – the sounds of the carnival – rose and dragged Laela out of her head. Sluggish, it took her a while to realise a shift had taken place; the human sounds – squeals and peals of laughter, chattering, whooping – that peaked and dipped over the cheerful lilt of the fairground music, had morphed into screams, terror-edged and panicked. The carnival now resounded with bloody discord and it swept like a wave from one unseen epicentre outward, horror rippling across the village.

Laela's eyes flicked back to the place where her mother had been, but nothing stirred. Sirens called out from a distance, and Laela's attention snapped back to the carnival. She pulled at her heavy limbs, urging them to speed over the dense grass until she was at the fencing. She slipped through and into the carnival.

***

Panic ruled. All about her, parents screamed for their children, who hid or stumbled or planted themselves in the crowds and wailed at the sun.

'Laela!' Elliott's arm swept her close into him. 'Stay close, love. We need to go.'

Jacob led them through the crowds. 'We can get through here, avoid the worst of it.'

Elliott nodded. They followed close behind Jacob, Elliott never releasing his grip on Laela's damp palm and Sam, roughed-up and hangdog trailed after them. They passed through the roped boundary around the carnival and headed for home. As she craned her neck, Laela caught sight of a deluge of people, held off from a centre point, like a gathered circle kept at once at bay and drawn close by the heat of a fire.

'Don't look, love. C'mon.'

Elliott's voice was gruff, his mouth a grim, pinched line, and she let herself be led. As they rounded the bend for home, police cars were arriving on the tarmac by the field, their sirens mingling with forlorn cries and wailing.

~ II ~

CHAPTER TWO

And they seem not to break; though once they are bowed
so low for long, they never right themselves.
— Robert Frost

Laela climbed high into the oak, scaling its limbs until they stretched into the purplish haze. She had the village spread out beneath her; the only rivals to her freedom of the sky were the trees and, in the near distance, the pointed spear of the church spire.

Beyond it, loomed the crooked remnants of the old bell tower. She had all but dismissed what had happened with her mother, almost convincing herself that it had somehow been part of the madness of the carnival, of her birthday. Perhaps, she thought, it was something she had created as a defence, to block the uncomfortable truth. A protection. She'd read about that.

She eyed the bell tower suspiciously, but no bells rang out and no human-shaped shadows slipped into view. She shouldered the confusion aside and rolled another cigarette, watching the smoke curl from her lips to the leaves above. Besides, she thought, when *hadn't* things been confusing?

She hummed with the wind and closed her eyes. Around her, the space filled rich with birdsong and the scuttling of small mammals.

She tried to forget. Out to the east, the village was murmuring its weekday song, ready for the final cadence before the evening. She studied the view, trying to ascertain if death had brought any change to the village, but it strode steadily on, any difference hidden among the necessary beat of the everyday. She thought of Mira and the way her lips pressed against each other when she was trying to figure something out. She pictured how her long hair slipped around the curve of her neck as she studied whatever textbook page was open in front of her, falling from the clasp and releasing her scent. *And she'll never be interested in a motherless headcase like me*, Laela thought.

* * *

Laela saw the Stranger long before her father did. She shifted from her perch, edging out along the boughs to escape their density. Curiosity trumped sense, and her foot snapped the hollow of dead wood. With a sickening lurch, she swung from the branch, one leg hooked to keep her from falling. The cigarette fell from her lips, hitting the ground in an eruption of embers and ash. Her stomach filled with a flurry of butterflies, but underneath the fear, she savoured the rush, the joy of close-up danger.

She hooked a second heel onto the branch and hauled herself up, laying her belly flat to the tree's wide stable limb and peered across Jacob's roof to the village street beyond. It made her think of all the times she'd sat up here with Jacob by her side. She loved him. Not like *that*; even if he wasn't gay, she didn't see him that way. His gruffness, his brutal honesty was such a rarity in the village where people tended to sigh and cock their heads or turn from her in pity. *Poor motherless mongrel*, she heard them think. But she and Jacob shared everything: smokes, grief, secrets, fights, laughter, danger – nothing was off limits.

They often sat side by side in one of their hideaways, battering around edges of their hurts. She remembered how she'd leant over the same branch years ago and seen Jacob, head in his hands, after his dad had locked him out of the house. She'd invited him over to her side of the wall and they'd climbed the oak, smoked, and talked. His dad, Jacob had said, had burst into his room looking for smokes. Instead, he'd caught Jacob eyeing pictures his dad didn't approve of. It hadn't gone down well.

'Me too,' she'd said.

'Yeah?' he'd replied.

'Well... sort of. I mean, if someone's hot, they're hot, right? My dad doesn't exactly care. About much, actually... And me being into *whoever* wouldn't really faze him. Sometimes I think he'd trade me to get Mum back.'

The remembered conversations drifted away and Laela realised she'd lost sight of her target. She scanned the village. There. Across the village's main road, just visible past the corner of Jacob's roof. The Stranger had her back to Laela, her tall frame slightly bent. Laela strained to see the woman's face, but a cherry tree, useful for sweet, moist bites in summer, obscured her view. All she could see were bare bloodied feet beneath shrouds of coloured fabric, feet that seemed to drink in the black of the tarmac on which they stood. The feet turned. Laela's heart skipped. A forceful squeak emanated from a villager's garden gate as it was wrenched shut. Laela could almost hear its owner's reproachful complaint – Not our kind.

The Stranger crouched down, the coloured fabric kissing the road, the woman's face almost visible beneath the boughs of the cherry. Laela strained to see, nearly forgetting the fall she'd scarcely avoided just moments before. Swathes of amber hair mingled with the black and blood. The head raised, snapped up to face Laela. The distance between them was far – further than either she or Jacob could pelt cherries or their juice-stained stones – but the Stranger's eyes pierced across the village street to Laela's bough, and in an instant, Laela saw the Elders from her dream, remembered the black ash smeared upon their faces and a witch's blood on their hands.

She felt raw flames and crackling heat and saw hands reaching out to pull her into a fire. She saw her mother and the black wings of crow and felt the chime of ancient bells in her bones. Her world became smoke and ash and bitten tongue and deadened land and skin and bone and prayer and curse.

And then it was gone. The Stranger was gone.

Laela's heart pounded in savage pulses, each beat blinding. The face of the Stranger, the clever angles and storm-filled eyes, had imprinted their ferocity upon her. Laela's hands were shaking, but still, she pushed herself up with flattened palms, and climbed even higher into the swaying boughs, hoping for another glimpse.

Instead, all she saw was her father's van, following the road as it wound through the village. She kept her eyes on him as he crossed the river that babbled around the feet of paddling children and the slick feathers of ducks laden with scattered grain. In summer, children would spend hours playing in the cool waters, losing time and paper boats and toys to the river's flow. The jetsam would wash up where the river dwindled to a stream, just past the cemetery.

Beyond there, the river then curved along the outskirts of the village and through the woods at the northern edge of Laela's garden. Once past the quiet of the birch grove and its shadows, it carved its way through field and dale, beyond even Laela's keen sight. The road, similarly, petered out as it bent around the village limits, branching off and diminishing to a pothole-laden dirt track as it approached her house.

But Laela's father still hadn't left the village. His van's grumble softened as it came to a halt in front of the churchyard wall. She craned her neck, but all she saw was her father's back as he leaned toward his window, deep in conversation, but she knew in her gut what she could not see: that beside the van, talking in low murmurs to her father was the Stranger.

Laela didn't wait to have her suspicions confirmed. She shimmied down the sheltered shadows of the oak and onto the cooling grass. The sound of the van could be heard rounding the road through the woods, the noise getting louder and louder as they neared. An electric twinge ran through her. The anticipation grew. She could feel it spreading, out of control, unchecked and rampant. A wild thing in her chest lurched toward the oncoming Stranger and yet she found herself rooted to the spot. She just... waited.

The van's tyres crept off the tarmac and crept along the dirt track. Laela could now see the Stranger sat beside her father, those storm-filled eyes piercing and unblinking. She didn't know if she should be scared, whether she should grab her father and run, but she saw his face through the windscreen, set in a jaw-locked smile, his eyes confused, glazed? and she knew in her gut that any attempt to run would be hopeless. Whatever was about to happen was inevitable. Inescapable.

The engine was cut. The doors opened. They both stepped out.

* * *

The back of the house stood basking in the sun's diminishing warmth. Its thatched roof burnt a fiery rusted red at the tail end of daylight, drinking in the summer's heat before dusk's arrival. The trio had settled in the kitchen, sprawled around the battered wooden table that was scattered with the remnants of a feast. Elliott and the Stranger were batting words and sputtered laughter back and forth across abandoned plates whilst Laela watched and felt a knot of apprehension in her belly tighten and flex. It was surreal, and far from putting her at ease, the familiarity between her father and the Stranger only served to heighten Laela's panic.

The Stranger laughed and seemed to conjure flickering shapes from the air by her fingertips. Laela's father was talking excitedly now but Laela's ears would not catch up to understand the conversation. She felt lost, a sleepwalker, as though she were trapped in a dream from which she could not wake. The two voices rose in unison and broke into more raucous laughter.

'Do you two... know each other?'

For a moment, everything suspended and the warm, glowing scene seemed like a perfect sphere of happiness in front of her that Laela could not enter. The two of them turned to stare at her. She felt like a splinter being pushed from the warm flesh of a body. The air was rotating specks of dust in shafts of streaming light, their dances wending their way around the figures at the table. Laela's father wiped a mirth-induced tear from the wrinkled pouch under his eye and, seeming not to hear her question, examined the bottle that lay between them.

'Ah, wonderful... Shall I fetch us another? Laela?' She nodded a reply, mute and automatic, and off her father left with jaunty steps to collect another bottle.

They were alone.

The Stranger turned her hooded eyes to Laela and Laela realised she could not tell how old she was. It was as though each time she looked at her, her eyes glanced off her skin, and were allowed to land only on those blue, piercing eyes. Her voice, though, was like a sheath of ice.

'Your father doesn't remember, nor should he. *You must.* Outside, under the stars of midnight.'

'Remember what? Listen, I don't know what the fuck you're doing, but –'

Footsteps. The Stranger stared coolly back and touched a finger to her lips, removing it as Laela's father made his reappearance in the kitchen. He proudly presented a fresh bottle of his self-brewed honey-dew. The Stranger reached out with her glass in hand, the other giving a flourished gesture of thanks, all trace of urgency and her cryptic words gone, and Laela wanted to scream, to demand someone tell her what was happening, what this woman had done with her father, what all these mysterious messages were about.

She wanted to break the odd normalcy of what surrounded her, even if it meant smashing plates and throwing things at this stranger, this woman who had come into their house un-welcomed and bewitched her father, confused Laela... But she didn't. She sat motionless and heavy with questions as the others continued with chat of this and that – Laela's father's work around the village, his skill at having re-thatched their roof himself, and Laela's upcoming stretch of summer holidays – until Elliott and their guest were talked out and silence fell like soft snow on the room.

The evening drew in around them, and when the last of the daylight had been shuttered out by the night, Laela's father declared it was time for bed. He summoned her to fetch fresh bedding from the airing cupboard with which to make up a bed for the Stranger on the sofa. The sofa, too, was dusty and very much well-loved, but with the clean sheets spread over it, there was a semblance of comfort. The trio bade their goodnights and made their ways to their respective beds.

On his way to his bedroom, Laela's father, who seemed obliv-ious to the strangeness of the nameless guest, paused at Laela's bedroom door to give her a kiss on her forehead, as he used to when she'd been a child. She noticed a glint in his eye. From this, at least, she took some comfort, knowing that, whatever the future may bring, her father had found a joy in the evening, which would spread into the coming days like a ripple on a smooth pond.

What she didn't know yet was how much he'd need it; they both would.

* * *

After her father had pulled the door to a creaking close, Laela slipped with the silence of secrecy from her bed and lit the can-dle on her desk. Its orange tongue licked through the sculpted shapes of its holder and sent the shadows flickering in elongated dances over the pale walls. She kept on the jeans she'd worn to explore the sunlit hours but left her feet bare, their black soles smearing their mark on the bedspread. Outside, the owls hooted their evening sentinel, and bats like whipping black gaps in the sky flapped their nightly scavenge over the dark world.

Laela continued to watch the distorted forms of the candle's patterns as she lay on her side on top of the sheets, mulling over all that had happened, and what stood before her. Who was this strange woman lying on the sofa downstairs?

Should she follow her bizarre request and meet her outside *under the stars of midnight?* Ridiculous, Laela thought. But her mind continued to whirr around the possibilities, and before she'd made a decision, she dropped beneath the surface of the heady waves into a fitful sleep. Once more, she found herself in the village of years long since passed, with the Elders. Watching them trap the Witch.

* * *

With magic, they bound the Witch to the roots of the yew. *You have brought harm to our clan,* they said. *This is your punishment.*

Laela knew this story now, as though it had been a bedtime tale whispered in her ear all her life: *They shed her blood and took her power and held her on the edge of life. Under midnight's new moon, they deadened the land around her, ensuring nothing remained on which she could feed. At last, they covered the yew with shadows of magic, hiding her from innocents.*

They left a guardian to tend the tree; and with each guardian's death another takes their place, ensuring the Witch is kept impotent, the small ember of life within her preventing death, preventing rebirth.

* * *

When Laela woke, the pale moonlight carried its silvered glow in thin shafts across her eyes. She told herself that it was its light, rather than a strangely natural assertion that *it was time*, which had awoken her. In the gloom, she stretched out and checked her mother's wind-up watch that lay next to her bed.

It was an illusion of choice, she realised. Somewhere in the fabric of the cosmos, it had been written already, and now that she stood at the fork in the road, on the brink of stepping one way or the other, she knew the paths to be the same.

With furtive steps, she hastened out of her bedroom, gliding over the floorboard which grumbled were she to land weight on it, and down the stairs, once more avoiding the steps which would, with squealing complaint, betray her descent.

The Stranger was not in the makeshift bed. The ground floor of the house lay open, empty. Waiting. Summer's merciful cooling breath snaked its way through the open kitchen door and Laela followed its source, pausing to run her fingertips over the wood of the kitchen table on her way, as though it were a talisman bound to bring her luck.

Midnight struck as her feet padded over the damp grass. Its chime reverberated around the indigo sky and its twilight companion. Magic turned the air to thick wads, their encircling oppression at once stifling yet pure, like the heaviness in a world awaiting a storm. It carried the sweet perfumes of honeysuckle and figs, and a hint of something that Laela did not recognise.

It was this enigmatic scent that Laela followed. Wisps of it trailed in the night across the garden and to the outer reaches of the grass, where it swooped under the arms of the oak and beyond the glinting silver of edge of the birch groves. The knot in her stomach tensed and curled and twisted around her insides, and Laela began to imagine that she could see the Witch's face from her dreams watching her in the darkness. Hesitation stalled her step. *What if it's a trap?*

Everything skipped and juddered and the landscape looked suddenly altered, hostile, and Laela wondered if she should turn back, wake her father, tell him that she'd gone out into the night and the Stranger was something different than he thought, something evil. The world sucked in a breath and waited for her choice. The bats and owls and night creatures stopped and there was, beyond the rushing of blood in Laela's ears, silence.

But what had her mother said? That Laela must *stop her.* Surely that meant Laela should go on? Her mother's apparition, however real it had been – and it was beginning to look like she hadn't imagined it – wouldn't tell her to do something she wasn't capable of...

She flicked her lighter and dragged on a roll up, swinging between fear and curiosity. She squeezed her eyes and begged the universe to make her decision for her, for some potent sign to force her onward, but nothing came. Instead, she reached into her intuition. When she opened her eyes again, she was re-solved. The moon was glowing with such ferocity, adamant that Laela should find her way, and the flitting bats and their darting dives spurred her forward toward the susurration of the stream and its pebbles and the gleam of the grove. She felt impelled, and she could not step off the path that laid itself out before her.

Laela took a slow step and felt dank marsh underfoot, and gathered her bearings. She was at the edge of the birches, where the water seeped to breach its banks and formed pools around the twisted roots of the trees. She squinted, eyes adjusting to the grove's deeper level of night. At her feet, the stream cut the woods in two and spat moss upon the rocks that adorned its flow. Pigment lost in the moon's luminescence rendered all in the murk-dappled wood grey and chrome.

Nothing stirred. Nothing breathed upon the earth. Silence swamped her lungs and eyes and then, as if in answer to a prayer unuttered, the sharp nip of that unfamiliar scent rose again and guided her over the smooth, flat pebbles to the other side where the trunks spared a small patch of land and the Stranger sat behind an ochre fire, head bowed. Laela wondered as she approached how she had not seen the fire's glow from across the stream.

'Sit.'

Laela touched her fingertips to the wet earth; steadied herself as she knelt in mirrored kind to the Stranger. Perhaps she was going to die here, she thought, but at least she'd have some answers. The smell was pungent. Its acrid scent filled her nostrils and stirred lurkings in her belly.

'Are you here...' Laela faltered. 'Is this something to do with my mother?'

When she received no answer, Laela dared to draw her eyes from the fire to the Stranger's face, but the woman's eyes and body were closed, her state trancelike. If she hadn't been so scared, if Jacob had been by her side, perhaps Laela would have laughed. But nothing felt funny now. The Stranger moaned, deep guttural grievings more akin in sound to the wild savagery of a beast in despair than a woman, and Laela felt the trembling of the ground beneath her body, a trembling fuelled by the moans, as though the Stranger was connected to the earth itself.

The fire thrived between them, suddenly raging and pitching as if billowed by a carnivorous wind. It roared and burned a hoarse scream along the skin of them both, singeing hairs and swelling in turmoil to mix with the putrid stench upon the air.

'Elder kin.'

The sounds stretched out and wretched. Not the voice of the woman who had shared their food and sat at their table. Laela wanted to run, but found herself held immobile as if her body were weighted to the ground.

'We speak to you as one, through the tongue of this vessel. You cannot remain unsure. The time for doubt is passed.'

The Stranger's head flung back and exposed a pearlescent neck. At its base, heavy raw scars rendered black showed their stark defiance. Her voice flung low snarls to the wind:

'Your magic is escaping and must be cast back.
The streams and twigs and mud shall rise and carry what's yours to
her, *and with it she will destroy you.*
For you, she will come,
But not before the rest is burned.
Claim it back or the evil will rise again,
As it did before your mother's final days,
When the blackness ruled.'

The Stranger lunged out an arm across the flames and seized Laela's wrist in a vicious hold, her trance-like state gone, her eyes painfully locked on Laela's. Laela struggled back, digging her heels into the dirt to escape the fingernails that dragged through her skin like hooks through the flesh of a fish.

The hairs of the Stranger's arm began to singe first. Still, she gripped Laela's arm. Her skin bubbled and spat until the uppermost layers began to peel off, slipping from the limb in sickening globs. Laela's eyes were fixed in grisly enchantment, but the Stranger paid it no notice. She clutched at Laela now with both hands until their brows were touching. Laela could still smell the herbs lingering under the reek of burning and began to sob hot, sizzling tears. She wanted to escape. She felt her own arm beginning to burn and wished she hadn't come, that she was still in her bed watching the candle flame.

'This is real, child. There is no escaping. Listen to your mother. Visit the Ancient Hearth. *Stop the Witch.*'

She held Laela's arm still as Laela cried out. The fire was eating into her skin, a pain beyond anything she'd ever felt. Though she wrenched and kicked and tried to get away, the Stranger held strong.

'You must remember,' she snarled.

And with that, at last, the Stranger released Laela's pinned arm. She fell away, nursing it, then watched in horror as the Stranger pitched forward into the fire, seeming to embrace the flames. They crawled over her neck and face, fizzling with excitement, drinking her in, but the Stranger didn't fight. Instead, she held her body still until there wasn't an inch of her skin unconsumed by the hungry blaze, and twisted her head to lock eyes with Laela, mouthing her final words again and again through disintegrated mounds. *Stop the Witch. You must remember.*

Laela froze, unable to do anything but watch the soundless mouth until it ceased to move. Then, under the night and its blank eyes, Laela slipped from consciousness and fell to the damp ground beside the stream, her own limp form a strange alteration of the seething and spitting body in the fire. Only the occasional twitching of the limbs of the fire-dancing corpse moved in the silent hours.

~ III ~

CHAPTER THREE

'Listen to the trees talking in their sleep,' she whispered,
as he lifted her to the ground. 'What nice dreams they
must have!'
— L.M. Montgomery, Anne of Green Gables

For two weeks, Laela and her father didn't leave the house. The doctor treated and bandaged her arm, prescribed antibiotics when the infection came. It spread and seethed and soon her flesh was hot with fever. She lived for a fortnight in a half-life of dreams and sweat while Elliott lived in a world of guilt and fear.

Over the years, in his blackest hours, Elliott had bargained with the devils in his mind to return his wife, even at the cost of taking his daughter. Now he looked set to get the bitter half of his wish. He barely slept, and ate little. His time was devoted to the care of his daughter, as though he could atone for all the terrible things he'd thought.

The doctor returned to re-bandage the wound and monitor her fever. Jacob visited. Neighbours with part compassion, part curiosity delivered pots and trays with pies and stews that her father could not get past her lips. She burned and writhed and shivered, and he felt powerless.

And then, at last, it began to subside. The doctor noted that her temperature was falling and her pulse steadying. But he saw the carrion hollows of Elliott's eyes and prescribed him rest and sleeping pills, which Elliott declined. Eventually, it was Penny-Jane, the postwoman, who intervened.

Elliott had answered the door in his pyjamas, the thin fabric hanging off his frame with the impossibility of acute weight loss in a matter of days. His eyes were red and raw, his skin sagging. He slumped against the doorframe until Penny-Jane softly brought them both inside.

'She's been shrieking in her sleep,' he said through thickly gummed lips. 'She sees something terrible, or thinks she does. It's so bad that she screams at me to make it stop, but I... She calls for her mother... I... I don't know how...'

Penny-Jane smothered him in arms and stroked his hair like he was a child, rather than the man of forty-four that he was.

'Shh now, there, love. It's just dreams. She'll be round soon, Doc said, you'll see. Then you can put this whole business behind you. Although,' she bit her lip and lowered her face to his, peering into his watery eyes, 'seems to me you'll frighten her half to death if she sees this mug, look at you!' She cocked an eyebrow. 'How about a bath?'

Whether he saw sense or whether he just wasn't up to Penny-Jane in full swing, he nodded his head and allowed himself to be traipsed up the stairs and sent into a skin-reddening hot bath. Afterwards, he sat down at the kitchen table and took the weight of his head in his hands.

'How long was I out? An hour? God, I feel like hell.'

Around him, Penny-Jane bustled and busied and fussed. When he spoke, it was to the placemat in front of him. 'I dreamt of her, Pen. Violet. I saw her face and she was asking me something but I couldn't hear what it was, and then I was being dragged away through the woods until I couldn't see her at all.'

Penny-Jane stared hard at his face until hers finally softened. 'Oh, love.' She bent over the table. 'It can't be easy. Little un' must've brought back some memories of what happened... but it's all so long ago.' She patted him on the back and straightened up. 'Can't go getting lost in the past, eh? Doesn't help for nothing now, does it?'

'I know, I just... it felt urgent, you know? Like I was supposed to do something. Like I was back there and I should have done something.'

Penny-Jane put the pots down on the stove with a resolute clatter. She spun round, holding the oven mitts like a weapon. 'Now listen here, you. Doc said that there was nothing that you could have done for Vie, nothing at all. A natural way for her to go that was, giving birth to that little joy machine of yours. We are where we are. And let's stick with that.'

Resigned and weary, Elliott mumbled a retreat and went to check on Laela. She was sleeping with a peace she'd not known for days.

Penny-Jane came to join him. 'See, little love is doing fine. And all the better for you. She's lucky to have a father that cares for her so.' She squeezed his shoulder then paused as she questioned whether or not to ask. 'Do you know who that woman was? That was there that night?'

Elliott shook his head. 'Jesus, Pen. I don't know.' He studied Laela's face and wondered how he could have let a stranger come into their home and do this to his daughter. 'I felt like I did. Like I'd known her forever and it was safe, you know?' His forehead wrinkled and he felt the guilt swell into his chest. 'It must sound crazy now.'

Penny-Jane smothered a twitch on her lips and shuffled him from the living room, once more resuming the gentle clatter of busy-making to drown out the voices in his head.

* * *

Laela was in darkness and falling. Around her, demons swirled in suffocating clouds, filling her lungs with stale noxious air, drowning her from the inside. When she clawed at their faces, all she saw was the skin-dripping face of the Stranger, the flesh melting from her skull as she mouthed stop her, over and over. In the distance, bells sounded.

Then it went quiet.

Laela was walking through snow. The cold bit at her bare feet. Up ahead, a bird waited, its feathers as intensely black as the snow was white, its eyes staring placidly into her. It was leading her up a slope to where the ground's crest met the sky, to where she knew she must journey.

Either side, trees lined her way. They were thin and brown and had no substance; she knew that if she could turn her head, they would leave only sparse impressions on the searing white blanket that surrounded them, but she couldn't control her eyes. Instead, they kept sliding away from where she wanted to look, making her stumble.

Her vision juddered and now the dream-snow came up to her waist and she was wading through its thick, syrupy embrace. She couldn't keep her head upright; it bent over her body and swayed from side to side with every lurch. She wanted to run. Her legs felt numb. Her arms went limp. Her mind was screaming. But her body wouldn't help itself. She dragged one leaden leg to meet the other, then forward again with the next.

As Laela took the next step, the ground opened in front of her. She tried to throw herself to one side, but gravity seemed to draw her into the sinkhole, and she felt the dizzying descent into nothingness. Over and over everything flipped and spun until Laela couldn't tell where her body ended and air began. With sudden force, the hole in the ground spat her out onto barren ground. Laela saw she was at the foot of a tree. A dead tree. It smiled when it saw her looking.

She clawed her way to her feet but roots crept up around her ankles and bound her. With pained effort, she drew her heavy head to look at the Tree. Its splintered, ragged arms were spread open, reaching to the air in vengeful lust. The twisted trunk arched its back as if the sky had tried to wrench it from the earth, leaving spirals of branches at its head and the underside of its ripped roots exposed. The gnarled face stared out at Laela.

Shall I tell you a secret? it said.

Big dead eyes sparked and bled, and Laela knew unquestionably that the Tree was no longer confined to the world of dreams, but that its roots stretched into reality. Its voice scraped at her skull.

This one will die for me.

It whispered a name, and bells rang.

~ IV ~

CHAPTER FOUR

"When you walk to the edge of all the light you have and
take that first step into the darkness of the unknown,
you must believe that one of two things will happen.
There will be something solid for you to stand upon or
you will be taught to fly."
— Patrick Overton

When Laela was strong enough, Elliott helped her outside so that she could sit on the grass under the oak's shading arms as he whittled and sawed and carved. It was like the old days, he thought, when Laela was no taller than his knee and their time was spent almost ceaselessly side by side, exploring the world that became new when he looked at it through her eyes.

He let the boys come to visit – Sam with soft words and books and sketching supplies, and Jacob with tales of playground fights and pranks. Elliott ushered them away whenever Laela's laughter turned to a weak smile and then, inevitably, sleep-laden lids, but, gradually, her health returned and Elliott went back to work leaving her under Jacob's watchful eye.

'I'll be working in the village, up at the Henderson's if you need me. You be sure to call me if anything happens, okay, Jake? Anything.'

Jacob gave a characteristic shrug. 'Sure,' but there was a sincerity there that reassured Elliott, who knew that if Jacob could be trusted with anything, it was Laela's wellbeing.

Elliott pulled Laela to him, his voice and his hold urgent. 'You two look after each other, now. And stay in the garden until I get back, just this once. No wandering off, okay?'

Laela poked her tongue at him. 'I'm fine, Dad. *Love you*,' and with that, she was off.

* * *

They were well above the platform of the tree house before they heard her father's van trundle away. Laela was staring into the distance, eyes hovering somewhere beyond the church. Jacob gave her a prod in the side.

'Jammy shit, missing the last two weeks of school.' He plucked a cigarette from his pocket and waved it at her as he spoke. 'I didn't even get that when I broke my arm.'

Laela shuffled her feet so that she was bracing her back against one of the forks in the branches. She picked at the scab on her wrist. 'Dad was probably a bit scared after what happened with my mum, that time of year and all.'

Jacob scuffed at a loose piece of bark with his boot and pulled back to the safety of trading insults. He dug her in the ribs again, this time with more gusto. 'Pff! Skiver!'

'Hey!' Sam's voice spun up through the tree.

Laela lowered the fist she'd prepared for Jacob and switched it out for an obscene gesture. She peered past the layers of leaves. Sam squinted up at them, the hand that sheltered his eyes not quite covering the newly-formed scar he'd acquired while trying to outrun his own panic at the carnival. It sat along-side the old one, the crinkled marks nearly touching, but where Jacob wore all of his scars with pride, Sam only pulled his fair hair further over his face in an attempt to cover them.

'Hey yourself!' Laela called. 'Coming up?'

Sam shook his head and jabbed a thumb. 'I've got these two to look after.' Behind him stood two dungaree-clad kids, their fat knuckles bunched around a dripping lolly. In their free hands they wielded wooden boats, which they intermittently used to half-heartedly batter each other. 'We're headed to the river, want to join?'

'Why hello there, Master and Little Miss Henderson.' Jacob doffed an imaginary cap to the children. He mimicked Sam, ges-turing with a thumb at Laela. 'Can't. Got this one to take care of. You could hang here?'

Behind her hand, Laela winked at Jacob.

'*Fuck off*', he mouthed.

'Nah. These two are fit to burst. Better get them somewhere they can let off steam,' Sam said. 'Well, see you.' He took the kids in tow, each giving a sticky-handed wave as they left.

'Jesus,' snorted Jacob when Sam had gone. 'He's collecting so many scars he's going to be unrecognisable by the time we leave school.'

'Like it stops you wanting to snog his face off.'

'Yeah, all right, dickhead. How about you with Jude What's-his-face in Geography? Or bloody Mira? Who's the real slut here?' When she didn't reply, he flicked the lighter in front of Laela's face. 'Hey! Where you at? You've been staring at that field all bloody day. What is it, zombies? Vampires? Bit sunny for vampires right now, mind you.'

Laela conjured a smile that wouldn't have fooled the Henderson kids. 'Nothing. I thought I saw something, before, that's all.'

'Right. Well, was it food? Cos I'm starving.' He began climbing down. 'Let's go eat.'

Laela reluctantly made to leave her perch. Jacob was already well beneath her, slipping from branch to branch with ease. She made to follow him, then paused. A sound, low and mournful carried across the village. *Bells.* Twelve strikes and each one made Laela more certain that they weren't coming from the church, but from the old bell tower.

'Hey! Can you hear that? Jacob? *Jacob!*'

This meant that the events of her birthday had actually happened, that Laela *had* seen her mother, that she could be waiting for her right now, just the other side of the village. She began scrambling down the oak, catching her knee as she went, not caring if she bled, nearly missing holds, and then she stopped. The church bells, she thought. Once they'd rung, her mother had vanished. And how long had the interval been between the ruin's bells and the church's? Only a matter of minutes. Even if she sprinted, she'd never make it in time.

'Fuck,' she hissed.

She drew in a breath and focused. If she couldn't get to her mother, she'd watch instead. She clambered back to her vantage point and trained her gaze on the ruin, tracing the stone's corner down to where it met the grass. Was that a shadow? A crow? It was too far to tell and then, before she could figure it out, the church bells rang.

They ate in silence, Laela with her eyes constantly on the kitchen clock, wondering how she could escape and get to the ruins for the next hour. Jacob administered a sharp reprimand with his fork. Her distraction had not gone unnoticed.

'What the hell?' Laela said, rubbing the smarting skin.

'Come on, then.'

'What?'

'Let's find out what's going on.'

'*What?*'

'I heard the bells too. It was weird. I mean, they're probably just testing them or something. Or the mechanism got all screwed up, I dunno. But if you're gonna be a weirdo all day I'd rather go find out what it is.'

Laela stared at him.

'Do you want to go or not?'

They used the oak to clamber over the wall. Moss dragged green streaks down the bellies of their shirts as they landed in Jacob's garden. Jacob's mum was out at work, but his dad finished early in the afternoons, so they crept past the curtained windows of his house.

Once clear of the garden, they ran along the village road and up through the rows of houses and their uniformly neat trellises and hedges of laurel and box, careful to avoid the street where Elliott was working. Laela's body felt feeble from the days of enforced rest, but she pushed on, striving to keep up. They ran until they reached the outer boundaries of the graveyard, where they staggered to a halt, panting.

Jacob looked at his watch, peering sideways under a graze in the glass he'd acquired after an experiment with fireworks.

'Ten to.' He sighed and slumped down on one of the gravestones. 'At least we'll be ready.'

But they wouldn't be. They were at the wrong place, Laela knew it, but how could she tell Jacob that they needed to be somewhere else? She'd sound mad. She looked up at the church and its bell tower, tall and gaunt in the afternoon sun. The spire seemed aggressive – detached from the nature around it – and the ornate housing of the bell beneath it seemed ugly. It was nothing like the empty, strangely beautiful ruin only a short sprint away. With growing dread, Laela watched the long hand approach twelve. To think she'd be so close to her mother only to miss her again was unbearable.

But one o'clock came and went with nothing remarkable, the tin and copper of the church bell nodding dutifully between its brick housing. Perhaps she was wrong – perhaps it only happened on certain days or times or when she was alone but no, she'd seen her mother earlier, or at least she'd seen something. And she'd heard two sets of bells. That she was sure of.

She began to fidget, wishing Jacob wasn't there, trying to conjure up ways to get him to go home, to leave her to the ruins and her mother. Even the prospect of disappointment should her mother not appear seemed more palatable alone. But he stayed steadfastly by her side, refusing to abandon his role.

'Do you think Sam might feel the same?' he asked, scuffing the toe of his trainers into the dry grass.

Two came and went. Frustration grew on both sides, and Jacob, having had no good reason to come in the first place, implored her to go home. He'd begun to regret his decision, worrying that Elliott would discover their absence, and while Jacob wasn't a stranger to trouble, the idea that he might make Elliott upset produced an uncomfortable sensation in his stomach.

'Then I'll just have to come back tomorrow,' Laela had replied, and Jacob had weighed it up and settled on one day of bollocking rather than two.

Then the resounding moan of bells marking three o'clock rang out, but not from the bell tower above them. Jacob, mouth open in confusion finally said what Laela had known all along.

'They're not coming from the church.' He looked around. 'Where are they?'

Laela knew, and there was no point pretending she didn't. She ran.

'Hey! Where're you going? Lae?'

But she was off, sprinting past crumbled graves and moulding flowers.

'Hey!'

Laela's feet pounded over the field and then she was scrambling over trunks and brambles, a mere stone's throw from the rock beneath the ruins, but too late. The church bells chimed. In the diminishing echo of the final bell, she saw the outline of her mother sat upon the rock and as silence returned, the image faded into transparency.

'No!'

Laela felt as though something necessary, something meaty had been ripped out of her. To have *seen* her, to know she had been there just seconds before, if Laela had just run fast enough, if Jacob hadn't been there...

'No. I need you to be here, I need you to tell me what the hell is going on. I *need* you!'

The colour drained away from the world, replaced instead with jasmine and flashes of bubbling skin, near-moonless nights and the silent, burned lips of the Stranger. Her mother's words came back to her, and she repeated them to herself in frantic whispers, trying to figure out whether they felt like something she'd really heard, or if she'd made them up. Made it all up.

Find the ancient place, beyond the veil.
Listen for the drums.
Take the ash from our fire and cast it into the Hearth.
I'll see you under the next new moon.

Was it a new moon? She had no idea. And how long did one last? How long until the next one? She felt broken – empty – with nothing left in her to process what was happening. Jacob caught up, red-faced and puffing.

'Hey, Lae–' he noticed her face and grimaced. 'What's got into you?'

Laela said nothing. She felt as though she were trapped behind a cloud, thick and pervasive that had rolled in around her, and that its grey walls made reaching anyone beyond it impossible.

Help, she cried from her invisible prison.

Help.

'Hey, Lae, come on–'

Jacob strolled over to her and half-playfully bumped a fist onto her shoulder. It was too much. She tried to find a way for everything inside her to come out in neat little lines and words and actions, but she couldn't, so she kicked him, hard, much harder than she'd meant to.

'Fuck *off*!' It came out high and strangled.

He didn't. She saw his face change from concerned and playful to mad as hell, incensed by the throbbing pain in his shin. But he only took a slow, deep breath and raised an eyebrow at her. The pits of his eyes kept their kindness. She did it again, and again, beating him with her fists when kicking wasn't enough and – at last – she watched the adrenaline surge through his fight-ready body.

Good, she thought.

He launched himself at her, grabbing her arms and pinning them above her head. She tried to wrench her way free, but he was older and stronger. He sat on her chest, pinning her effortlessly.

'Let me go!' she yelled, struggling against his weight, relieved at last to have something to rail against. She thrashed her legs and felt her knees connect with the back of his rib cage, and it felt good, as though all her pain and anguish were there, made solid in Jacob's body.

'Not until you tell me what's going on.' Jacob increased the pressure on her arms. 'Tell me what's wrong, Lae. Talk to me.'

'Let me go!'

He pinched her wrists, drawing blood. 'Talk to me!'

She kneed him again, hoping she could hurt him enough that he'd leave, rather than keep asking her to do the one thing she wanted to do more than anything else but couldn't.

'Talk to me!'

She gave up. Her body weakened.

'Come on, Lae. We tell each other everything. Bloody everything! Although I'm starting to regret telling you about Sam, the amount you take the piss about it.' He tried a laugh.

Laela began to sob in frustration, no longer trying to escape, just wanting it all to be over. Just wanting to crawl into her bed and sleep.

'Lady Lae?'

'I saw my mum.'

'What?' He shifted some of his weight onto his heels but didn't release her. 'What do you mean, you saw her?' He gripped her arms tighter, pressing them into the dirt. 'Shit. Look, can I let you go, or are you going to kick me again?'

She shook her head and he released his grip. They sat facing each other.

He stalled, not knowing what to do, and eventually pulled a crumpled cigarette packet from his pocket and handed her one. 'Tell me.' His blue eyes, tinged with concern, levelled hers.

For a moment, they sat in silence and did nothing but watch the smoke curl upwards.

'I saw my mum.' Laela said eventually. She spoke quietly, forming the words with care. It was absurd, hearing herself saying it aloud for the first time. Utterly mad. 'She was there. I saw her. I saw her and then she... disappeared. I, I did, Jacob, don't look at me like that, I'm telling you I *saw* her!'

Jacob bit his lip and wrinkled his nose. 'Okay, Lae, okay...' He looked around as if suddenly uncomfortable, exhaling smoke deliberately. 'Let's head home, shall we? Your dad'll be back soon and I promised I'd keep you out of trouble.' He pulled Laela to her feet, but she didn't want to move. Instead, she stared wild-eyed at the landscape around her, lost. He tugged at her T-shirt.

'I saw her at the carnival, too. She told me...'

'Jesus. C'mon,' he said gently.

He took her hand and began leading her back toward the church. She gazed back at its ruined counterpart, keeping it in focus until its stone disappeared behind the yews of the grave-yard. They made their way home through the village, Laela with the occasional glance behind her and Jacob with deliberate care not to let go of her hand, as if doing so would be to release her to the demons he imagined pursued her.

Neither said a word until they were inside the quiet of the kitchen. Jacob watched the driveway from the door and waited until he saw the van pulling up.

'I'll be off, then. I'll see you tomorrow. Take care not to run off without me.' But his voice had no mirth left and the wink he gave was mechanical.

Laela said nothing, but continued to stare at the grain of the table as he slipped away quietly, retracing their earlier steps and scaling the wall to his garden.

Elliott stepped inside and cast a quick, vacant smile at Laela. His face was ashen. He ignored the mud he trailed into the house and went through to the living room, sitting on the sofa with his head in his hands.

Laela felt anxiety jolt through her. Had she been seen? Could Jacob have said something?

'Laela.'

Her dad patted the cushion next to him, and she followed and sat, trying to think up excuses for why she'd left the garden. She worried at her lip with her thumbnail until her father gently took her hand in his, wrapping his fingers around hers. They were like cold stone.

'You've got to listen, love. There's something I have to say.'

Laela felt the sweat on his palm slide over her knuckles and her stomach lurched.

'Two of the Henderson kids were playing in the stream.'

Laela took a moment to catch up, adjust. Then she nodded, relaxing a little. She wasn't in trouble. 'They were with Sam,' she said.

And then her father looked at her and she knew. She imagined the Henderson kids with their little wooden boats, paddling with their trousers rolled up above their pudgy ankles, wanting to know why their boats with their coloured sails weren't drifting downstream. She pictured Sam at the carnival, how he'd paled at the thought of the ghost train, bent double to fit inside the fortune-teller's caravan, how she'd taken his hand and run and run... *We're headed to the river, want to join?*

And she thought of Sam's face letting water slip by its edges, blocking the river's flow.

'Laela, I'm so sorry.'

Her father couldn't get the words out. He couldn't tell her, but it didn't matter. She knew what her father was trying to say. She knew because it had been whispered to her, from the snarling hole in the dead tree. A grim prophecy that had taken her friend.

Sam was dead.

$\sim V \sim$

CHAPTER FIVE

Things
that can't move
learn to see.
— Louise Glück, The Wild Iris

The new moon swallowed the sky. Under the rooftops of the village, there were sombre meals and furtive prayers of gratitude that *it wasn't ours.*

That night, Laela was plagued by horrors. Again, she returned to the Tree with its gaping mouth. This time, it seemed that it could reach out its tendrils and grab her. Again, she found her feet swamped and heavy. The carrion crow screeched in on a thunderclap, spreading its great wingspan across Laela's vision and blurring her world ink black.

She woke with the sheets damp and her chest heaving. The night with the Stranger rushed back to her as she crept with silent footsteps through the house. Her father's door was swung wide; as Laela watched, his chest rose and fell to the rhythm of his snores.

She skipped past creaking boards and into the blackness of the living room. Her eyes adjusted so she could distinguish between shadow and object, and she weaved with ease through furniture to the fireplace. She touched her fingertips to the mantel, feeling its wood sigh in response, then knelt in its mouth. The scent of ash and wood smoke lingered on stone. Laela's disbelief at what she was about to do rose and then quailed with the memory of Sam. What more had she to lose?

She glanced over her shoulder and held her breath as she listened for footsteps or her father's shifting weight, but heard nothing. From the pocket of her pyjamas, she pulled a small, drawstring pouch, given to her by her aunt for a birthday years before. Laela smiled as she remembered the garnet studs that had once had their home in there, and how they'd found their way out of her ears and into the river as she was swimming.

The stone offered rough kisses to her hand as she scooped some of the soft grey ash into the pouch. She gathered kindling and logs from the fireside and slipped quietly from the house.

Barely a sliver of moon lit the night. Through fingers of wych elm and oak, dapples of streetlamp fluttered onto the grass. They caught bare toes and snippets of fabric as Laela slunk through shadows to the grove by the stream. She came to a halt in front of the spot where the Stranger had lit her fire. The earth was still scorched there. Laela trembled with the memory of snapping embers and burnt flesh but she steadied her breath, steeling her mind and her body against its urge to panic.

She took the knife her father had given her, struggling not to think of the dread she would cause him should he find her gone, and kindled a fire the way he'd taught her, striking the blade against flint until she saw splinters of light. Owls kept watch and offered mournful cries as she coaxed the fire into being. When tendrils of smoke rose to greet their call, Laela leant back against the silvery trunk of a birch, following its branches up into the sky.

Find the ancient place, beyond the veil...

She allowed her eyes to close, and felt the heat radiating from the flames mingle and chase the dank air.

'Mum, I don't know what to do. I need your help...'

The fire sputtered as she stared into its crackling mass. Embers danced under scabs of ash and became Sam's face staring back at her. *She'll kill again.* Anger lurched through her, an easier, more palatable emotion than the guilt, than shame. How could she know what to do?

Laela stood, spat into the fire and left. She blundered from the birches and into the pine forest. Its smell danced lightly through the air and gradually she found her anger subsiding.

By the time she got to the road, her mind had cleared, but still, she walked on, her feet knowing a purpose her head no longer held. The cemetery was quiet and beyond that, the fields, too. She waited. At last, the absent bell carried its midnight herald and Laela turned on the spot to glare at the bell tower and its rock. As she watched, shadows melded together, spooling and swelling and catching the moonlight until they absorbed the silver and spun it into the shape of Laela's mother.

Laela wanted her to speak. To help. Why was she silent? Laela felt the familiar anger rise and burn in her chest.

'I don't know what I'm doing. I've got no idea what's going on. Why won't you give me answers? What's with all the cryptic bullshit from you and others? Why won't anyone just come out and tell me what's going on?'

She didn't move when Laela stepped closer, didn't say anything.

'Why won't you help!'

Her mother stood silent, eyes sad and palms upturned. Laela couldn't take it anymore. The pounding in her chest was louder than her own voice and each breath seemed loose and devoid of air. She felt her legs buckle and she fell into her mother's arms, unable to find the energy for anger or the strength to fight the tears. 'It's not my fault that Sam died! Tell me it's not my fault.'

Her mother held her, still wordless. When she pulled away, Laela saw her own hurt mirrored in her mother's eyes. It seemed to take her great effort to speak.

'There is no one who can show you, Laela; you must find it for yourself. Find it before the next new moon. You are brave, my love, remember that. Don't be afraid to burn.'

The church bells echoed the ruin's midnight toll and as they rang, her mother kissed Laela's forehead, then faded until she was no more than a whisper upon the chill wind.

***

The day, when it dawned, was a shadowy repetition of its predecessor. The sun shone, but its warmth seemed absent. Laela's father went off to work and left her with Jacob, this time holding her a little tighter and a little longer before he left. Jacob wouldn't talk about the day before. For both of them, the thought that Sam was really gone was too large to take in and so they sat under the oak, numb with shock.

Laela wanted to mourn Sam's death, to share the loss with Jacob, but guilt swallowed her whole and she found a barrier between her and Jacob that had never been there before. Surely, she thought, if she could get him to understand then he could help, they'd be in it together and they could stop whatever terrible thing it was that was happening. He'd know what to do. She tried to broach her secret. It sounded garbled and rushed but she just needed to get it out so that it was done and she wasn't alone again.

'Jake... I saw my mum again. Remember, I said I saw her before, only I wasn't sure because of everything that happened afterwards and I thought I may have gone a little mad... well, I saw her again last night and I know it's real. She said... she said I've got to do something. I think what happened with Sam...'

His eyes were cold steel discs. She trailed off.

'Making up weird shit about your mum is one thing, but if you talk about Sam again, I'll box you.' He shuffled his feet in the dirt and sighed. 'Christ. Look, I know you're going through...whatever... at the moment, but that's not OK. And don't tell your dad what you pretended to see. It'd mess him up.' Jacob ran his fingers through his hair and tugged at a handful. 'I'll be back in a minute.'

Laela said nothing but she felt her cheeks burning crimson and hot. She watched as he picked up his shoes and walked inside. It was minutes before she realised her jaw was still clenched and her palms ached from where she'd dug her fingernails into them. As she brought them up to her face to examine the red crescents, a shadow emerged from between the shade of the birches. The carrion crow glided to the ground with unmeasured fluidity; shades of deep violet shimmering through its plumage as it fell, like a raindrop of oil through a shaft of sun. It watched Laela with clever ash-white eyes. With a cock of its head, it opened its black beak and shattered the humdrum quiet with a rough-edged cry that shook the leaves and the blades of grass.

Laela, a reddened knee pressing into the dirt, felt her heartbeat quicken. This time she was not afraid. This time she didn't back away. They stared at each other, Laela wondering if she would soon feel the sharp attack of its beak or if, as she remembered from her dream, the crow was a messenger, a guide to be followed.

She trusted instinct, and as the crow launched itself into the air, Laela sprang into a sprint, head down and fists clenched as they darted through the silver trunks of the birches and leapt the breadth of the stream. The crow stayed in steady flight ahead of her, guiding her path. This time, the route to the bells led through the woods behind the house, following the stream and passing it, crossing over the marshes and the fields until the village lay behind her and the church spire stabbed the sky to her right. The crow swooped and fell from the air. It seemed to conjure a cloak from the wind and spun it around until it was invisible.

Laela was alone on the plain. With flooding drab of grey, clouds began to streak darkness across the land. She waited. Minutes rolled by, and Laela reclaimed a steady breath. She began to feel the ache in her feet from where she'd run barefoot over sharp grass and rock. The crumbling tower stood as it had before, the fragments of its previous life scattered around it like offerings. The bells from its replacement tolled their hour. She knelt in front of the rock. Nothing happened. And then, as if brought by the wind over the field, Laela felt someone behind her.

'Mum!'

She turned, but it wasn't her mother.

Jacob's eyes were sad. He crouched down next to her and wrapped his arms around her back. 'I know you miss her, Lae. I know you wish you'd got a chance to know her but... she's gone.' She felt his lips on her cheek. His breath was soft. 'Come on,' he said.

She shook her head, but was too tired to fight.

Laela sat, shell-shocked and numb, cloaked in Jacob's arms until long after the clock rang out for seven. The sky began to darken with rain clouds. Slowly, they made their way home, dragging her aching and mud-spattered feet through the dirt until she could make out the shape of her father's figure in the orange glow of the kitchen doorway. Jacob left her there.

'Jesus, Laela!' Elliott's haggard face was pinched with fear. 'I thought you were gone, I thought... Oh God, you're home, that's all that matters.'

She allowed herself to be held, murmuring, in turn, her assurances that she wouldn't run off again, empty apologies for frightening them and a plea to be allowed to go to bed. That night she heard the voices of her father and Penny-Jane cresting and lulling, her father's torrent shushed and soothed by quiet reasoning. Laela crouched on the landing, letting her body become absorbed into the shadows of the banister.

'You know, when she wasn't home, I went looking. I found ashes in the birch grove.' Laela could hear the sadness in her father's voice.

'From when that woman was here?'

Elliott grunted into his mug. 'No. It was fresh.' The worn creases around his eyes caught the light. 'I mean, what does that mean? Is she trying to deal with something? Why would she try to re-play that?'

Laela saw pale trembles of tears spill down his face.

Penny-Jane caught his chin. 'Hey. You don't know what goes through that girl's head, and nor do I. She's been through a lot, that's true. But children recover, quicker than we do. Try not to worry.'

'I want to make sure I'm doing the best I can for her. I feel like I've failed her, Pen.'

'Oh, tosh.'

'We're not as close as we used to be. The connection, it's gone, and I don't know how to get it back.'

Penny-Jane grimaced but let her hardened exterior relax. 'C'mon now, lovey. That's not the case. She loves you.'

'She does. But she's growing up. And she's been through so much. Sometimes I wonder what Vie would say...'

'Violet would say you're doing a damn good job.'

'Am I?'

The look on Elliott's face broke Penny-Jane's heart, and she reached for something to say, some comfort to give. 'Look, if you're really worried about her, you could have a word with Mattie. She used to be a nurse up at the old... *hospital.*'

Penny-Jane flinched even as she spoke the name. Mattie Emmerson made her uncomfortable – as did the psychiatric hospital at which Mattie had worked.

She wasn't the only one. Up on the banister, Laela shuddered.

Elliott looked unsure. He drained his mug and let out a heavy sigh. 'Maybe I'll talk to her in the morning. See if she's got some free time to spend with Laela.'

Laela bit her lip and spilled hot tears onto the landing carpet. She slunk back to her bedroom, silently closing the door behind her. In an echo of her memory, she heard the reverberations of her mother's voice as she drifted to sleep.

You are brave...

~ VI ~

CHAPTER SIX

Laela didn't make it into Mattie's house. When she arrived, the crow was already sat on the fence post, scratching at the wood with hooked steel claws and watching guardedly. Laela pondered for a moment that it might not be anything to do with her mother, or the Stranger, or the odd things that were happening, but when she tried to pass it to ring the doorbell it unfurled, beating its black wings in front of her until she retreated. She halted at the gate. It returned to its steady position, a look of unequivocal urgency on its features. *Now*, it seemed to say. *Go now.*

Shuffling came from inside the house and then, from behind the door the sound of a chain being withdrawn. The crow cocked its head at Laela, waiting for her response, her decision. She heard the lock cycle through the chambers and knew that any second the door would open and Mattie Emmerson would usher her inside, into safety and away from the visceral danger she was otherwise surely headed into.

She turned and ran. Wing to wing, Laela and the crow fled to the wilds, her hair streaming from her braid and catching the scents of summer in its tangle, the crow's black cloak sucking in daylight as it flew. As she ran, she left behind the thoughts of her father and the desire to reassure him. She abandoned them as she abandoned the notion that she could hide from what was happening.

She let the moment grab her and truth lead her and then they were into the dark of the woods and their cool shelter. Tall pines bore their scent on a gentle breeze, but after only a few minutes walking their numbers dwindled and thinned and Laela found herself in a clearing, sunlight drifting down onto grass. Ahead, the crow scratched at the ground where the green grew patchy.

Now. Here.

And suddenly something in Laela understood how to get to the Ancient Hearth. It made its home in her stomach and spread its intuition through her bones. She let that something guide her hands as she gathered dry, brittle branches from amongst the undergrowth and stacked them above kindling of bracken and snapped twigs. She'd known all along, a knowledge that fear had covered but now, with so many dead her fear sank and determination rose. She glanced around and pulled the lighter from her pocket.

Don't be afraid to burn. You are brave.

Her hand didn't tremble.

She lit the pyre.

The wind came and fanned the fire, letting it leap and dance. Smoke mingled with pine. Laela watched as the flames steadied. She inhaled the fresh scent of the woods and closed her eyes, then stepped forward into the fire. Instinct brought her arms up to cover her face and she felt the heat sear her legs, scorch through her shoes. She smelt her hair burning, felt the flash of heat against her cheek and in her nostrils and fought to keep from running, from leaving the pain and the smoke. She held still until she could no longer stand.

When she came to, she was in a different world.

* * *

Laela checked her arms for burns and found none, and her face, when she ran her fingers over it, felt smooth. No damage. She felt a small rush of excitement that it had worked. That she was *there*. But where was that?

The landscape was steeped in the deep violet hues that come with the twilight hours, the shadows deeper, more pronounced. They seeped into the trees and left dark pools around their base. Tall pines asserted their silhouettes against the sky, their elegant shapes reaching for the night, but it wasn't the forest of the village, Laela was certain. This place felt different, eldritch.

She got to her feet and walked further into the darkness, beginning to trust her instinct over what was laid bare in front of her. After a few paces she was rewarded: amongst the pines a light escaped, flickering its tongue over rough bark and needled fronds. It pulled her toward it, its promise of secrets revealed luring her in.

Underfoot, discarded limbs and fingers of the trees relented and snapped as she pursued the light. As she neared, the scent of pine gave way to that of bitter herbs, the same peculiar aroma that Laela had smelt at the Stranger's fire. She struggled to keep her pace steady, wanting as she did to run toward what she knew would give her answers, and then, as if fashioned from nothing more than air and shadow, an entrance-way solidified ahead of her.

Two vertical slabs of granite reared up from the ground, meeting the thickly woven thatch of a conical roof, underneath which firelight flicked its tongue, beckoning for Laela to step through and greet it. Inside, the glow scarcely penetrated the recesses of the timber. Spirals of smoke stung her eyes as they wound their way up to the pinnacle, smudging into the shadows. Around the fire were laid skins of deer and bear and wolf and sheep. Laela lowered herself onto a pelt and waited, settling herself into the impossibility of the situation. Opposite her, the dimness of the woods outside stole across the threshold and joined the shifting dark inside.

Laela brought her gaze to rest steadily on the white embers, watching them peel and flurry and blaze until, in the gravid quiet, instinct told her she was not alone. Almost as soon as that thought was fully formed, figures emerged, bleeding from the shadows, and took their place on the skins around the fire. Their forms were unstable, insubstantial, impressions of grey in a flickering shadow world. Elders.

One stepped into the centre. Laela could see her clear-cut and sharp, though the others were still blurs. Her weathered face held carved lines of hard toil and stories of mountain and tundra. In her hand, rested a drum. She raised it high over the fire, allowing the rising smoke to dance across its veined surface; skin stretched taut in her hands of leather and bone. The susurrations of the shadows ceased, and a heavy, heady silence filled the space.

The old woman stamped one bare foot in the dirt and flung her head backwards, releasing a primal bellow into the air. Her wild hair whipped its strands through the smoke as she began to work the drum with her hand, spinning it around her as she stamped and sang and struck with rhythmic certainty. Others around her joined their voices to hers, and the air became thick with ancestral power.

Laela gave herself to the Hearth. The drum beat into her bones, the old woman's hands like horses' hooves beating the land, singing the earth. Laela knew its beat, and she knew its language. She let a warrior's yelp cut the night and felt the power of her ancestral blood pounding through her veins. It felt like home and sorrow and strength. It held the heathered dawn and sea-struck crags and black moonless nights filled with winter's wind. Frost and fire and stag and stone beat through her. Thunder drum broke her down into shadow and flame and there she was, whirling around the crackling fire with sister and shaman, Elders – a tribe thought long dead by the world but known by the land to course through its very heart.

Quick tongues blessed the fire, and all that danced around it. They spat into its core and let the fire spit its blessings back onto their skin. The ground shook under their stamping feet and trembled its throaty thanks through their flanks. The eaves of the stone roundhouse were filled with smoke and song, and prayers sung and spun around the Ancient Hearth. Laela felt it consume her, every part of her incandescent with the rhythm.

Then the dance began to slow, the pace dwindling as the flames lowered into the stone-bound hearth. The shadows seemed to return to the recesses and shelter of the corners, and Laela was left alone with the steady beat of the drum. Their footsteps slowed as they brought the song to its end, the beat not ceased, only quieted into the pulse of heart and blood, hidden within their skins.

Ask the fire, ask the fire, ask the fire...

The old woman took her place on the reindeer hide opposite Laela, dropping her drum to the ground and her eyes to the fire. Laela lowered herself onto soft fur, the world inside stone now silent but for hearth and breath, and, just as she had suddenly known how to get to the Ancient Hearth, she found she now knew what she must do. She drew the drawstring pouch from her pocket and waited until the flames sank into the embers and the fire was quiet, fierce. She offered the ash to the fire, watching how the heat danced under the scabs. Words came, but she spoke to a place in the Hearth that needed no crude tongue-language. Still, she asked aloud.

'What must I know? What does my mum want me to learn?'

She glanced at the old woman's face, but it remained expressionless, so she brought her gaze back to the embers and gradually, patches and patterns became distinct and began to move about in fiery whorls like silhouettes against a red moon. Faces rose and fell until one loomed up at her, eye sockets ablaze but the bones defined. And then her mother's face was there, smooth and pale with wrinkles around the eyes that Laela always thought from photographs would be laughter lines. Laela's Aunt Lorna, now only the stuff of memories and seldom sent birthday cards, sat in the armchair of Laela's living room.

She spoke to Laela's mother. The sounds from the fire image trembled as though from underwater.

'She'll need to know, Vie.'

'She won't. Not if I succeed – there'll be nothing to protect the village *from*. I'm not having my daughter raised by some melancholic.'

Lorna's shoulders rounded with defeat. Violet left the fire and sat beside her sister.

'That's not who he is. It's not who I want him to be for our daughter.' She stroked her hair. 'Please, Lorna, you have to do this for me. If I die, Elliott mustn't remember the truth. It'd eat him up. And I want Laela to be free from all this, have a fresh start.'

'But it's our duty...'

'Oh, damn our duty! This thing is taking lives, Lor. Elliott doesn't understand, but you *must*. More people will die if I don't kill it now. And if I succeed, Laela never need know that she's one poor wretch in a long line meant to keep it at bay because there will be no evil in this territory to protect anyone from. Don't you see? I want what's best for her.'

Lorna shifted slightly in her chair. 'She's not just that, though is she, she's–'

'He can't know, Lor. Promise me that. Make it like I never existed.'

'Bu –'

'Please. She deserves to grow up happy.'

Lorna studied her hands in the firelight. 'He won't forget you, Vie, not completely. His love's too strong. I'll...' She sighed, resigned. 'I'll make you normal in his memory if that's what you want. No magic. But...'

Violet nodded. She hugged her sister. 'Thank you,' she whispered.

As Laela watched, the scene in the living room blurred and then reset. This time, Laela's mother was alone. She gazed into the fire, her eyes burning up at Laela across time and death.

'Laela. I don't want you to be frightened. I hope you don't end up seeing this. This isn't a life I would want for you. I want you to be free. This lineage of death and duty ends with me. I'm creating something new for you: a life without the limit of obligation.'

The fire crackled and spat a flash of hot ember onto the hearthstone, making Laela flinch away. When Laela looked again, the image of her mother had gone. The embers burned themselves into nothingness under her gaze, and then flared back to steady flames.

'Where's she gone? Is that it? Tell me!'

Across the Hearth from her, the old woman remained still and silent. Wind lifted ash and scattered it over the granite stones. From the woods outside it brought the clear scent of pine and earth on rain-strewn dusk. The dim intimacy of the fire and her mother's memories were gone; whatever message she had been meant to get was over.

Laela sat there, absorbing the fire stories and her mother's words. She felt hollow, as though learning a fraction of the truth of it all had exposed the vastness of what she did not yet understand.

So, her father didn't know. He really believed her mother had died in childbirth rather than... well, Laela didn't know the details but she knew it was the Witch. Her mother had died trying to kill the Witch, trying to protect Laela and the village and everyone beyond the confines of their land. Because that had been her job. And it was now Laela's duty. She sat a while longer trying to piece together the information, but the smoke was beginning to make her feel sick and her head cloud over and so she bowed to the hearth tender and made her way out of the roundhouse.

Dew soaked her feet and brushed wet kisses against her ankles. By now the land had turned away from the sun and watched the rise of the moon, her crescent beam picking fronds and needles from the forest and adorning them against the world of greys and blacks with a silvered touch. Laela kept walking until something shifted, whether in her head, or in the world, she didn't know. But before she had time to place it, she was walking back through the trees near the village.

Shouts punctuated the stillness of the woods. A blanket was thrown around her shoulders and a voice, distant yet loud all at once called out, 'She's over here!'

$$\sim \text{VII} \sim$$

CHAPTER SEVEN

Fear is a vile thing, and is at the bottom of almost every
wrong and hatred of the world.
— L.M. Montgomery, Emily Climbs

Elliott took in his daughter's ripped clothes and the ash-grey streaks on her face and pushed away the helping hands that had gathered around her. She followed him home, unsure of how to talk to the one person in the world she felt she never had to. They ate dinner in silence. They made it as far as the stairs on the way to sleep before they found a way to cross to the other side of the unnatural gulf that had widened its jaws between them.

'Didn't fancy going to Mattie's then, huh?' His easy smile struck bright and solid in the dim of the hallway. She shook her head.

'Look, I don't know what you're going through... I can't imagine... But I'm here if you want to talk. Or don't want to. Or, I will be, anyway.'

He paused, studied her face. Her hazel eyes were the same as they had always been. She was there. He knew her. He made sure those eyes came back to his before he continued. Made sure his voice was staid.

'I'm going to finish the work I have up at the Stevenson's – you might have to spend a day or two with Mattie, but that's it, I promise – and then I'll stay home for a bit. I figure... this could be the last summer before you get caught up in other things and have your own adventures, and I'd like it if I could be around more. Make the most of it. And, maybe, we could ride whatever this is out together?'

He watched his daughter's face break into a grin and felt relief pour into his heart. Elliott held his daughter and knew that although strange things may come and shake and rattle at their bones, nothing would break their understanding.

* * *

Laela's sleep that night was troubled with nightmares. They drifted in and swept their fingers over her vision until she could see and feel nothing but their imposed reality. In her dream, it was winter in a faraway land, long ago. Frost reigned and sucked at the air in lungs until ribs threatened to crack from the inside.

Their heavy trudge fell on the snow. Some were in boots, others barefoot. Blood fell from the raw soles of feet and left a crimson trail in the pure white blanket that covered the earth. Laela knew that this was her family. Some were old: gaunt faces harangued by angst. The Elders carried infants in their arms who wailed in the cold and steamed their distress into clouds. Laela walked alongside them, over the fields, through dim shadows of trees and then, in sunlit procession, the path started to widen, and familiar mounds and landscape emerged from out of the pallor.

They climbed up the incline to the edge of the village. Laela saw the bell tower standing tall and intact above the roofs of the houses. No smoke breached the sky from their chimneys; the village was deathly silent, and the land around bereft of life.

A grey fog rolled out thick over the low-lying lands of the green, tumbling from the woods beyond. Laela watched as it unfurled and spread its fingers over the streets and houses. It snuck between fenceposts and enveloped doorways and windows. Landmarks disappeared. All was wraith-white and ghostly.

Laela could hear slitherings and scuffles in the mist but saw nothing. Nothing but white cloud surrounded them. It closed in on the travellers, threatened to engulf them but none stirred. They stood in defiant stillness against the enemy they had stalked for so long. The world took pause and then, in the eerie blank, a scream sounded from the direction of the houses. Laela awoke in her bed, gasping for air.

* * *

Two hotbeds of magic had crept up in the village, like wells of molten power spurred into existence... by a third.

The girl. Laela. Her sister's child.

Clearly no longer such a child.

Lorna felt them swelling amongst the land but could not yet tell what they would bring, nor how powerful they or the girl would grow to be.

In the quiet of night, in stone, she waited.

~ VIII ~

CHAPTER EIGHT

Laela sat folded into the sofa. Elliott gave a sly wink from behind the cover of the doorway and grinned. 'I'll be back before sundown. You know where food is – help yourself to whatever you can find. And don't feel you have to stay until I'm home, Mattie. Thank you again for watching out for Laela.'

Mattie sniffed. 'I should think we might have to visit the grocers or pop back to mine for proper *foodstuffs*.'

Elliott contained a laugh and sent it into the frayed denim of his jeans as he tugged at the laces of his boots. 'Lae's lucky to have you around, Mattie. Nothing beats home-cooked food and fresh ingredients.'

A snort escaped from Laela.

Mattie peered at her over the grey steel rims of the spectacles wedged onto the bridge of her nose. She sniffed. Laela picked at the bits of loose stitching on an embroidered cushion, allowing the small bits of thread to float through beams of sunshine and out to the kitchen. She wasn't feeling brilliant about being left alone with Mattie but she desperately wanted her father to feel assured, so she stayed silent. Mattie sniffed again and gave a curt nod.

Elliott straightened and murmured a goodbye into Laela's hair. 'I'll see you later, love. Be good.'

Laela pulled her father into a hug, taking a moment to nestle into his chest. When she released him, his face had relaxed into an easy smile.

'Right. I better get on.' He let himself out into the daylight, feeling the warmth spread through his fingers and into his mood.

Laela listened as the van's engine grumbled and faded and her father was gone.

'Laela...'

Laela kept picking. She didn't want to give Mattie one reason to think she needed any kind of intervention but *fuck* did she want to throw something at her.

'Laela!'

Laela watched from under her eyelashes as Mattie stood and pulled an orange plastic container out of her cardigan. She placed the pills deliberately on the coffee table and knelt down to glare into Laela's face. Laela smelt peppermint and boiled foods and wanted to scream. Instead, she picked.

'Laela, your father wants you to take these. They're medicine, to make you feel a bit... calmer.'

Laela felt a jolt in her stomach. Her dad wouldn't do that. He wouldn't...

'He's worried. We all are. But...' Mattie sat her weight next to the pills on the low table. There was a pause as Mattie surveyed Laela and Laela stared back stonily. 'If you were to tell us what's going on, perhaps we could help. And then you wouldn't need to take pills or be locked in here; you'd be free to play outside with Jacob...'

Laela looked up at Mattie, ready to snarl, to fight. She wasn't trapped. She had her way out.

Mattie continued, 'If you told *me* what happened, perhaps I could help.' Her eyebrow raised and Laela was sure she caught a glimpse of what might have been a wink in anyone else but in Mattie, could surely only have been a twitch, a muscular spasm or nervous tic and not a gesture of friendliness. She stayed quiet.

There was a long pause where once again both sides surveyed the other. Then, Mattie threw up her hands. 'Heavens, girl. *I saw.*' There was no smugness, no sign of gross satisfaction, just truth growled out amidst grey hair and spectacles. She went on,

'When you left my house, I followed you. I hid in the treeline and was about to drag you back by your scruff when you vanished, well, when you seemed to set yourself on fire. I ran towards you, thinking I could stop you and then, nothing! Not even a single shred of you to be found.'

Laela felt her cheeks going red. She hadn't considered what it would look like if someone saw her. Mattie ploughed on, sinking her neck into her shoulders like a vulture assessing its prey.

'I'm an old woman, and far too nosy for her own good, so I've seen a thing or two in my time. Your mother – she used to pull stunts like this when she was a child. So, I figured, must run in the family. But your father, he doesn't know, does he?'

Laela tried to look impassively blank, but beneath the surface, her heart was racing. Someone else knew her mum had been a witch? A guardian? Whatever. Someone else might believe her.

'When he got home, and you still hadn't come back, I had to tell him *something*. And then he wanted to search the woods, sent out half the village to look for you... Caused him quite a scare.'

That struck deep. Laela paled and forgot her silence. 'I didn't mean to...'

Mattie sighed and shuffled her weight onto the sofa beside Laela. 'I know. I told him I'd lost you. Couldn't find you, which wasn't quite a lie, I suppose.' She took off her glasses, made a show of polishing them with a hand-stitched handkerchief. 'Look, I'm not stupid. I notice things. People have started to die. Not many folks were here when it happened before, and those that were for some reason seem to have forgotten.' She eyed Laela. 'But I remember. And I know your mother somehow made it stop, so –'

Laela cut her off. 'It's happened before? When?'

Mattie smiled, her lips a grim line of satisfaction. 'Before you were born. The deaths looked accidental, or like suicides, but there were too many for it to be a coincidence. So, I kept track.'

* * *

The Witch inhaled, remembering what it was to feel the cold, dank touch of the earth and its hollows.

She felt for her arms, but there were none. In their stead, thick, rotten branches stretched out into thinly spun twigs, their weight barely held in the naked boughs. Her breasts were changed into bark, rough and dead; there was no trace of the woman she once was, save her arching spine, now the curved trunk twisted like the animal in pain she had been when they had bound her here.

I remember, she thought. *And I am coming back.*

She felt down into the earth, where faint traces of the magic that had rekindled her strength still lingered. Still further she went into the earth's depths, and she began to feel the churning of the earthworms and the maggots, the desperate seeking of scavengers, and the freshly dead leaking their lifeblood into the ground. But nothing compared. She could taste the potency of the magic that dwelled in the house by the woods. She hungered for it. And she hungered for vengeance.

* * *

It took Laela a while before she understood what she was staring at.

'These are the records of patients admitted during the months your mother was pregnant.'

They were back in Mattie's living room, photocopied papers strewn across the carpet.

'This was back before I worked exclusively in the psychiatric ward. In the early months, there were only a few isolated incidents – an overdose, a hanging... and then it was like a switch flipped and suddenly the casualties started streaming in, once a month, but more involved and each case more –' Mattie spread her hands, searching for words. 'Violent. Grotesque.'

Laela shifted, uneasy.

'I'll admit, I was fascinated. Our village, so quiet, so,' she laughed, '*tedious* in so many ways, to be transformed into a hotbed of suicide and murder. I couldn't understand it.' She eyeballed Laela over the rim of her spectacles. 'I suppose I was able to retain a certain distance from everything that was going on, and with that I could study the patterns objectively.' She laughed again. 'I must sound heartless, I know, but,' she shuffled the papers with an extended finger, alighting on one and handing it to Laela, 'as you'll see, I wasn't able to keep that distance for very long.'

Laela scanned the words.

Emmerson.

Mattie barked a dry laugh. 'My son. I'd had him young, out of wedlock – those things weren't cared for in the village at the time. Now, of course, the world being what it is, there's much more leniency. But I kept him. Loved him. He was my world. His death, I... It ruined me, for a while. I don't suppose I've been quite the same since.'

Laela didn't know what to say.

Mattie shook her head. 'The other staff, the head of the hospital, the police, the rest of the village, they thought it was all very strange, but they couldn't find a connection. Investigations were done, of course, and then, as time wore on and no answers were found, everyone set about forgetting. Until there was only me. Only me who knew there had to be a link between them all – and only me at home. The other families, wives, husbands, mothers... they weren't interested in what I had to say. Most moved and I daresay moved on from wondering. Me, I,' she shook her head, her eyes misting over. 'I couldn't. I had to find answers. I had to know. I transferred to the psychiatric unit as soon as I returned to work but by then it was all over. Your mother was dead. You were born. The murders stopped.'

Laela bit her lip, trying to take it all in. She studied Mattie's face as she spoke, trying to imagine the grief and torment she'd been through, so similar yet worlds apart from Laela's own.

'My mother,' she began, not knowing how to tell Mattie everything she'd seen and heard in the fire of the Ancient Hearth, not knowing if by sharing her secret she'd cause herself to be judged as mad – because it sounded mad, it *felt* mad to Laela – but all she knew was that the woman before her had suffered, that she'd looked for answers her whole life, and she deserved them.

'I saw something.'

And she told Mattie Emmerson everything she knew about the Witch, her mother, and the Elders.

When Laela was done, Mattie silently walked to the kitchen, returning clutching a tumbler of amber liquid, which she knocked back in one gulp. She stared at Laela from across the room.

'If I hadn't seen what I saw – your disappearing into flames, your mother's odd behaviour, the bodies all those years ago – I should think you were playing a cruel game with me.' Her eyes dropped to the bottom of the glass, her thumb tracing the patterns around its edge. 'As it is, I believe you. And I think that's possibly far more terrifying to admit out loud. For both of us. Because I think up until now, you weren't really sure about whether you believed or not. And now you do... well. You know you're the one that has to do something about it.'

Laela's stomach flipped. She nodded. Sharing the truth had made it real. She could no longer harbour the hope that she was crazy; she had no option but to figure out how to stop a seemingly unstoppable killer that no one would believe existed.

* * *

Laela watched the moon grow fat from her window. With every day that passed, she felt horror creep further up her throat. She watched the dwindling light of the moon until it was only a sliver that separated her from the black that seeped at its edges. Time crept past, yet she did nothing. So, she waited, knowing only that she mustn't let something terrible happen.

$$\sim \text{IX} \sim$$

CHAPTER NINE

*With their bodies these women form gateways into the silent
lands, a hidden landscape where the dead journey.*

— Carolyn Hillyer

The Witch felt her power rising in the black night. She
stretched out her senses, looking for the broken homes, the
unjustly treated, the beaten and the neglected, the sick, the corrupted. The mist rose from her branches and leached out into
the night. There was no light to catch it; no moon shone to cap-
ture glints of the drifting motes and spores as they spun their
way across the land from the tree and stole into the village.

Only one could she take. But soon, she thought, *soon* she
would be strong enough to take all that she pleased.

She rifled the houses and ransacked the beds until there, in
the darkness of a dirty kitchen, she found her *one*. He was tired.
She could feel his weariness and taste his regret. It ran in rings
throughout his body, and when she crept inside his lungs, he

did not fight. She shrugged on his body and felt his skin tighten around her.

As one, they left the bottle on the table next to the empty, hollow glasses and went upstairs. Their left hand carried a knife they'd slipped from the kitchen drawer; as they passed the window of the landing, its blade gleamed yellow and cold in the diluted lamplight.

In the bedroom, the Witch noted the female in the tangle of bed sheets, saw the pain in her heart too and thought about how she could take her – and the child she sensed in the room down the hall – at the next new moon.

She held the knife handle steady in the man's hand and climbed onto the bed. She felt arousal stir. She tightened his body around herself, feeling her magic possess every atom, moving his limbs as though her own. They clambered quietly around the sleeping figure, placing one knee either side of her chest and lightly fingering the sheet around her face so that it pinned her head.

They woke her up with a simple kiss.

Her eyes showed terror, agonising and beautiful. They stuffed the sheet into her silently screaming mouth and took the blade. Beneath their legs, they felt her buck and wriggle, straining to escape. But they held on. The woman soaked the mattress with her urine as the knife blade touched her throat. She hardly resisted when they turned the knifepoint up and placed the handle between her teeth, making sure her jaw, though shaking, clamped tight. Her mouth held the blade steady.

They lowered themselves so that their eyes were a hair's breadth from hers. And then they dug the blade into their throat and slashed. Blood gushed over the woman's face and soaked red the sheets. It dribbled down the handle of the knife and stained the woman's lips and teeth.

The Witch gurgled laughter through the blood, feeling ecstasy flood through her. She savoured the death until every last drop had gone from his body, and then shed the man's limp form, and spun back to the Tree in turning, delighted whorls of dust, filled with the glorious power of stolen life.

* * *

In the black of the new moon, Laela slept. Something dark and teeming rattled past the house through the woods.

The phone rang. A body left the house. An engine hummed. Laela slept on.

Sometime during the blue hour, coloured lights flashed through the window of Laela's bedroom and sent their sploshes of panic onto the ceiling: prickling, artificial blues stark against the hue of the world before dawn.

The flashes roused Laela from her dreamland and brought her senses staggering into the waking nightmare. She kept the bed sheets pulled up tight as armour around her torso and opened the window further. She peered out into the morning. All seemed quiet. Laela felt the wooden ridge of the window frame dig into her ribcage as she strained to see past the garden wall. The lights were the other side – one, maybe two – sets of flashing blues, and the roof of an ambulance nosing out from the eaves of Jacob's house.

'Oh, god.'

Laela scrambled into jeans and a T-shirt and flung aside the pillowcase that was still stuffed under the door. The candle still smouldered, flashing orange and hungry onto the wood around it. The wax had melted and pooled onto the bedside table. It splattered onto the wall as she blew out the flame.

She heard the kitchen door open and squeal shut and she stopped, waiting. Footsteps resounded through the house. One set heavy but sure, the other light but tripping, unsteady. The latter set halted downstairs, whilst the ones that Laela assumed belonged to her father ascended the stairs and then joined with other noises. The airing cupboard door opened, and Laela heard a tumble of linen spill out, and a soft *shhp* as Elliott pressed the stiffened door back into its frame.

Laela held her breath as the footsteps spiralled back in to meet one another in the space beneath Laela's bedroom. She heard her father's voice rumble in the depths of his chest, the words indistinguishable, but the steady warmth spilling out into the rest of the house like the glow of firelight.

She waited under the covers for her father to come. He didn't try to slip past into his bed, which he must have been long craving. Laela smelt the faint hints of sawdust and beeswax and sweat and smoke that made up her father's scent and wriggled her shoulders until she sat upright in bed. The door opened and in the dim light her father – part shaped silver, part silhouette – took gentle steps into her room. Dawn was stretching her arms and had begun to light the land with crimson, but for this house, the blue hour still lingered. Elliott was almost ghostly, faded. His jaw was darkened with stubble that seemed to hang around with the gloom etched beneath his eyes. He swept his hair back from his face and smiled at her. His face was the ash of a fire long cold.

Dad?' she enquired into his eyes, but she knew what was coming.

He sighed, weary.

Laela waited, a sick lurching feeling tumbling around her stomach.

'Something happened...' His voice trailed away as he turned and clicked her bedroom door closed.

'Someone's dead, aren't they?' She heard panic rising in her voice, but she didn't care, she hated the waiting, the fidgeting around the truth.

Her dad sighed and knelt in front of her, raising a finger to his lips. 'Jacob's dad was found. The police were asking me if I'd seen anything, heard anything. Lesley – his mum's in tatters, asked if we'd take Jacob in for a couple of days while she sorts herself out. I said we'd be happy to do anything we could to help, under the circumstances. What do you think, Lae? Spare some room for your friend?'

She nodded, unsettling tears.

'Oh, sweetheart.' He patted her shoulder and squeezed it. 'I've made up the bed on the couch for Jacob. I doubt he'll get any sleep, but we should try not to disturb him for a bit, eh?'

Laela nodded once more and wished terribly hard for things to be back the way they were before her birthday.

When her father left, she lay still on the bed, fully clothed and empty.

***

Laela couldn't sleep. The day following Jacob's arrival – the hours following the death of his father – had been muted as though life were a furtive thing to be kept hidden. She waited until she was sure her father was asleep, or at least locked in his room in silence, and made her way downstairs. Jacob lay on the sofa, his breath soft against the cushions. But it was a sleep of exhaustion rather than peace, and the pain etched into his face wasn't diminished by darkness.

Laela slipped past him and prayed neither he nor her father would wake before she returned.

***

The lights inside Mattie's house were out and the village lay dormant, waiting for morning.

Laela knocked, quietly at first and then urgency took hold and she hammered at Mattie's door, the sharp noise biting and echoing around the silent streets.

A light flicked on upstairs, followed by another downstairs, and then the clunking sound of locks opening. Mattie peered through the gap in the door, wary and behind the safety of the security chain. Her mouth upturned when she saw it was Laela who stood shivering despite the heat of the night on her doorstep. She raised an eyebrow.

'Wait.'

The door was closed once more and the chain released, and then Laela was inside Mattie's house, quietly worrying at a fingernail, unable to speak.

Mattie ignored her for a while, going through the ritual of lighting the gas and heating milk on the stove. She set a steaming cup of cocoa in front of Laela and screeched a chair out from under the table. She took a deep breath.

'I've heard, obviously, about Jacob's dad. He must be distraught.'

Tongue still bound, Laela nodded.

'You suspect, as I do, that it was this *evil* – the Witch – that did it.'

Laela's lip quivered and Mattie watched a tear escape and roll down her cheek. She reached across the table, feeling as though she were reaching across a rift as apparent and daunting as a chasm, and clasped Laela's hand in hers. 'What's happening isn't your fault. None of this is predictable. There's nothing you could have done, no way you could have known.'

Mattie gripped her hand until Laela was forced to look up into Mattie's fierce, grey eyes. 'There is entirely no use putting any more burden on your shoulders than already rests there. Do what has to be done. And to do that, you can't carry guilt. You have to drop that right now.'

The words made sense, but in her heart, all Laela saw was the pain she had caused.

'Snap out of it. Think of a way forward,' Mattie implored, grasping Laela's hand. 'Do you think you could go back to the place in the woods, with the fire?'

Laela's face crinkled.

'Well, there's no use waiting for your mother to appear; someone else may be dead by then.'

* * *

The Hearth was quiet. No shadows danced or crept about the stone circle. The drum was silent, but the old woman sat, tending the fire. Her long white hair hung in bedraggled locks about her shoulders and lifted in the currents of air rising from the Hearth. Laela caught the scent of bitter herbs and burning oak. She sat. Ash from her hands fed the fire, and she waited, asking the same question over and over: *What's happening in the village?*

No flame memories appeared. Laela tried again.

What do you want me to know?

This time, her mother paced in the living room. 'We can't kill what's already dead...'

The picture skipped. Her aunt squatted before the fireplace and pressed tears from her eyes. 'We don't *know* anything. How are we supposed to do this if there's no evidence of her punishment left? You want to just try re-binding her...' And then the image faded into the flames once more.

Who?

A dozen voices gurgled from the fire; moment on top of moment shuddered and scraped across one another.

'The Witch.'

'...the Witch...'

The Witch.

Laela looked at the old woman opposite her. She faced her silently.

'Is that it?' But the woman stared impassively through her, continuing to stoke the flames with a long, gnarled stick.

'What then? How do I defeat her? What am I supposed to ask?'

The fire burned on.

'What am I supposed to do? Why is nobody helping?' Her heart pounded through her; she could feel its tremble in her breath and without warning her anger boiled over. 'Why can't you help me? All you give me is cryptic messages and dead people. Why is this happening? Why can't you just –' Laela sat down, legs suddenly weak, her anger gone. She held her head in the heels of her hands and wept, huge, grievous, gulping sobs shaking her body. She let everything pour out into the dirt.

When she was done, she felt the emptiness in her filled by the steady crackling of the fire. She inhaled the heady scents of smoke and wood and allowed the wretched feeling in her stomach to subside.

The old woman's voice rasped.

'You are here because you are a part of the ancient pact made with the Earth, left here by the Elders to guard and protect the people who dwell in this land and drink from her waters. We are your tribe. We cannot spare you, sister. The world is in need of your magic. Do not relent until your duty is done.'

The stone took in the words in silence. Laela brushed the tears from her face. 'I – I don't think I can...'

'Mourn your life if you desire. But you are on a journey. Embrace it, or the Earth will suffer her greatest loss.'

~ X ~

CHAPTER TEN

"A Witch is born out of the true hungers of her time..."

— Ray Bradbury, Long After Midnight

Sometime during the sunlit hours, the hard shrill of the phone rang out. Laela crept from her room across the landing to listen at the banister, but all she could make out were rumblings from her father. His measured footsteps paced the floor beneath before creeping up the stairs past Jacob. Laela didn't bother to pretend she hadn't been listening and was grateful Elliott didn't pretend that everything was fine.

'Last night Lesley wasn't feeling too good. Penny's asked me to pop over to check in on her –'

The scrunch of gravel alerted them to the arrival of a visitor. Elliott descended wearily to open the door and Laela, already feeling the surge of expectant panic, stole along the landing to peek out of the small, round window of the bathroom.

A police car idled outside, but her father didn't invite them in; instead, they stood and spoke under the eaves of the house where Laela couldn't see them. It was a dry summer's day, but the wind shook the trees and snatched at the policewoman's words, carrying them away into the woods. Some minutes later, building dust clouds marked their retreat as the tyres churned the dirt of the driveway. Laela waited until they had gone before tiptoeing to the kitchen door where her father stood with ashen face.

'Lesley's been taken away,' he said. 'She... I was too late. They said she'll recover, but...'

***

Days passed in blurry grey. Jacob spent most of his time sat in numbed silence, not feeling the minutes move or seeing the world as it buzzed around him, his thoughts constantly revolving around *What if?*

He hadn't been allowed in his parents' bedroom since his father's death, and his mind tortured him with possibilities that perhaps none of it had happened, that maybe his dad would come back, calling out in Laela's kitchen and apologising for being late home from somewhere they hadn't known he'd gone. Maybe even his drunken stumblings and creativity with his belt would have been welcome. Maybe.

Laela stayed by his side and moved her bedding downstairs. At night, each of them lay quiet, listening for the other's sounds of sleep, until Jacob thought he was alone in the waking world and he could sob into his pillow unheard.

Late one afternoon, Penny-Jane scuffed at the doorstep with her boots. Whispered words caught in the air and drifted to Laela like dandelions on the breeze.

'Nervous breakdown, they think...'

'...she's in hospital...'

'...get away from it all... new perspective...'

Her dad made some phone calls after that, shutting doors behind him with the slow squeeze of the handle. When he came to find her and Jacob, it was with a forced smile and a voice like a fishhook swathed in saccharine.

'I've booked us a holiday. Us three. Somewhere we can relax for a bit.'

Jacob's eyes slid towards Elliott but seemed to stare through him. 'What about my mum?'

'She's still not feeling well, Jacob; she's getting some rest. It'll do everyone good to have a break.'

Jacob's fists turned white at the knuckles and then the strength seemed to drain out from him. 'Okay,' he whispered.

His resigned shoulders sloped over his body as he shuffled from his perch and dragged himself up the stairs. Laela looked at her dad. The sickly smile vanished from his lips, replaced instead by fragile exhaustion.

'Where are we going?' she asked.

His mouth was a pinch. 'Aunt Lorna's.'

***

That night, Laela listened for the steady in/out breath that followed Jacob's muffled sobs, then stole from her bed.

The dim woods that surrounded the roundhouse were still, the fabric of the night dense, allowing the air to carry the scent and sound of the crackling fire to Laela's ears. She followed the soft glow into the quietness of the roundhouse and sat in front of the hearth, the cloth of her pyjamas scuffling as she pulled the refilled ash pouch from her pocket.

The old woman looked on, silent.

Laela spoke to the fire, her voice low but certain. 'I accept what I am. And I seek guidance.'

But this time, no faces appeared; the fire had no stories for her. Instead, only a letter, written on parchment, hung in the blaze.

'Take it,' rumbled the old woman.

Laela hesitated, before remembering the fear she'd felt the first time she'd entered the portal fire to the Ancient Hearth, and how now she didn't even consider being afraid of it. She extended her hand to grab the parchment but immediately withdrew. This fire was not like the portal fire. It was beyond anything she'd ever felt. This fire housed a heat that screamed into her bones. She looked to the hearth-tender, but her face remained inscrutable.

Laela thought of Sam and Jacob and took a deep breath. She'd come so far, and she didn't know if she'd be able to return to the Ancient Hearth while she was at her aunt's and so, as if from above herself, she watched as she plunged her hand into the fire once more. The pain ricocheted up her arm and into her chest. She steeled herself and reached in further still to seize the parchment, at last feeling the dry paper almost cool against her fingers. When she drew her hand from the fire the flesh continued to burn, the skin smouldering.

The hearth-tender spoke before Laela had a chance to break the seal, a kindly hand raised. 'Take it with you to the house on the hill. They will help you there.'

Laela opened her mouth to ask, but thought better of it. She knew she would find out soon enough. She stashed it unread in her pocket and, with its vicious edges dug into her thigh, walked away from the Hearth, trudging through her heartache, connecting one sole with the earth after the other in a stumbling, ungainly dance, which the moon looked down upon and yearned to repair with comfort.

~ XI ~

CHAPTER ELEVEN

Life is sweet. Life is also very short.

— Natalie Merchant

The next morning, the attic was dredged, and Laela's dad appeared with dust-coated bags and a pair of cases. Socks and underwear and sandals were thrown in from great heights and grimaced at in their shambolic bundles. The routine of holiday brought with it echoes of excitement, and shortly behind that, guilt.

Both Laela and Elliott accompanied Jacob to pick up a selection of his things, the three of them driving the solemn route through the woods without the disturbance of words. It was as though arriving at an unfamiliar destination. Each took a moment to steel themselves before leaving the safety of the van and making their way up the paving stones to the house.

Inside, the air was caked with a sour blend of stale smoke and wine-soaked mourning. They picked their way through the jetsam – glass from broken bottles mingled with shattered photo frames; forgotten meals turned ashtray for ground-in cigarette butts; a shirt, crumpled but placed carefully across the arm of the sofa; and a belt, its leather worn and scuffed, its buckle cold and heavy.

Jacob's eyes rested on each object. It felt too open, his home life too plainly laid out for Laela and Elliott to look at, and he wondered now at how much worse it felt than the jokes he'd made over cigarettes to his friends. But perhaps they didn't see what he saw. Perhaps it wasn't all spelt out as obviously as he thought, and all they could see was an untidy house, each individual crime or indecency blurred into a blanket mess.

He caught a sideways glance at Laela and knew at once that wasn't true. Her face showed the connection from bottle to belt, and he felt sick that all his inner life stood naked around them. He walked on. At the foot of the stairs, he found the light switch and trailed his fingers along the handrail as he ascended, the chips in the white paint stretching like open mouths growing progressively wider as he neared the top.

He felt his heartbeat quicken even as he tried to avoid looking at the entrance to his parents' bedroom. He forced his legs to move past it to his own room, keeping his eyes fixed on the puckered carpet. He slogged his schoolbooks out onto his bed and stuffed a collection of underwear and clothing into his bag, managing to not think as he did. When he was done, he slung the backpack over his shoulder and walked along the landing.

Elliott had followed him up the stairs and was stood in the main bedroom's doorway, trying to appear relaxed. He put his hand out as Jacob tried to push past him.

'I have to,' was all he had to say for Elliott to lower his arm, and then he was there.

The sheets had been changed, although Jacob doubted his mum had slept there since his father's death. There was no sign that spoke of what had happened, no blood or remnant, and when Jacob paced the carpet, the bed didn't jump at him, it remained steady, normal, not the scene of his father's suicide at all. The chest of drawers where his mum hid her cigarettes and booze money was the same. The curtains. The walls. Nothing changed, yet everything altered.

He circled the room once more, taking it all in, feeling miles away from his body, and then left.

* * *

They departed the same day. Laela's hand was raw from the fire the night before, and she tried to hide the bandages with which she'd covered it with the pulled-down sleeve of her jumper. Jacob soon found sleep, with ear and cheek flattened into the glass of the window.

Laela sat in between the others and gazed at the road ahead, lulled by the van's steady thrum. She longed to be able to tell Jacob what was happening, even tell her father, but that wouldn't be fair. And they'd never believe her. In sporadic moments her chin would drop to her chest as she dozed off, only to reawaken with a jolt and a renewed tugging of her sleeve. If her father noticed these panicked scrabblings, he asked no questions: grief brought blind spots.

They sped past stalls of fruit, and flowers on lampposts. Buzzards spiralled. Each background blurred into the next. Dirt-greyed walls became tree-lined roads and they, in turn, opened out into vast green spaces where the sun alighted onto every blade of grass and coloured the wings of soaring birds with rainbow fire.

Rain sped down as they approached nightfall and their long-awaited destination. It splashed and hammered on the roof of the van and soaked away the caked dust and dirt of the city's smog and country lanes. All around, puddles formed giving the appearance at times of it being a great black river that they traversed, rather than a road.

Street lights were scarce now; the only light was the moon's waxing crescent, her wolfish grey grinning lopsidedly at the stars and the vast world below them. Laela felt safe, secure in the knowledge that the Witch wouldn't strike until the new moon, and the revelations of the previous week gave her a sense of hope: more answers would help her save the village.

Houses were passed with less frequency, and only the occasional yellow glow of headlights ruffled the darkness. The road turned to track, horned with lumps of compressed dirt that popped out and marked the verge in speckled patterns or crumbled under the weight of the spinning wheels. The land began to drop away at either side, descending into a deep gorge on one and a lush, tree-flooded valley the other. Under the moonlight the track was pale, flowing down like a river over the black hills, then rising up toward the shining stars. Miles of hills and roadside were left behind, abandoned to their musings.

They rounded a bend, Laela's father hunched over the steering wheel to squint ahead. Its path descended once more before climbing up and thinning out into nothing more than a bare smattering of hard earth amongst the green either side, and at the peak of the hilltop stood a house. It reared over the land and water with a haggard stoop. Laela's heart pounded through her chest as she thought of the hearth-tender's words.

As they closed in, she examined her aunt's home. A squat, rounded lower floor gave way to a thin tower, stretched forty feet above the land. It appeared to rest onto a bulky second story on one side, as though it needed to lean on it for support. Atop the tower, glass-filled walls sloped up to a point: the crown of the lighthouse. Its face eyed the crags that surrounded it, and its back looked over the bubbling cauldron of sea with undiminished pride. In an alcove in the mound of earth, a garden thrived amongst the wilderness; tender trees waved their welcome in the darkness. Laela picked these out and whispered to her father in wonder. Their appearance – so incongruent with the setting – mirrored the fragility of the house.

Elliott parked the van in front of the dry-stone wall. The rain fell heavy on their heads, but the taste of salt filled their lungs and spoke to their bones, and the travellers perked up with the cold of the rain's touch. They huddled beneath the porch and waited as Laela's father tapped on the wood, the rain driving in in sideways sheets and soaking the door.

Minutes went by, and the three shivered in the wet landscape. And then, above them, a light went on, casting an amber radiance in the recess. The door flung backwards, and the smell of bread and burnt wood crashed into the damp night.

Aunt Lorna struck a wild picture in the entrance-way: streaked hair and billowing shawl as though a hoard of imps danced below her arms. Laela noted the long, straight wooden staff of smoothed ash that Lorna gripped in one hand as though, despite the appearance of bright strength and energy, it was the only thing keeping her upright.

'My darlings! Come in!'

With her beaming face and radiant warmth, she was almost impossibly different from the Lorna of the fire-image. She ushered them inside, brushing onto the floor the droplets that had settled themselves on shoulders and backs.

'Come by the fireside, warm yourselves! Dinner's in the oven, and water is hot, ready for baths.' She turned her bright, glinting eyes to Jacob and leaned her weight over her walking stick, causing the firelight to dance across her cheeks. 'You must be Jacob, lovely to meet you. Lorna.'

* * *

The rain battered the roof and windows, but the glow of the fire and the abundant flickering candles seemed to guard the inside of the house from the lashing torrent and chill. Jacob, freshly washed and dressed, returned and curled up on the sofa. Laela followed suit and sat by the fireside on the sheepskin rug next to the cat, who stretched and slunk around her shins before bounding up to Jacob. It nuzzled at him with its grey head, twisting and pushing its face into Jacob's hand, and then stared up at him unblinkingly with huge, ocean-steel eyes when Jacob's hand hung unmoving from the cushions.

Lorna turned, 'He's magic, that cat – always knows when I need a cuddle.'

Warily at first, Jacob fingered the soft fur around its neck. The cat promptly leapt up and wound itself into a ball in the curve of Jacob's stomach, purring.

'Thanks for taking us in, Lorna.' Elliott sighed. 'It's been a long month. We really appreciate the break.'

'And I appreciate the company. It's a beautiful world from this vantage point, but it can get mighty lonely for a person.'

The cat looked up with narrowed eyes.

'Anyway, who's up for some homemade pie? Everything's fresh from the garden.'

She flapped an oven-gloved hand as steam rose out of the oven, sending the aroma of pastry wafting out into the house. Laela couldn't shake the thought that this Lorna seemed a little *too* perfect, and the sounds and smells of the lighthouse too comforting.

'There's no ceremony here, loves. It's self-serve. Come dig in.' Lorna plonked the steaming oven dish onto a cast-iron trivet next to a stack of plates.

Laela waited until the others had served themselves and then piled a plate high with pie and greens, her hunger overriding her suspicions, relishing the way the steam seemed to soothe her tired eyes.

As they ate, she studied her aunt from across the table, taking time to note the further wrinkles and greys that adorned her appearance since the memories in the Hearth's fire. There was something in her eyes too, although she couldn't place it. It was a something that waited, crouched – not yet unkind, but with all the desperation that hinted that it could be. She wanted desperately to ask her aunt about everything. She *needed* to. But how? When her father and Jacob were here, and everything was already so steeped in chaos and grief?

Elliott broke the silence. Jabbing his fork at the food he said, 'This is delicious, Lor.'

Lorna turned not to Elliott, but to Laela. 'If you look after the land, she'll provide you with all that you need, and more.' She winked.

By the time the china of the plates resurfaced, the moon had taken her place high in the sky. She presided over the oddly shaped house on the edge of the cliff and watched, amused, as the wind buffeted and the rain caressed with fervent ardour the slick black of the roof. Inside, the children were yawning, and their eyes found the path to sleep an irresistible one. They allowed themselves to be led from table to bed.

'I've set you two up in the lantern room. It's not fancy, but it'll suffice for now.'

Up the stairs they spiralled, wending their way past landings and passageways until they reached a small room at the upper-most point of the tower, Lorna seemingly untroubled by the effort of climbing, while Laela, still not fully recovered, found herself panting and the muscles in her legs burning. Its walls – snowflake-white – held their curves around several arched windows looking straight out into the black night and the endless stretch of ocean. The rain strummed her sweet refrain against their panes and sent sploshes bouncing off the outer window ledges into the water, land, and roof below.

Two beds faced the stairs, their heads by the outer walls, their bodies lined with thick, soft bedding and pillows. On the opposite wall squatted a chest of drawers, and next to it, a desk. Between the two sides, partially covering the wooden boards, lay a rug, its thick tapestry in parts worn bare, but still generous in its colour.

Lorna walked the few paces across the room, the wooden stick striking the floor every other step, and lit a candle in the alcove of each window above their beds.

'I've left the glass bare, no curtains here... so expect to be awake with the sun.' She was slowed now, as though the trilling Lorna of earlier had been an act and now, in the dark, she could shake off a little of that pretence. 'Goodnight, my sweethearts.'

She smiled indulgently at them and descended the stairs, leaving Laela and Jacob surrounded by the night sky.

They listened to the receding beat of the walking stick, sank sleepily into their mattresses and stared. Above them, white clouds, brilliant against the black velvet night, sped past, offering fleeting glimmers of stars. They saw now that the whole pointed dome of the lighthouse was bare glass, save for a metal ball in the centre. The barrier between them and the night was thin and clear, casting them into the infinite deep of the sky and her charms. Laela lay awake for some time, watching the scudding and twinkling and beaming of the celestial dancers, but it was Jacob who lost himself up there, in that space, that vastness. He let his hurt melt into the endless, and when he did eventually sleep, it was quiet and dreamless.

* * *

Lorna retraced her steps back to the ground floor. The firelight had dwindled, and the shadows had crept further from their corners. The remaining glow was thrown out onto the sofa and the figures seated upon it; Elliott had moved and was lying back amongst sunken cushions with his feet up on the low table and the cat purring with contentment on his lap. They looked up at her as Lorna allowed the final stair to creak under her step. Elliott's lined face beamed.

'This cat is incredible, Lor. I swear his fur's changed colour since we got here. What's his name?' Elliott asked as he scratched behind the creature's ears.

'It changes,' she said. She glanced at the clock on the driftwood mantel, 'You could probably call him Midnight.'

She tightened her grip on the hard wood in her hand and felt about in the dark for throwaway conversation. Instead, something too big, too laced with feeling emerged. 'Elliott, I'm sorry I stayed away for so long. I found it too painful to see you and Laela; I couldn't stop thinking about Vie, I was driving myself mad, and –'

'Hey, it's okay,' Elliott murmured, getting up. Lorna felt his hand on hers as though it burnt through years of ice. 'It was a hard time for all of us, Lor. You did what you had to.'

Lorna felt something in her heart break a little further and hoped Elliott would misread the pain on her face for that of uncomplicated grief. She turned away, letting his hand drop, and began fussing at the cat's cheeks.

'Shall I put another log on the fire?' he asked.

Lorna examined his voice for a trace of suspicion then shook her head. Collected herself. 'No, thanks. I think I'd better get some sleep.'

Elliott yawned and stretched. 'I should, too. Did you say I was on the second?' He smiled warmly at her, and Lorna felt herself condemned.

'Mmm.' She found the nerve to plaster a smile on her face and look him in the eye. 'I'll show you up –'

'No bother. I know the way.' He bent and kissed the top of her head as he walked past her to the stairs. 'You get yourself some rest, Lorna. You've been an angel to us all. We can't thank you enough.'

Lorna's smile grew weak once more, but she managed a feeble, 'Goodnight.'

She watched Elliott's back as he ascended the stairs, his broad shoulders disappearing as the steps spiralled into the dark above.

'Hey, you.' She turned to the cat. 'Go see he gets himself some good rest, eh?' The cat eyed her suspiciously. 'I know,' she said. 'I promise I'll get to bed soon.' Midnight rubbed his head affectionately against her knuckles and then slunk dutifully after Elliott, up into the silent tower.

For a moment, before she became aware of the faint mutterings of the night, a relaxed hush pervaded. Lorna peered toward the upper rooms and landings of the lighthouse and listened. All seemed calm. Quiet. Then she turned her back on the stairs. She placed her staff carefully against the wall and, standing on the lowermost step, spread her hands wide and slow in front of her.

There, in the gloom, an archway formed. The stitching around its edges looked frayed, Lorna thought. *Time for a repair.* She should do something about that soon. At her feet, where the living room floor usually was, the familiar steps of cold stone emerged, leading down into darker depths. She picked up her staff, flicked a hand, extinguishing the flames in the fireplace, and descended through the doorway, sweeping it closed behind her.

~ XII ~

CHAPTER TWELVE

> Because no retreat from the world can mask what is in
> your face.
> — Gregory Maguire, Wicked: The Life and Times of the
> Wicked Witch of the West

The rain continued to tap her melodies onto the lighthouse, swelling the belly of the land below. Elliott, weary, accepted Lorna's offer to stay for a few days. Necessity, however, meant that he spent the first morning hunched over the phone, making funeral arrangements for Jacob's father. He'd tried to finish his task before the rest of the household were awake, but had forgotten that business hours seldom coincide with the stealth of early morning.

He sighed and abandoned his work, heating water on the stove, stooping as he did so to look out of the kitchen's narrow window. Dawn had come, and the red sun burned away the rain, yet a few scattered clouds still clung to the sky. The light seemed to set them afire. Through their blaze, gulls swept and glided and dove. He was still half-watching, lost in thought, as the kettle's sigh became an urgent whistle. Elliott slid on his boots and took his mug of coffee out into the light and watched as its steam rose and lost itself in the dawn breeze.

'Morning!' called Lorna.

The cat bounded back to her and wove through her booted feet, catching the folds of her open cardigan on his tail. Her face was ruddy, glowing with exertion. She cradled open baskets, their handles resting heavily and awkwardly on her forearms.

'Figs,' she said, presenting Elliott with the sight of the fresh, ripe fruits, in such abundance that they were almost spilling from the baskets. 'Help me get these inside?'

'Sure.'

They strode their muddy boots into the alcove of the front porch and left them there to bask in the sun until the mud dried and flaked. They set the baskets down on the kitchen counter, and Elliott somehow found himself washing fig after fig as he and Lorna talked.

'Thanks for giving me a hand.' Her voice dropped, 'How are you doing, Elliott? Really.' The kitchen was quiet apart from the gentle stream of running water, and the soft, barely-there sounds of the ocean outside.

'We're managing. Recent events... It's... hard. What Laela and I have, it's wonderful. I don't know many parents who end up with such a relationship with their kids, certainly not Jacob's folks...'

'I don't need to tell you that he's lucky to have you. They both are.' She carefully smoothed her thumb over the fabric of the tea towel. 'Laela's a miracle, Elliott. And she's grown that way because of you. And what you're both doing for Jacob... It's lovely. I'm sure his mother will appreciate it, when she's in a better state.'

Elliott stepped back from the sink and ran his hands through his hair. The sounds of movement way above them indicated that Laela and Jacob were awake and would soon be descending upon the quiet of the kitchen. He pressed the base of his skull into his palms and sighed. 'I have one more call to make; they weren't open before. The kids... Jacob shouldn't hear this.'

'I'll take them out,' she said. 'They can come with me for the morning, give you some time to make arrangements.'

He nodded, and the muscles of his mouth returned it to the grim line that had become its norm in recent days. Lorna caught his hand in hers and pressed figs into his palm. 'Eat.'

He nodded again.

'Elliott,' she said, eyes serious and fixed. 'I'm sorry I left you both. I'm going to try to be there for you from now on. I- I'm glad you called.'

Elliott's smile filled with warmth. 'Me too, Lor. It's been good seeing you. And having someone I can rely on.'

* * *

Laela and Jacob had enjoyed the morning's clear view from the lantern room. The ocean stretched beyond the horizon to where the sun turned the water into liquid fire, matching the blood orange sky. They had watched birds soar and rise on thermals and catch leaping fish in their hungry beaks. The cliff edge beneath them curled around to the west with jagged teeth and steely greys. To the left, the hungry waves ate into the rocks, and, following the circle of the lantern room around, at the final point of the compass lay the garden and then the hinterlands, disappearing into distant greens punctuated with bright yellow gorse. Laela tried to goad Jacob into wanting to explore, but to no avail, so they traipsed downstairs to the kitchen.

'Hey, love,' called Elliott. 'Jake. Sleep well?' He noticed the pools of greys and purples had subsided a little under Jacob's eyes, but he still carried a weariness in his face and limbs that would take more than one night's sleep to heal.

Lorna was rinsing figs in the kitchen, putting the clean ones onto a linen cloth on the counter to dry. The wind had spun her hair so that it looked like a swirl of gunmetal waves laced through rays of sun that bobbed as she busied herself.

'Fancy a walk on the beach, you two?' she called over her shoulder.

Laela glanced at her father, who stayed, elbows resting on the breakfast table, hands occasionally fluttering across his mouth. He looked like a wavering eye in the midst of a morning storm.

'You ready, Dad?' she asked, noting his bootless feet.

'Mm,' he grunted, then reworked his face into a smile. 'I have a few bits and bobs to do here first; I might catch up with you later. You three have fun!'

'Get your coats then,' Lorna's voice carried from the hallway. 'You'll be blown about – summer's not quite as forgiving in this wind!'

They gathered their things and followed Lorna out of the house and into the bright, breeze-blown morning.

Without the shelter of the house, the wind was strong; it blew and buffeted them around, exposed as they were on the cliff top. They followed the track east until it dipped and suddenly disappeared, and Jacob elbowed Laela, nodding to Lorna's stick and muttered, 'How the fuck is your aunt going to make it down there?'

Laela, shocked by Jacob having spoken, opened her mouth to respond; but before she could, Lorna had gracefully climbed down the track and vanished from sight. At first, there were a few cautious steps from Jacob and Laela as they followed before Lorna re-emerged again, leading them around grassy tips and down the steep descent. The zigzagging path was no more than a foot wide, and riddled with small rocks. For another half an hour, they scampered and wove and jumped down the cliff path, taking care when they stumbled on loose rocks not to follow them as they tumbled over the edge. Lorna never put a foot wrong.

At last, the solid path beneath their shoes gave way to fine, buttermilk-coloured sand. Here the waters did not crash, but instead lapped gently, leaving frothy kisses on the paleness of the beach. Lorna bent down and removed her shoes. Laela and Jacob did the same, and soon they were all walking along the hard, wet sand, enjoying its roughness on the soles of their feet, skipping backwards whenever a wave brought its icy fingers too high, and dodging the scattering crabs left beached by the tide.

They walked away from the water's dark line and sat on a large, flat rock, smoothed over the years by the ocean. Lorna splayed out cheese scones and fresh figs, and soon there was the approving silence of satisfied hunger. Gulls with yellow eyes watched with unreserved keenness for crumbs that could be scavenged later, the bolder ones making hopeful and aggressive swoops.

As the meal tapered off, the picnickers idly contemplated the grey ocean and her white-crested waves. Occasionally, a fish would break the surface, to which the ever-hungry birds would flock in squawking mass.

After the food was gone, Jacob began to fidget. He went off to investigate the bounty of rock pools that lay farther along the shore. Laela lent her back along the smooth rock and allowed her eyes to gently close. Suddenly, she felt a sharp pinch on the burnt skin of her hand. She tried to pull down her sleeve to cover it, but too late.

'It seems we need to discuss a few things,' Lorna said.

With deliberate care, she examined Laela's hand and removed a small glass bottle from inside her coat, its contents disguised under a blue veneer. She pulled a cork stopper from the top with her teeth, and Laela tried to jerk away as her aunt spattered droplets of liquid on the burn. It smarted.

'Wait.'

The pain was almost unbearable, a searing wave cresting over the steady agony she'd had since reaching into the hearth fire; but as Laela looked, the skin knitted together, the red blisters smoothed and paled until no trace of the burn was left. She scrambled back, but Lorna's grip held her.

'How did you... How is that even possible?'

'Healing herbs,' Lorna said, with a grin that didn't quite reach her eyes. 'It's like nothing ever happened.' Then her grip tightened. 'It must have been awful for you, Laela, all those tragedies. And finding out about your mother's death like that... I would have liked to have been able to tell you myself.' She looked Laela in the eye but there was something shifting, artificial beneath her gaze. 'I bet a part of you wishes you'd never remembered.'

Laela watched Jacob throwing pebbles into the waves and wished that he were close enough for her to shout to. Lorna leaned in close until Laela could smell the woodsmoke on her hair. 'That's all your mother wanted for you – a normal life. And you were happy, weren't you?' She studied Laela's face intently.

'I think so.' Laela's wrist was released and she rubbed it, edging away from her aunt. 'But now... Now I have to figure out how to stop the Witch. Only no-one will really tell me what I need to do.'

Lorna nodded. 'Elder Law states that a witch must grow by discovering things for herself. Help must be minimal. I'm sure it's frustrating, given the circumstances...'

'Jacob's dad died.' Laela's voice was hardly a whisper above the sea-rolled pebbles. 'And Sam.' She felt anger flare. 'If they know everything, if they're so powerful, why couldn't they have intervened? Why didn't they do something?'

Lorna gave a bitter laugh. 'It doesn't work that way. A portion of us are reborn to protect the world. The rest aren't *here* in this realm anymore. For them it takes a great amount of magic to sustain a presence here.' She eyed Laela. 'You'll have met one of them... she appears when it's a witch's time to begin a journey or take over a territory.'

Laela nodded, the pieces falling into place. 'The Stranger.'

Hand in pocket, Lorna played with the stopper of the second vial. The hidden vial. The one she would have no choice but to use. 'She granted me responsibility for the coastline and its inland moors. Your mother was given the village where you now live. We each have our appointed land, over which we have power, indeed, the only place we have power.'

The moment was close. No Elliott, and Jacob wasn't near enough to stop her...

'We're the descendants of a sacred line. Our task is to observe, and to protect, where necessary, the balance. We use our knowledge of the world's hidden mechanisms, and pass down wisdom to the new-borns, to ourselves. When we die, our spirit returns to the earth, and we are reborn so that we may continue to perform our duties. And at the end of our earthly service, we are released from these bindings and return to the source of all things.' And sweet, sweet ignorance. Just like Violet would want...

'My dreams,' said Laela. 'I've seen myself, in the village sometimes with others I think – or I feel – I know, but it's before roads and the village of this time, and we're walking across the snow.'

'Some of us may get glimpses back into our past lives. Your dreams are harmless enough. They tend to pass once you become aware of them, of who you are. Perhaps, though, they have served their purpose.' She began to twist the stopper from the glass. If she got her here, now, it could be so quick... It could be over in moments.

'And what about my mum? Is she dead, or a ghost?'

Lorna's chest turned to ice. Inside her pocket, her hand went still. 'Your mother?'

'She's barely said anything but... Wait, I nearly forgot.' Laela fumbled in her coat for the folded paper she'd got from the Ancient Hearth. Gulls circled overhead, their intermittent cries piercing the low murmur of the sea. 'The hearth-tender said to give this to you – yours is the house on the hill – that you'd help.'

Lorna gathered herself. The contents of the second vial were ready to spill out, to do what needed to be done but... *Later*, she thought. She could always do it later.

She pressed the stopper firmly into the neck of the glass with her thumb, and then reached out to take the parchment from her niece's hand.

~ XIII ~

CHAPTER THIRTEEN

And hand in hand, on the edge of the sand,

They danced by the light of the moon.

— Edward Lear, The Owl and the Pussycat

'How's it going then, Tom?'

The sky was sallow-grey, and Elliott had driven through the day's long hours from the old lighthouse to where his van was now parked on the driveway of Tom Whitley. Both he and his vehicle looked worse for wear. 'Penny-Jane phoned and said there's been something up with my pipes?'

Tom Whitley knitted his eyebrows together and sucked the yellow dusk air in through his teeth. 'You not been by the house yet?'

'Thought I'd pick you up first.'

'Ah, you trust my judgement, I see.'

'I trust the best and only plumber in the village when he tells me I got a burst pipe.'

'Flattery won't get you a discount, Elliott.' He chuckled. 'Let me get my things together, I'll follow you.'

'I'll get a pot of tea brewing.'

Tom laughed. 'I wouldn't count on it.'

Elliott swung himself into the driver's seat and felt the miles of road he'd put behind him leech at his bones, and suddenly the journey home seemed longer than a few minutes. He'd rounded the corner of the main street before he heard Tom's engine growl to life and the plumber's van's tyres roll out of the drive.

And then he was on, out of the village centre and nearing the woods that bordered the road that led to home. It felt an age since he had been there. The sun had started to creep down behind the hills, and to his right, Elliott saw its glow flutter auburn on slivers of the woods, and burn the ground at the feet of trees a rusted amber.

He had the window open, the scent of summer grazing his face and teasing his hair. Then, through the window's open jaws came the cry of crows. His eyes followed the sound to the right of the road, where trees met tarmac at the foot of the hill. It was lined with a darkness that was dense and watchful; black-shadow sentinels with bright metal eyes.

Elliott slowed. They seemed to be waiting.

The van juddered to a halt, the ratchet of the handbrake bringing the road through the woods to silence.

Behind the line of crows, the woods went on, stretching up into the hillside; but to the left, where their mirrored counterparts should stand, there was nothing but white mist. White obscured the trunks. All white. Like the clouds had sunk to the ground, and the world was all the wrong way up. Elliott's only reference point was the very tip of the canopy, a thumbnail-strip separating the white of the forest realm from the clouds of the sky above. And then it was gone.

Elliott studied the blank mass. The village, situated as it was in a scoop of land between hills, often found itself cloaked in mist and fog, particularly when autumn had taken hold. But this didn't feel right to him. It behaved differently. It *behaved*.

He shook it off and put his paranoia down to being road-tired. His hand reached for the gear stick, and he allowed the van to move up to second as he switched on his high beams. The mist began to curl outwards from the treeline. It reached out onto the road. It began to seep towards his van. Elliott laughed at his own jolting reaction as the crows took to the sky like sudden splashes of ink thrown into the grey heavens. Then the engine stalled.

He took a deep breath. Steadied.

Elliott knew the woods, and he knew human nature. He knew how people panicked and lost themselves; familiar routes distorted under the lens of fear.

The mist had closed behind him now, like skin healing up over a wound.

Elliott fumbled to restart his engine, telling himself he was only anxious to see home, but there was only a repeated rasp that led once more back to that oppressive silence. He leaned back in the driver's seat, hands smoothing along the steering wheel and listened. Noises from the village filtered around in the mist, contorted and echoed and amplified like kaleidoscopic images. He tried the ignition again.

Nothing.

He heard a rumble of tyres and engine behind him and flashed his lights.

'Hey! Tom!'

The rumble slowed, like thunder falling asleep. Elliott opened the van's door and stepped out onto the road he couldn't see. 'Tom! My van's given up. Too much for one day, I think. Well, for both of us... fancy giving us a ride?' Elliott strained his ears. But there was no response, only, in the distance, a peel of church bells.

'Tom...?' But he couldn't even hear the church bells now. The mist had grown so dense that Elliott was sure that if he let go of the driver's door, he'd lose his van.

'Well.' He reached into the glove compartment and felt for the flashlight. He tried to force this to be casual, a normal event, but fear had struck his vocal cords, he heard it in himself. 'Looks like it's the long way round.' He pushed the van door closed behind him and pocketed the keys. He'd left his hazards on, and their muted orange flash hardly dented the white, but it felt to Elliott like a silent scream, a warning, for him to go back to his van; to not leave his one point of reference and safety in a deformed world of mist and uncertainty.

The woods were cotton-thick and quiet as he stepped off the road and into their silence.

* * *

The fireplace was cold stone and grey open mouth, but the sun burned on the cliff top around the lighthouse, and the cool of the living room offered welcome sanctuary.

'Can we talk now?'

Lorna looked up from her work and plastered a smile on her face. 'Where's Jacob?'

Laela shrugged. 'I think he's upstairs. I sorta lost him after lunch. My dad?' She walked around the table and looked at the herbs strewn across it. Lorna had picked a selection and pressed them into a bunch in her hands, which she was looping around with thin, red cord. At each turn, she paused to pull the thin red line tighter around the bundle.

'He left a note. He's had to head back to the village, something about burst pipes.'

Laela felt a knot in her stomach tighten. She watched as the chaos of colour – purples, reds, greens – were woven into a thick, tightly packed stick.

Her aunt glanced up. 'He'll be OK. The moon's still waxing so the Witch has no power.' She continued, occasionally flicking the length of cord around one extended finger, until only an inch remained to be bound, like a sun-tinged oil slick at the tip of a torch head.

Laela raised an eyebrow, surprised by her aunt's matter-of-fact claim. The cat appeared in the doorway. Lorna gave a slight bow of her head and smile as he trotted off up the stairs. 'Now then,' she said, leaving the red thread and herbs.

'Let's talk.'

* * *

At school, Elliott had learned that Heaven was a cloud-bound kingdom in the sky. And so, as a boy, if the day brought mist, he'd be terrified to leave the house, afraid that he would inadvertently step into the afterlife and Death would snap him up. His mother, somewhat differently minded to the school, had at every opportunity afterward taken him out into the woods and mountains, in all conditions, until he was at ease trekking across barren ridges above the clouds, and in dense forest, or marshlands beneath the stars; navigating the land with a healthy respect for the wilds, and not one bit afraid of death or stumbling into *Heaven* by mistake.

The tarmac's uniform flat gave out to the uneven floor of the woods. Leaf and twig rustled and cracked underneath Elliott's step and provided him with his only orientation. The mist felt dense as he breathed in. *Fog?* He couldn't remember what the difference was.

He'd tried to keep heading west from the road, and hoped that soon he'd either hit the boundary to the house or something else he'd recognise that would lead him home. He crept on through the trees, pressing his palms into rough bark to steady himself, and made sure with each step that the ground underneath was solid enough to take his weight. He asked himself if perhaps his slow movement was because he wanted his footsteps to be inaudible, undetectable. But to what?

A cracking from the woods made him freeze. Elliott held his breath, waited, his ears pricked and head turned with blind eyes in the direction of the noise. The woods were silent, too... listening. Bracken and undergrowth snapped; the sound cut Elliott on his back like a bite of static.

'Hello?' he called. He noted how the mist clamped those tentative syllables into its white. More creaks and cracks struck out from where he supposed the trees stood. Elliott felt the pounding of his heart in his ears, its drumbeat growing louder and more erratic, and the shape of his breath following into disturbed disorder.

He told himself not to panic. Panic leads to rash decisions, and that'll get a person lost. He slowed his breathing and checked his phone for signal. He wondered whether Tom Whitley would still be there by the time he got back to the house, and then allowed himself to grumble about how tedious it would be if he missed him. He almost smiled to himself in those woods, in the mist, at the bizarreness of it all.

He checked again, but his phone's screen showed no bars. He hoped Tom would wait.

And then, as his eyes slid from the phone to the ground, he saw something slither.

Follow me home, it said.

Creaks of splintered trees echoed like laughter around the wood, and a wild thing yipped in pain, and Elliott knew then the words he had heard were as real as the sounds in the woods and that *something* was here and it was calling to him.

Follow me, it said.
Follow me.
And he followed.

* * *

Laela followed her aunt to the foot of the stairs.

'You asked me about portals.'

Lorna ushered Laela behind her, so that they stood on the bottom stair, facing down into the living room. Laela recalled standing next to Jacob at the foot of his staircase, daring each other to jump from higher and higher steps, until Jacob had broken his collar bone.

'In our tradition,' her aunt continued, handing Laela her walking stick, 'we call them doorways.'

Laela watched as her aunt spread her hands slowly through the empty space before them. Her fingers seemed to catch on something in the air, and suddenly, the image of the living room was split, like a curtain had opened in the world.

'You can find the threads that make up the world's fabric and drag open the seams.'

The opening was a doorway, a portal, and it brought shadows, cold stone and the smell of damp. Laela felt her stomach lurch as she realised that she was now simultaneously at the foot of one staircase and the top of another.

'That's a fixed doorway,' her aunt said, her breath sounding slightly more laboured. 'It's easier, or rather energetically *cheaper* for me to have a permanent, hidden doorway than to have to go through the process of making a new one every time. This one's getting a bit tatty – I'll have to reseal the edges soon or it'll collapse.'

Lorna prised the walking stick from Laela's fingers and stepped through the portal, ducking her head under its arched roof. She beckoned for Laela to follow, which she did, albeit with hesitance. Once through, the doorway started to seal behind them, its edges disintegrating, crumbling in on themselves, the particles reforming as old stone in darkness.

'Where are we?' asked Laela. The closed portal took with it the light. In the perfect darkness, waves crashed and shuddered somewhere above or around, and the scent of the sea stung her nostrils in the salt-hardened air. Laela heard the scuff of a match. Its light threw itself against the sides of the stairs, and

Laela saw roughly hewn rock around her. 'Are we underneath the lighthouse?'

Her aunt walked on. 'We are very far from anywhere you know at all. Watch your head.' The steps turned to uneven floor. The roof of the passageway cut down sharply, forcing Laela to crouch to pass. Her aunt's voice had lowered, and Laela heard whispered incantations. As she rose out of the passageway, shadows shifted and dispersed. A light source bled out into the space. Laela stared at it: a saucer of hollowed blue glass hung, suspended by woven silver threads. A dazzling white orb burned, cradled in its recesses, and to Laela it looked as though someone had plucked a star from the night sky and held it captive there, cupped in deep blue.

'There's an Elder lodging perched on a rock, in the middle of an ageless sea. We're in the depths of the island on which it stands. Underneath its secrets.'

The starlight caught every corner. It looked as though dripped crimson stone had made the cave; solid fingers hung like pendants, almost mirror-cast reflections of the floor-grown towers that stretched and rose to meet them. The outer walls rose upward into shadow, ending in a place that Laela could not see, and neither starlight nor firelight touched its limits. In the core of the room, half-swallowed by a ring of stalagmites, was a bright hearth in which a steady fire burned.

'It's beautiful!' Laela breathed.

Her aunt smiled and turned to a large wooden cabinet. She leant her staff against the cabinet's side and removed two mugs from the shelves and began plucking herbs from drawers and jars and filling a copper kettle with water. 'I thought it was incredible, the first time I saw it.' She hung the kettle over the fire and gestured to the back wall, which Laela's curiosity hadn't had a chance to take in. Under a mouth of rock there was a crescent of red sand, and in its arms, a pool, serene and flawless. 'The lagoon leads out to the ocean, should you be able to hold your breath so long as to swim it.' She threw a handful of pebbles into the water, the stones falling with a soft *plonk, ploosh ploosh*. Electric blue sparked.

'Magic!' Laela said.

'Not quite,' her aunt laughed. 'Bioluminescence.'

Laela scooped a handful of sand and poured it into the water. An underwater flow glittered downward to where it hit the lagoon floor, making it seem as though it were made of starlight.

'They're plankton. Living creatures. Remarkable, isn't it?'

Laela nodded.

'But we didn't come here for that,' said Lorna, the words uttered gently but the accompanying smile not hanging quite right about the cheeks, making Laela acutely aware of their isolation and the insurmountable distance from anywhere familiar. She felt the butterflies in her stomach stir and she realised that while she didn't trust her aunt, she might be closer to getting answers now than she'd ever been.

They left the lagoon, Lorna motioning to where cushions perched on woven rugs beside the hearth. As Laela sat, Lorna poured hot water from the kettle into the mugs and handed her one.

'Thanks,' she said. 'You were going to tell me about the Witch. Who is she?'

'Show me the letter first.'

Laela bit her lip. 'You *will* tell me afterwards,' she said, reaching into her pockets to finger its bent ears.

'Yes, yes. Come on then, let's have a look...' Lorna's eyes flitted over the pocket that Laela's hand fumbled in. 'Give it to me.'

Laela felt her lips dry, and her tongue stick to the roof of her mouth. She drew the letter from her pocket. 'I'm not su–'

Lorna snatched the paper from her fingers, her hand trembling as she tore the envelope and ripped the edges and creased deep folds into the letter with a fearful grip.

'Is this it?' Lorna was shrugged inside a skin of mania.

Laela nodded.

'This is all she gave you? Nothing more?' Lorna's voice had turned high and strangled. She turned the paper over and over in desperate hands. Spittle flew from her mouth. Laela shrank back. 'Nothing?' she said again, in that cracked voice.

'No – that's all that came. I haven't touched it... I haven't opened it, I swear.'

'Damn!' Lorna put her head in her hands and let loose a muffled howl. Her body, curled over itself, remained eerily still for some moments and then, as though jerked upright by some compelling force, she stood, eyes wild and jaw clenched.

She picked up Laela's mug and dashed it against the wall of the cavern, the contents hissing as they spattered out.

'What... what *was* that?' Laela dragged her eyes from the smouldering shards of the mug and looked up at her aunt who now stood, defeated and weary beside the fire.

When Lorna spoke, her lips trembled into a smile. 'I lose everyone.' She eased herself once more to the floor, looking suddenly pained. 'Your mother, my husband. I lose the ones I love. I get left behind. And when they return, they are not the same. There is something... unfinished about them.' She looked at Laela at last. 'Your mother's final request was to make you forget, make your father forget. And I thought perhaps, even now, if I bound your magic, or removed it, the Witch wouldn't be able to find you, and you could be happy and I... I'd have fulfilled the one thing my sister asked of me.' She glanced sadly at the piece of paper in her hand. 'But she doesn't want that now. She wants *tradition*.'

Laela put her hand on Lorna's arm. 'What does it say?'

'Take a look for yourself.'

She reached for the paper, gently easing it from Lorna's grip.

Lorna, she needs you. Help her remember. Help her know who she is.

'Fifteen years and that's all I get.' She began dabbing the dark crescents under her eyes with her sleeve. 'And *I know* that message would've exhausted her magic but...' Lorna turned to Laela, eyes blazing. 'Wait. You said something. On the beach. You said, *she's barely said anything.*'

Laela felt the heat rise in her face. 'I've seen her,' she blurted. 'My mum – she appears sometimes. Though she doesn't say much. I, I thought you knew?'

Lorna shook her head. 'So that's what it was,' she said, now staring into the fire as though the chaos of the flames might help her order her thoughts. 'I felt her. But I thought it had to be you, or some sort of echo. I thought I was losing my mind.' She shook her head again, the fragility gone. 'So, she's *back.*'

'Only for a few minutes...' Laela traced the words on the paper, wondering if her mother's handwriting was the same as it had been before her death. 'She never has time to say much.'

'Where? Where is she? When does she appear?' Every word surged out before being reigned in, as though each time Lorna opened her mouth her heart could spill onto the floor.

'There's a ruin on the outskirts of the village.'

'I know it.'

'Every third hour, a few minutes before the church bells ring out, there's another set of bells. I can't see them, but it sounds like they come from the ruins, like an echo of the bells that used to be there. My mum, she appears in the few moments between.'

'Between the past and the present.'

'Yeah, it's not all the time though, it's only some days,' she said, and felt an echo of hurt. 'Lorna, was that... were you going to poison me?'

'No!' She spread her hands, ready to justify, to fight, and then crumpled. 'My sister, that promise, it was all I had left of her. I'd never do anything to hurt you. But I'd tear this world down if that's what she asked me to do.' She raised her eyes to Laela's. 'I'd make you forget if she asked me to.'

Laela sat quietly mulling it all over. It was almost unthinkable, that she could have come so close to being ignorant of it all once more. To losing her mother again. but Lorna was all she had. She studied the lines of her face, more deeply etched now than she'd seen in the memories of the hearth fire.

'Will you help me?'

Lorna heaved in a breath. 'I'll help.'

* * *

Elliott heard the skulls of dead creatures crunch under his boots. He was stumbling forward, hands outstretched; he feared what could be behind rather than what lay ahead of him, and so he lurched wildly from step to step, trying to outrun his imagination. His fear pushed him onward through the trees, blind step and ragged breath guiding him.

The mist was closing in on him now, scratching at his face and lungs and he was running, not feeling the impact of branch and leaf and thorn as he fumbled through their tangle. On and on he ran, convinced that should he stop he'd be a dead man, that Death would find him in the trees and mist, and that up ahead, impossibly, he'd find shelter, he'd find home.

And then, a light. It burned through the mist with a jaundice-yellow glow. Elliott latched on to its beam and hurried, helter-skelter for the light. And then the toe of his boot dug into something hard and unbending, and the heels of his hands found the burning graze of tarmac.

Tom Whitley's laughter rumbled down at him.

'Hey, slow down there. You can't run in this weather – visibility's a goddamn joke.' His outstretched hand reached out from the mist. 'You alright?'

Elliott let Tom haul him to his feet and rubbed the bridge of his nose.

'Uhuh. Yeah.'

He looked back and saw the mist hanging thick and low beneath the treetops. He'd circled back around to the road. Tom Whitley's van was parked with full beams blazing next to his own abandoned van.

'Just need some sleep, that's all.'

His mind felt an unexpected horror curl over and nest into his thoughts.

'Mind if we take your van, Tom? My engine needs a rest.'

'So do you, it seems. I'll give you a lift back, but let's save taking a look at that pipe 'til tomorrow, huh?'

Elliott gave a grim nod. He felt his friend looking sideways at him as he slammed the passenger door closed behind him.

* * *

'Tell me. Does she appear around the same time as the deaths?'

'I hadn't thought about it, I guess.'

'Jacob's dad... that was recent, wasn't it? How many days ago?'

'Nearly a week? Six days ago, I think.'

Her aunt nodded and gave a rough grunt. 'The new moon.' She spoke almost to herself. 'There's a grace period around the new moon. Three days which lend themselves to a gathering of energy. It should be a resting time, a healing time. But it's also when the land is at its darkest, unwatched. It's during this time that things can slip through the gaps. And it would appear that during these three days is when both your mother and the Witch can gather enough energy to manifest themselves physically, The Witch to kill, and your mother to warn you.'

Laela felt a slick river of ice in her stomach. 'Are you saying they're linked?'

'Your magic has gone uncontrolled for years. It's seeped into the land. The Witch has used it to regain her power. Your mother, I don't know... Perhaps her return is triggered by a combination of your magic and the Witch's. But they've both used you to get a foot back in this realm.' She paused, allowing Laela to absorb the information before she spoke again.

'Laela, the Witch has a connection to you.'

Heart pounding, Laela could barely stammer out the words, 'So, let's *un*-connect me.' She felt sick. She wanted it out.

'It's not that simple. If we tried to do that now, the Witch would overpower you; there's a chance she'd take over your body and you'd be nothing more than a vessel, trapped, and then the Witch would be free to walk the world and do whatever she likes.' Her brow knitted and she idly flicked at a piece of ash that had fluttered onto her sleeve. 'No. You need to learn to control your magic. It'll stop her from taking any more. From getting stronger.'

Chaotic bursts of colour swam around Laela's head. She couldn't focus. 'No,' she said. 'This isn't happening. This isn't real.' Numbness crept up her cheeks. The thought of the Witch – the thing that had killed Jacob's dad and Sam – was *inside* her, connected to her somehow, was too much to bear.

'It's not happening.'

'Laela, I'm sorry. This can't be easy.'

'No. I'm going home. None of this is real. It's fine. It's fine.' She stumbled from the fire to the passageway, her shoulders and elbows catching glances of rough stone. 'Let me out! I need to find Jacob. Let me out!' She was scrabbling at the stone, trying to open the doorway that led back to the lighthouse and its living room. She could hear her own voice shouting. 'Let me out!'

'Hey, Laela, look at me, look at me.'

Lorna clasped Laela's hands and tried to hold her from throwing herself against the impassive stone. 'You're going to be alright. It's all going to be alright. Listen. I promise.' She locked eyes with Laela. 'We can do this. *You* can do this. It won't be easy, but I know you can.'

They sank down onto the rock, Lorna cradling her niece's head in her arms.

Eventually Laela spoke, her voice quiet, 'My mum. You said she can only do so much, that it uses her magic. Do you think she'd spend more time with me if she could?'

'Oh, Laela,' said Lorna, softening. 'You were everything to your mum. She'd move the universe to spend more time with you.'

***

Inside, the confines of the van shrank. Elliott watched in the wing-mirror as the sight of his van disappeared from view. Tom cleared his throat.

'You, uh, you sure you're okay, Elliott? That was a terrible business with Don...'

Elliot grunted. He watched the white as they rolled past almost inscrutable shifts. Shadows? Shapes? *Blood on bone and mist,* he thought. *Why did he think that?*

'...kind of you to take in young Jacob, 'specially after all that happened with Laela. Mand said if there's anything we can do, just give us a call. You know where we are.'

Blood on bone and mist.

'Yeah, sure. Hey, Tom? Could you let me out here? I think I could use the walk – been cooped up in one of these all day.'

'Are you sure? I gotta drive past yours anyway.'

Blood on mist.

'Yeah. Drop me here. My legs need the stretch.'

It's watching me.

The door had clunked open before the wheels stopped turning.

'Hey! Elliott! Your flashlight!'

It's watching me.
It's watching me.

~ XIV ~

CHAPTER FOURTEEN

Not everybody wants to be looked at.

Everybody wants to be seen.

— Amanda Palmer, The Art of Asking

'Your mother was six months pregnant with you before she learned the truth about what was happening.' Her aunt spread newspaper clippings over the ground.

Man's body found in woods after fatal overdose.

'By then, the Witch had grown strong.'

Local police officer found hanging.

'Your mother, she hadn't seen it, that it was all messed up and bound to you, we thought it was a coincidence. Hoped it was.'

Vicar found in rectory with bleach burns around mouth.

'But every new moon there was a death – or a suicide, supposedly.'

Teacher killed boy, eight, before taking his own life.

'She feeds off their deaths. Uses their energy to regain her strength.'

Camping hell for family found murdered. Father found with throat slit, prime suspect.

'And if she could add fear to the mix too, well. It only led to more victims ready for her to take possession of them. Your mother knew she had to stop her.'

Run of suicides turns village into horror town.

Teenagers found with fatal knife wounds in stomach.

Children's terror as mother slashes own throat.

More dead following 'gas leak' in local school.

'We came up with a plan.'

I heard the Tree screaming your name.

'Violet – your mother – died re-binding the Witch to that tree. She didn't tell me what she was going to do. We'd discussed it before, came up with a way of doing it. But she promised she'd tell me before she did anything.'

Let me tell you a secret.

'But when I got there, you mum was already so weak... She made me promise to keep it from Elliott – to hide the violence of her death from him, from you, so you two would be happy. So you could have a normal life. I, I made him forget.'

This one will die for me.

'Laela?'

Laela's face tingled. Her hands buzzed at the end of arms unfelt. The world shrank to two pinpricks of colour in front of her, Lorna's voice and the crackling of the wood on the fire distant and stretched. She tried to speak, and her senses slid away.

* * *

Lorna lowered her niece's head to a cushion and dragged a blanket over her body. She stroked the hair from Laela's face, watching the shadows flit and stutter over her pale skin. Beyond the steady swell of her rib cage, Laela's feet were tangled around the book, the open pages still showing splashes of red on the sallow blues of faces and limbs. Lorna stretched over Laela's side and slid the book toward her.

The firelight picked out headlines and clippings that Lorna begged her eyes not to be compelled to study, for the words shaped moments in her mind – moments of death, of violence, that she wished she had not seen. She looked from their grim lettering to Laela and saw the remnants of Violet in her cheeks, and in the dark caves that held her eyes. She stroked the mirrored shadows of half crescents beneath her sister's child's heavy lids.

Clawed feet clacked on stone behind her. She turned to face the cat, whose presence seemed to augment the sadness in her heart, as though by him bearing witness, the tragedy came more sharply into focus.

'She's so young, I forgot, she's just a child.' The cat nuzzled into her and she let her face fall into his golden fur. But it lasted only a moment, and then he pulled away. Lorna sighed. She knew, yet still, she asked, 'What, Noon, what is it?'

Her heart sank as she heard the reply.

'Watch her. I'll go alone.'

* * *

When Laela woke, she found soft, warm fur curled up in the hollow of her stomach, sending snuffled snores out under her armpit. Their breath gently pressed rib and fur together, and Laela felt the ridge of the cat's spine rise and fall with her own.

The fire warmed her back, coaxing her body to allow itself to sink once more into cosy darkness. But her mind began to tick over. It started to fumble with words and colours and shapes and, though she couldn't make sense of them consciously, the mechanisms of her body twigged and her breathing drew sharp and fast, her muscles switched on and carved her limbs tense and alert, electric shocks of adrenaline skipping through her.

The cat shifted, stretched out long against her stomach and exposed his soft neck. Laela fingered the silky patch behind his ears. She looked at his face and found herself smiling at his contentment - and then her eyes skipped to where the box lay closed on the stone floor. All at once, the images she'd pored over with Lorna came flooding into her mind, and with it came scents of hot blood, wet and slippery and metallic, fading ashes and salt and smoke and death and broken bones and chaos.

She felt the cat twitch and then the gentle pressure of its paw on her arm. She looked into his pale blue eyes. He blinked slowly, and then sauntered to a patch of deerskin by the fire, leaving the path between Laela and the box open, clear.

Laela propped herself up on an elbow, noting the slight bruised feeling, and reached her fingertips of the other hand out. She hesitated, eyeing the spilled contents of the mug Lorna had given her. What if she didn't? What if she was just on a holiday at her aunt's, and in a month's time she went back to school having spent a summer playing with her friends? But the cavern loomed reality around her. There was no shred of normality here.

Laela studied the images. She met the gaze of corpse and bereaved and did not blink at the blood, nor at the implements of murder. She read article and summary, taking in details and speculations and the annotated red scribbles, which spun like crimson spider webs across the pages. She lifted another edge of paper.

To my darling Laela, it read.

She felt sick.

Should my plan not be a success, I pass this knowledge on to you...

I hope you will never have to read these words.

Laela looked at the cat, who was licking himself in front of the fire. He turned for a moment, then devoted himself to his grooming. Laela bunched up her legs and pressed a finger into the page so that she could trace the words.

Our family journeyed to the village, almost as soon as the Witch had been discovered. They had tracked her down, her movements across the continents marked with blood. The villagers were manic with grief. Almost everyone had felt the pain of loss by the time we came. She was stronger then. And so full. Her witch's belly grew and swelled until she was fat with the lives of those she had slaughtered.

After they killed her, our forbears encased the spirit of that wicked thing in the twisted skeleton of a tree. They drained the power from it and bound it to themselves so that it could not return without their knowledge. They bought the land that surrounded the Tree, ensuring that their kind would keep watch over its evil; that our lineage was to guard and to protect. Needless to say, when one thing is bound to another, the connection goes both ways...

By the time I was six months pregnant with you, the same number had died under the dark moon. Your magic must have been so power-ful... Your father and I debated what to do, but he feared for our safety too much to want me to put my life at risk, and yours. Aunt Lorna and I talked about it, too, but I suppose she was too protective of me to approve. They both love me so much.

I decided that I would sneak out and confront her, but the weeks dragged by, and the moon lost her light, and soon again, the Witch struck, and I did nothing.

And then one night I heard the Tree whisper your name.

And I know I must act, now.

I don't know what will happen tonight, but I hope I will bring you peace and that this page will be burned by your aunt, along with the rest of this book, its use having been removed. But if I haven't, know that I love you. And I did as much as anyone would do.

Laela re-read the pages until her eyes blurred.

I hope you will never have to read these words.

I hope I will bring you peace.

** * **

The wind whipped through Jacob's hair and teased his balance, as though testing his intentions, and his footing. The cigarette between his lips trembled with every gust. He'd wandered around the lighthouse, searching for Laela, Elliott, Lorna, anyone, and then, when the loneliness got too much, headed for the cliff path. The blue sea of the morning had swirled concrete grey and now crashed against the rocks, leaping at their faces with sprayed fingers of rabid foam.

He remembered the last trip he'd made with his parents to the beach. His dad had barked at him that Jacob was too old for building sandcastles, and his mother had lain there, smoking cigarette after cigarette, letting their orange tips starve in the sand. He tried to be sad about his dad, but he wasn't.

When he sliced through the layers of numb, all he could feel was relief. But when he let himself think about Sam, about what they had and what could have been... If he'd just said something. Been open. *Done* something. Maybe they could have been happy, and if not, then at least, maybe, he wouldn't be dead.

Jacob watched a teardrop plummet to meet the spray and realised he was crying. He couldn't remember the last time he'd cried in daylight. And then it all came out. And it wouldn't stop. And he wanted nothing more than a way out, to not feel this way, to make it end.

* * *

Laela wiped her cheeks and sniffed. Her mother's words had stopped. She flicked through the rest of the box, but the remainder of the pages were newspaper clippings and home-printed photographs of the crime scenes, obsessively cut out and stored by Lorna. She folded the letter until she could slip it into her pocket and replaced the rest of the contents of the box.

The cat winced as Laela tossed the box carelessly away from her, the sound echoing around the cavern, threatening to dislodge the pendants of time-dripped stone. Clippings and photographs spilled out as it struck the floor, the firelight catching the disturbed faces of the murdered. She rested her head onto her hands, feeling the muscles in her neck stretch and ease. The cat walked over and rubbed his head on the pointed bone of her elbow, and she let her fingers coil the fur of his neck.

'Laela!'

She started. A doorway appeared, and in its centre, Lorna crouched low, urging Laela to follow her. Salted wind gusted in and threw the upturned contents of the box around the cavern like confetti from a giant's hand.

'Hurry!'

Through the doorway, Laela saw that the sky had brewed great, grey storm clouds, menacing and edged with claws of slate. Her feet slid onto the grass as cold pellets of rain began to rap down on her forehead and strike her cheekbones. There seemed then to be a mountain range between her and the warmth of the fireside.

The cold pellets of rain stung and pricked her sluggish senses into waking. They were on the cliff behind the lighthouse. Jacob's back was to the water, but he was looking down, craning over his shoulder as he shuffled clumsily backwards. Lorna closed the doorway and grabbed her arm as she ran forward. 'He's been up here for hours. He won't come down. I can't talk to him, Laela. You have to do something, you understand?'

Laela felt the blood rush through her ears. She didn't understand. She could barely see.

'Jake?' When he didn't respond, she wondered if the wind had snatched away her words. 'Jacob? What are you doing? Come inside, I–'

'I don't know what to do, Lae.' Rain plastered his fringe into strips of black across his crumpled brow. His voice came out in juddered sobs. 'I miss them. I miss them so much, and I don't know what to do.'

Laela could see his breath bucking his ribs in irregular spasms. She inched closer.

'Why don't you come inside, Jake?'

'Everyone's left me, Lae. And where were you? I needed you, and you weren't there. I looked for you.'

'I...' She looked back at Lorna. 'I've been in contact with my mum, Jake. There's something going on, look Jacob...' Laela's throat closed as she watched her friend take another step backwards. She could feel the slick grass under her own feet and wondered if she were there to watch her friend die.

'What? This again? Fuck! You don't have to *lie*, Laela. Just say it. Nobody wants me anymore.'

'No, it's true, wait, Jake, I can show you, I... You've got me, Jacob. I love you. Trust me.'

'No. No...' As he shook his head, Laela saw his wild eyes under his fringe had turned blank and were unfocused. 'I've had enough. I can't take this anymore.' He turned to face the water. The rocks.

'Lorna, do something!' But Laela saw the same, blank stare that had fixed in Jacob's eyes mirrored in Lorna's.

'*Lorna!*'

Laela was shrieking now, but her aunt seemed lost in her own head, frozen, the last of her strength spent on clinging on to her wooden staff.

Laela felt the sounds scrape at her throat. Rain clung to the air. 'Jake, believe me, turn around, I can prove it all...'

'I don't care anymore, Laela. I've had it, I...'

Laela summoned everything she had. She didn't know what she was doing, but she felt the energy course through her, felt it snapping at her tendons and skin and gathering, painful ice building in the nerve endings of her fingertips. And then she released. She dragged her fingers outward. Her eyes were closed, but she could feel the doorway there in front of her.

Her voice hoarse, she managed only a throaty whisper. 'Jacob...'

He turned, and Laela saw the shock bolt through him as he realised there was now a path in front of him leading straight into a fire-lit cavern. She watched words form on his lips, but if he did manage any sound, the wind and rain whipped it out to sea.

'How is...?'

Laela watched as the world's gears moved in slow motion. A foot skidded on the grass. An arm flailed up as the rest of Jacob's body followed gravity, then a flash of skin and cloth, as she grabbed onto his wrist and pulled him onto the grass. He remained still beside her and Laela lay, heart pounding into the ground, fingering the dent in the mud where Jacob had slipped. She edged past it, the wet grass like a leathery tongue on her knees and peered over into the churning foam beneath.

'Laela!'

She realised how tired she was. Exhausted. Her body felt a dead weight, and she could imagine herself, passively, easily, rolling into the white foam and troubled rocks. Into rest.

'Laela! Come on!' Her aunt filled the doorway. She beckoned Laela back into the silent stone.

I can't, she tried to say. *Help me; I have nothing left.*

'Laela,' she hissed. '*Laela, close the doorway.*'

Laela summoned the last of her strength – strength she didn't have. She crawled to her aunt, and sealed the churning elements behind them.

~ XV ~

CHAPTER FIFTEEN

No true knowledge is ever reached without pain.

— Naomi Alderman, Disobedience

Laela felt hazy, as though she were looking at the world from the bottom of a pond. The cavern's heat felt oppressive, hostile, or maybe that was her own skin, she couldn't tell. She had removed herself from the heat of the fire, dragging her limbs slowly as though they were made of stone, and now sat by the lagoon, her bare toes curling into the wet sand.

She watched Lorna guide Jacob to the hearth-side and wrap him in dry furs and blankets. He had a stare that went well past the ground at which it was directed.

'He'll be alright,' Lorna said, crouching next to her and pressing a ceramic mug filled with amber liquid into Laela's hand. 'Drink this, it'll help.'

Laela shook her head. 'I can't, I'm too tired–'

155

'Drink it. I promise it's nothing strange.'

Lorna tipped the lip of the mug toward Laela's mouth, and, after a sip, Laela upended the rest. Heat, painful and vital spread through her limbs. The world shot back into focus. The drained feeling still sucked at her bones, but it no longer felt paralysing.

'It's the doorway. It takes energy to sustain one. Lots of it. You'll recover soon.'

Lorna returned to Jacob and gave him the same, and slowly, his eyes seemed to resurface.

Laela shifted over to where her friend sat. 'Smoke?' she asked, offering a battered pack of cigarettes. Jacob shook his head.

'Jake, I'm so sorry. I shouldn't have disappeared. I should have stayed with you, I didn't think.'

'I should have believed you, Lae.' He laughed, looking around at the cavern. 'I just thought you were, I dunno, making it all up... because of your mum.'

'I didn't believe it either, at first.'

As Laela said it, she realised that, until Jacob had seen it, she had allowed a part of herself to believe that it wasn't real. Now, though, there was no escaping the truth.

Lorna cleared her throat. 'Laela, Jake... We have to go somewhere, make a journey.' She spoke softly, but her voice was edged with a hardness that Laela understood stemmed from urgency.

Laela tried not to flinch at her aunt's hand on her shoulder. 'Where?' she managed, feeling a longing for her bedroom in the village and the quiet darkness found under her duvet. Jacob stayed silent, observing.

'Na'gathamuir. It's where we'll find the book.'

'The book?'

'Memories can be lost, altered, when we transition from one life to the next. The Elders have kept a written record of all our shared knowledge since we came to this realm. To keep it safe, its guarded elsewhere, in the hands of one of the Earth's greatest allies and fiercest protectors. We need to find out what our ancestors knew about the Witch.'

Lorna rose and crossed to where stone jutted from the cavern's side, and a cacophony of wooden shelves and drawers were wedged into the recesses. 'We need to take a gift,' she said, carefully sliding something out of a narrow, velvet-lined drawer. She held a small, spherical object up to the light, its colours fluttering and shifting. 'An offering worthy of knowledge,' she said as she wrapped it in the velvet once more and slipped it into her pocket.

'Laela?' Jacob whispered, his hand reaching for hers. She couldn't remember when he'd sounded so scared. 'What's happening?'

Laela didn't know where to begin. She was afraid it would be too much. 'There's a witch,' she said. 'A bad one. She's been killing people in the village and making it look like suicide.'

'My dad?'

'Yeah,' she said. She couldn't meet his eye.

'And Sam?'

Laela nodded, mute with guilt.

'And you are...?'

Lorna cut in. 'We're witches, Jacob. Guardians.' She stood, checking her pocket for the small sphere. 'It's a lot to take in, I know. It'll take some time, and I'm afraid we don't have time. Right now, we need information. Jacob, if you're well enough, we need to travel. Or... you can stay here if you'd prefer.'

Laela watched her friend nod slowly. 'I have to take some time to think,' he said. 'It's okay.' He squeezed Laela's hand, but she noticed he didn't look at her. Couldn't. 'I won't do anything; I'll be alright... by myself. Promise I won't do anything. I just want some time alone.'

'Sure thing, Jacob.' Lorna motioned to the cat. '*Afternoon* here will lead you back to the lighthouse.'

Jacob wrapped the blankets tighter around his shoulders and followed Afternoon, who by now was a bright ball of blue with golden streaks – the colours of a perfect summer's day. Laela watched them leave and wished silently that she could take away some of Jacob's pain.

'Laela.' Her aunt's voice cut into her thoughts. 'We need to go.'

* * *

Lorna had cut a doorway through to Na'gathamuir. From there, she said, the journey must be on foot. 'Sometimes sacrifice is the most trusted magic we have.'

The world they stepped into was drenched in light. It wasn't sunshine, Laela realised; but rather, the ground and sky and all in between emanated a vivid, pale light that at once burnt and froze her skin and eyes. She tried to shelter them with her hands but found that she, too, glowed with the same radiance, and her own touch burned.

'It isn't far. We'll be through to the path soon... if they'll have us.'

They were walking, although to where and following what route, Laela did not know. Lorna seemed familiar, although not comfortable with the journey; even with her stick her pace was hobbled, stilted. Heaviness still lingered and weighed Laela's limbs. It made progress slow and dulled her brain so that when her aunt began to speak, it took some time before Laela realised that she was under interrogation.

'What you did, Laela - it was impossible.'

'What do you mean?' The light was blinding her eyes, and aside from Lorna, Laela felt something probing the intricacies of her mind.

'Since the Witch was first bound, there have been restrictions on our magic. Each is assigned a territory to protect. A witch's power can only be used at full strength on her own land; anywhere else and she is weaker, limited.'

Laela could feel a presence growing stronger: assessing, analysing. It buzzed under her skin.

Her aunt continued, 'Casting a doorway is big magic, Laela. Even an experienced witch shouldn't be capable of something like that on another's territory.'

'I, I don't know how it happened, I...' Laela felt her aunt scrutinising her. All around suddenly seemed hostile, a void into which Laela was walking deeper and deeper with someone she didn't really know, couldn't trust.

'You're much stronger than we thought, Laela.' Her aunt's tone eased. 'That could be good.'

The light seemed to dim, and the travellers slowed their pace. Lorna tensed, then relaxed as the darkness intensified around them. Hazy wisps of shadow became contours of ground, and then black consumed everything but the path. 'We made it,' she said, exhaling with relief. 'Take off your shoes.'

The light was just enough that Laela could see to undo her laces; as she did so, she noticed that the sense of being furtively investigated had stopped, and the shadows were quiet.

When their feet were bare and their shoes hung from their fingertips, the path lit, its surface effulgent with the same light as they had encountered at the start of their journey but soft, constrained. They started to walk.

'Ow!' Where the sole of Laela's foot had pressed into the path came an electric searing sensation.

Lorna gave a grim nod but carried on, her gait slow and rigid, and when Laela looked, the soles of her aunt's feet were bleeding.

'Keep the question you need the answer to in your heart. What you want more than anything.' She walked on, not waiting for Laela.

Laela bent to examine the path. It was the colour of blood. It was blood. Congealed. Ice-hardened. *Sacrifice.*

She steeled herself and continued. Each step was the same agonizing, breath-taking pain that made Laela want to cry out, but she thought of her mother and how much she yearned to learn more of who she was. She focused on the path ahead. On what she wanted.

Before them, hundreds of metres ahead, hung a sphere of water: an elephantine raindrop whose waters trembled where they met the path in dense and murky smoke.

Laela's feet were raw. The skin felt as though it had ripped away, and with every step, a layer was lost to the path. She gritted her teeth. She held herself upright. The pain sent spasms of agony through her heart and snatched her breath.

You don't have to go on, little one. You could turn back.

She heard the voice the same way that she had known that she was being watched – below hearing, too subtle for ordinary senses, it was in her head and in her bones.

'I'll continue,' she said aloud. 'I want to gain understanding.'

The air sucked in a breath.

Your predecessors walked for lifetimes across tundra and plain to gain great wisdom, and while there is no snow nor ice nor rock here, I must create something for you to endure, something against which you must prove yourself worthy. So...

You walk their collective pain.

'I will continue,' she repeated, setting her jaw against the pain. She thought of Jacob, of his parents, of Sam, her mother, of Mattie and her son, of the village saturated in violence. And she walked on. She dug into her reserves, finding strength she didn't know she had. She fought the pain in her feet and the pain in her chest and the burning of her legs as though it were alive and she could kill it with her will.

But just as she thought that the end was attainable, the ground seemed to stretch and the path, prolonged, seemed too much to bear.

I can give you what you want.
I can make it stop, make you forget.
If you turn back,
I'll let you live unburdened.
You could be free.
I'll let you forget.

Laela wavered, the pain in her feet burning up into her legs. She forced herself to take a step, her whole body shaking with the effort. The hurt blazed through every cell, encasing her chest in swathes of scalding agony.

'I want the truth!' she yelled, no longer able to see the path ahead but staggering blindly onward, knowing that if she could just keep walking, she'd learn what happened to her mother, she could know her a little more. she could find out who *she* really was.

'I want answers.' And she knew then that she'd walk her lifespan if it meant she'd gain what she sought.

As soon as that thought had landed in her heart, rain-scent cooled her nostrils, and the light brush of smoke graced her cheeks. She opened her eyes and saw that the raindrop now rose above her, clear and shimmering. Alone, she stepped through the water and smoke and into its quiet hush.

'Well walked, traveller.' It was a deep voice, clear and resonant, lyrical. A throne of water, limpid and still held the speaker's face in the shadows, but their body, though mostly obscured, looked human-shaped. 'I'm afraid I can't apologise for your journey here. This is a place of safekeeping, secrets and truths; the path cannot be a straightforward one.'

'It was you... you were the one *analysing* me.'

Laughter came, pure and darkly delighted. 'Indeed, little witch, it was. You must expect to have your soul pried and tested if you go in search of truth.'

Laela was too tired and too scared to be riled. 'Where's my aunt?' she said.

Again, the throaty chuckle resounded throughout the raindrop. 'She is safe. As all things here are.'

Laela opened her mouth to speak but realised that she did not know what to say. She was exhausted. She looked down at her toes. The ground, now black rock and cool, eased their discomfort.

'Come,' the voice said. 'Let your feet be soothed by the waters.'

The speaker stepped down from the shadows and Laela stared. They were as though the rock and waters and smoke of the world had come alive. Their face was cut sharp, as though cheekbone and jaw had split from flint and, baking under a red-flamed sun, had sweated a sheen of skin. They – for Laela could not tell if her host was male or female – took her hand and guided her to where the pillar of water tumbled down to make a quietly murmuring stream. The shadows followed, smouldering around the crown of the smooth-carved skull like black flames.

The stream reminded her of the pebble-strewn brook in the shades of the birch grove at home but its waters, she saw, were purer than any she had seen before.

'Put your feet in.'

They sat on the edge, and Laela lowered her wounded, bloody feet into the biting flow. The current caught the cuts and tears and colours of her pain, carrying the crimson swirls downstream. Laela watched until the water ran clear once more, then peered at her companion sidelong and, she hoped, unnoticed.

Their flint-skinned body was swathed in an ocean swell that broke and trembled with their breath. Waves swept across the surface and left ever-changing patterns with retreat. Laela felt the brush of sea-spray lips on her ear,

Flint for skin, supple and black,
Maelstrom eyes, to find the heart of the world,
Hair of smoke and shadow and a winter's haar,
That is what the guardian of truth is made of.

Their eyes met Laela's curiosity with their own. One glacial finger touched her cheek. 'And you would be the witch who can change the world.'

'I want to help my mother.'

The creature smiled. 'And your village? And the rest of them?'

'I–'

'And yourself?' Their eyes flickered.

Laela thought. 'I need to know my history. The book will tell me.'

'The book? You think that who you are can be found in a book? In a history?' Their smile twisted wry.

'I hadn't really thought...'

Maelstrom eyes, dragging her in. 'You will need to know who you are, little witch, before this can be over. Before this can truly begin.' The creature lowered their legs into the stream until they stood, waist deep in the water. At least, Laela supposed that they stood, for where their body was submerged their form seemed to meld with the water and disappear into the transparent flow.

'Have you brought a gift?'

The sphere, Lorna still had it. 'I- my aunt has it.'

'That is *her* gift.' The corner of their mouth twitched. 'It seems that her heart yearned for some other knowledge than this. You must pay your own price.' The wreathes of smoke and shadow closed around the flint-held whirlpools seemed suddenly menacing.

'I don't have anything. I...'

The creature revealed sharp, river-cut teeth. 'Then you shall have to owe me, little witch. No matter. I am sure I will find something that you can give.'

Once more the fierce eyes turned upon her, and then the creature bled its form into the stream and vanished.

* * *

Laela sat on the bank, staring into the crystalline waters.

And yourself? You will need to know who you are.

I'm just a half-orphaned, half-gay, witch kid with no clue what I'm doing and death all around...

'Laela! Oh, thank god.'

Laela turned. Her aunt had appeared behind her, as had, in the centre of the raindrop's obsidian floor, a large tome. Laela got up. The heavy-headed feeling from earlier had passed, and now she felt instead every atom inside her vibrating, alert, bright.

Lorna looked pale, worn. She gestured to the book, laying one hand on its face. 'We must read it here – no-one can take the book from this place, save its guardian.'

Laela walked over, wincing as the soles of her feet caught on the stone. The book was old, its cover worn. She picked it up. Aunt and niece sat side by side, the large tome's great weight resting across both their laps. Laela fingered the rough leather binding. She pushed her skin into the cuts and curves, the indentations allowing her to merge with the book for their brief patterns.

'This is Elder lore,' said her aunt, prying the cover open. It released a musk scent of rusk and smoke. 'It embodies all that we have learned since our coming to the earthly realm. This is our safeguard against forgetting. In this book, all our knowledge is held.'

Laela pored over ink-scratched impressions of Elder Origin and herbal magic, physika and realm histories.

'We haven't time to study,' her aunt said gently. 'If you like, you can return here afterwards, but in the meantime, we have to deal with the matter at hand. I promise to help you, and I shall try to teach you everything of this that I can remember.' Lorna was earnest, genuine. Laela wondered what knowledge it was that her aunt had gained from the guardian.

'A chapter was written on the Witch alone. Your mother and I added to it, but the details of her history and the magic used in her binding have slipped from memory. If we can see what magic the Elders used, perhaps we can figure out a way to re-bind her or learn enough to separate your magic from hers...' Lorna stopped. Frantically her fingers rifled through the book.

'It can't be... It's gone!' All that remained were ragged page stubs where the chapter should have been. 'But no-one can take anything out of Na'gathamuir. How did this happen?' Lorna pushed the book to the floor and walked away, pressing her fingertips into her temples.

Laela flicked through the remainder of the book. She turned further pages over until the words ran out and only swirls of ink covered the page. And then they started to clear. Glyphs and runes began to dance in her head, swallowing her logic and knowledge and tapping into something deep within her. The letters begin to define themselves before her, the strange new language becoming all too familiar.

Lorna stepped closer, and Laela could feel her aunt scrutinising her face.

'Can you read it?'

'Yes, I, some of it...'

She takes the weak.

'What's it say?'

They bring her their violence, and she spins it in rivers of red.

'I, I can't say...'

You mustn't trust even those that are closest to you, for they too can fall.

'Sometimes we leave messages for ourselves, across time, but often they get lost.'

She kills at the new moon...

'This must be something you wrote to yourself. You must have been one of the original Elders who bound the Witch.'

...but as her power grows, she can possess, even in light...

'Laela, if you can read this, perhaps we could find a way to defeat the Witch.'

...the village is never safe. Daylight is no barrier. Nor is the full moon. She is no longer confined to the lunar darkness.

Laela's heart hammered through her chest. 'My dad! We have to go!'

'Laela? What's it say?'

'He's not safe! We need to leave, now!'

The creature of flint and truth emerged from the ground.

'You have your truth, little witch?'

'Please. I need to go. Now – my father's in danger.'

'I shall send you back. But I have thought of a gift that you can give me.' They stepped closer until ice and damp snatched at her skin once more and drew out shivering goosebumps.

'Anything. Tell me.'

Their mouth contorted as they stood, holding Laela in their stark and immutable power.

'You will return here, to me, knowing who you are. And we shall discuss the terms.'

Laela tried to squirm away, but the Guardian of the Truth's presence left her intentions inescapable, and her mind could only focus on her urgency to get back to her father.

'Okay,' she managed. 'I will. Now please, let me–'

* * *

'Hey, I'm fine, sweetie, what's up? You okay?'

The receiver kept slipping in her palm.

'Lae? You sound out of breath, hon, are you alright? Laela?'

'Yeah, Dad, I'm fine. Sorry, I just missed you, that's all.'

'Alright, well, hey, you take it easy now. I've got to stay here for bit, sort things out. You tell your Aunty Lorna I'll be back there to pick you up next Sunday, how's that?'

* * *

Lorna eased the receiver out of her niece's hand and left its weight stretching the ringlets of plastic-coated wire down the wall. She put her arms around Laela's shoulders and guided her to sit at the corner of the kitchen table.

The sound of the weather droned through the worry: the perpetual determination of rain set against rock. Lorna studied Laela's face, noting the bulge of clenched jaw and the way she seemed to stare through the table's grain, unblinking.

Every muscle remained fastened in place, and Lorna had to repeat herself to make sure her voice wasn't only in her head. '...it doesn't have to be hot chocolate; it could be tea, or something herbal, perhaps? I might even have a fizzy something in the pantry...'

She trailed off as she saw her niece's mouth start to work over inclinations of words, but all she could hear was the rush of the north wind and the rain as it plummeted from wind-borne clouds and buried itself into ground and brick.

'What was that, sweetheart?' Lorna gripped the underside of her chair and pressed her toenails into the flagstones. She didn't want this. Her sister's child stared across the table at her.

'Why didn't you help?'

'What?'

'If you knew the Witch was killing people, why didn't you help my mum?'

Lorna felt her body stiffen but tried to keep her voice soft. 'I, I did what I could love.'

'You didn't, she's dead! If you knew, why didn't you do something?'

Lorna could see her niece's fear, too bitter and cutting as it was, had turned into hard-edges and anger and tore through her young body like wildfire. She tried again, gently. 'I knew I couldn't do anything, Laela, not really. I was *there*,' she said quietly. 'Elliott called me in a mad panic; I knew right away what had happened. Your mum hadn't told me what she was going to do, or when. We'd discussed *possibilities*... I came as quickly as I could... but it was too late. She... died before I could heal her.' Lorna sighed, some of the burden slipping away as she confessed. 'I did what she'd asked me to do, and left Elliott only after I was sure the Forget-Me had worked its way through his mind and you were safe. But I couldn't come back, not after that. It was too painful, to be that close and having to watch my sister as she died. Seeing Elliott, seeing you, for a long time, it was all too much. So, I kept away.'

Lorna could see Laela taking it all in, piecing together the final moments of her mother's life, the details of her death and the aftermath that had left their family torn.

'But now the Witch is back,' croaked Laela.

'I wasn't sure if the power you held had been taken away in the binding. It was one of the things we'd discussed, your loss of magic – that it might be a possible outcome – and I thought, I suppose, I hoped, in a way, that it had been destroyed, along with the Witch. But we never thought... We didn't know this could be an outcome.'

They listened to the rain's soft drone and stared into the table. Laela's tremulous voice broke the hush. 'Why does it have to be me?'

Their eyes met, and Lorna wished she wasn't having this conversation. She cleared her throat, but her voice was barely above a whisper. 'You're the only one who has the right to perform magic there. No-one else would have the power that it would take to defeat the Witch.'

'But the Witch has power there! And I don't know anything! I can't do any magic! I don't know how to control what I have. Why can't someone else?'

She's a kid.

Lorna dug the heels of her palms into her temples. 'All I can do is train you, like your mother asked, and considering you can perform magic here, that should be pretty easy.' She tried to sound offhand, bright. 'You're already pretty strong.' But Laela's face was still grey; the fear-coloured face of an exhausted child who'd already lost so much. 'Laela. Look at me. You can do this. You have to do this.'

~ XVI ~

CHAPTER SIXTEEN

As she woke, a tumble of memories splashed their colours and sounds through Laela's head. Her limbs felt heavy, but not in the magic-depleted kind of way she'd come to recognise, but a sad lethargy which dragged at bones and weakened muscle. Each of the trio had gone to bed wrapped in quietness, with the insistence from Lorna that training should start in the morning. Laela and Jacob, too mentally sapped to do anything but concede, shuffled through the motions of breakfast, and followed Lorna into the cavern.

Jacob sat facing the back wall trailing his finger in the dark pool and watching blue sparks chase his skin. His silence remained intact; his feelings buried deep, but not bitterly. At least, thought Laela, he was happy to be close to the others.

'Right,' said Lorna, plonking herself down beside the fire, and leaving Laela standing in the middle of the cavern. 'Let's start with doorways, since I know you can already do that.'

Laela cleared her throat and tried to look confident. The least she could do for Jacob and his family was to make it look like she knew what she was doing. 'Sure.'

She closed her eyes and tried to remember what she had done the day before on the cliff, how it had felt to create a doorway, but everything in her head went white, and all that came to mind were imprints of colour in the light. She thought she could hear Jacob breathing, and her aunt shifting her weight on the cushion.

Come on, she thought. *Come on.*

She spread her fingers in front of her face and tried to imagine a doorway appearing through the world. Tried to want it. Tried to mean it.

Nothing happened.

She opened her eyes. Lorna's arms were folded, and Laela thought her face looked as though it had been gripped by fishhooks on either side of her mouth and yanked outward when her aunt attempted to smile. Laela's shoulders slumped. 'I don't know what I'm doing,' she admitted.

Lorna nodded and unfolded her arms. She called over her shoulder, 'Jacob, stay here, we'll be back in a while.' She raised an eyebrow at Noon. 'The cat will help you if you should need anything. Just ask.'

Jacob stuck a thumb upwards and continued drawing blue stars in the water.

* * *

'Time can be spun and wrung out, but never snapped. And there's more than one way to access a spatial location. Doorways can be fixed, hidden, created or spontaneous.'

Lorna parted a doorway in front of them and beckoned Laela to follow into the dappled sunlight. The pockmarked earth looked familiar.

'Hey, this is the hill in the woods behind our house!'

'I thought you could use a simpler starting point than being on someone else's territory.' Lorna smiled at her. 'Oftentimes it's easy to do something without thinking, in the midst of a moment that needs it. But you need to learn to have control, too, to perform magic at will. So, let's try again. Sit.'

'What about the Witch? Didn't past me or whatever say that she had power during the entire lunar cycle? Isn't this dangerous?'

'She's kept really quiet about it, if she is strong enough to act outside of the new moon. And if you can't control your magic, it's a guaranteed win for her - so, sit.'

The earth had grown warm under the sun's touch. Laela looked out over the valley of trees which, she knew, sloped gently downward to the road to home. To the left, she glimpsed the church spire and a smattering of gravestones, but for the most part, the village's houses and inhabitants were sheltered by the boughs and creaking limbs of the intervening woods.

'Forget all about doorways for now. Close your eyes.'

Laela let her eyes close. She could feel the warmth of the sun on the tops of her knees and her shinbones. Birdsong and scattered laughter broke past the susurrus of the day, but the scene felt surreal, as though she were still back in the lighthouse and merely dreaming of home.

'Clear your mind. Let your focus come onto your breath.'

Laela tried to clear her head, but thoughts of the Witch and Sam and her mum and Jake kept swirling around.

'You need your mind to be completely focused, Laela. If not, the path to the doorway will be muddied. Take a moment. *Breathe.*'

Laela breathed. She concentrated on the sound it made as the air rushed in and out through her nostrils, and after a while, she noticed it slow. She noted her mind was wandering less and her muscles seemed relaxed.

'Now, find the world around you, the stuff that holds it together. It criss-crosses threads everywhere, like a lattice of spider-webs. Pick a small point in that web and focus on it.'

Laela felt out in front of her, trying to pick out what Lorna was talking about. Something winged buzzed past, taking with it Laela's concentration. She brought her mind back to task. Then, as though layered underneath the air and sounds of the day, something emerged. At first, it was subtle. And then all of a sudden, it was everywhere, everything. A tightly woven mesh of thin-strand cobwebs slunk around reality. It held the shapes of hills, trees, sound, vibrations, Lorna. Everything.

'That's good.' Laela heard the smile in Lorna's voice. 'Now, choose a spot to focus on.'

Laela selected a spot in front of her at eye level and fixed her attention on it.

'Good. Now split your focus. Keep it trained on the patch in front of you, and think of a particular point in your garden. Make the image clear. Let it settle behind the fabric in front of you. Use your hands. Pick it open. Like you're drawing curtains apart, or making a hole in a cardigan. As the hole gets bigger, you'll start to see the garden. Don't stop until the doorway is solid.'

Laela's fingertips snagged on something barely tangible. She pressed into its edges, feeling them thicken and solidify under her touch, and she pulled. Through the gap in the threads, she saw the oak tree. She felt her hands tremble with the effort, but she kept going until the whole trunk could be seen. Her whole body was buzzing. She could hear her father whistling a tune somewhere nearby and strained her head to see if she could see him. Then pain shot through her arms and her aunt was screaming at her to *Get back!*

Laela opened her eyes; a churning mass of grey and black streamed from her hands with brutal anguish. She felt it rip and tear at her body, its force sucking her toward it.

'Close it!'

Laela tried to bring the threads back together, but it was too strong. She could hear her aunt screaming. She could *feel* the world, the whole planet, vibrating and buzzing and *burning*. Every creature and every stone cried out to her, grappling to grasp her as they drowned in the flux.

She squeezed her eyes tightly shut and scrabbled at the drifting threads with her hands, pressing seams inward and dragging them over the churning rift. And then a searing pain in her hands, and the tumult subsided.

Her mind, for an instant, hung its focus in the hidden workings of the world, then lurched to the ground with her, back into her bones, the exhaustion and the pain. Over the agony, Laela could hear birdsong again. She opened her eyes. Lorna sat on the grass, ashen. Laela tried to raise her head, but its weight was too much.

'Wh- what happened?' Laela gasped. Her hands felt as though they were on fire, but she couldn't bring them up to her face to see.

Her aunt was tight-lipped, and her speech clipped, as though she was looking for a way that her anger could not to rush out with her words. 'That was the gap between the fabrics of the world. The unseen that makes the seen. It's everywhere and, for the most part, harmless. But when you're trying to open up a doorway, you have to be certain. There can be no doubt. No fear. No distraction.' She crawled over the ground and squatted next to Laela to examine her hands. She was not gentle. 'What we're doing here is dangerous, Laela. It's not some trick you can show your friends or use to bunk off school. This is the very frame-work of the universe that you're screwing with. There's no room for mistakes.' Lorna tutted and dropped Laela's hands. 'I can't do anything with this. We'll have to go back. You can't train like this. Useless.'

Laela saw her aunt's frustration and felt her own nerves prickle in retaliation. She fought the heavy feeling in her body and dragged herself up until she was sitting. The effort sent her slumping forward over her legs. She looked down and saw swirls of grey burned into the flesh of her palm. The pain was raw and maddeningly urgent.

'It'll heal, in time. But it's a temporal scar, they don't dis-appear, and the pain will linger.'

Laela thought she detected satisfaction.

She rolled her head until she could watch the clouds scud their shade over the spire and treetops. She thought of Sam, and Jacob's dad, and the dead woman at the carnival, and of all the people she knew in the village who would lose their lives if she did nothing. There was so much riding on this. *Fuck.* 'Again.'

Her aunt snorted. 'Laela, you need to heal. You can't do anything like this, you're –'

'I can do it,' Laela growled. It took everything she had, staggering to her feet, but she made it. 'Again,' she said.

They kept on until dusk brought thin, chilling air that made the bare skin of Laela's forearms rise in bumps like the plucked flesh of a bird. Hunger gnawed at her stomach, and the exhaustion rose like waves over her, but she kept on. Blinking lights dotted the scene below, and she wondered if an evening like this had once preceded the Witch's attack on villagers; them making plans for the next day before retiring to bed, only to find death sometime in the night, cruelly and violently. She imagined the mist, hung heavy and low like cloud around the ankles of the village, and the curiosity that it would first inspire, changing to terror as the months wore on, as the link between the mist and death became obvious.

She'd held a doorway – coin-sized, but solid – by the time day drew to a close. But the success felt hollow, and she trusted neither her magic nor her ability to wield it.

* * *

The north wind shook the glass of the lantern room, and Laela tightened her grip on her shins, hugging herself further into her cocoon of skin and darkness. She felt tired. Her efforts from the previous days dragged at her bones, making her lungs pull at each heavy breath, and the thought of doing anything but lie there impossible. The room shuddered as another gust swept itself over the conical, throwing sea-spat droplets that held their origin miles across oceans against the glass. Laela watched them bulge into globules which, once their weight became too much, dribbled wearily.

Another heavy splotch had formed and begun to trickle when Laela heard footsteps. Jacob's reflection brought a pallid yellow to the glass and its raindrops in front of her. She wanted to turn around and face her friend but the guilt was too much.

My family is the reason your dad is dead, the reason you'll never hold the boy you loved in secret...

She stayed on her side, eyes on raindrops.

Behind her, Jacob cleared his throat. 'Um, Laela?'

She held her breath and then eked it out slowly past her pounding heart, hoping that it would look as though she were sleeping. She felt his weight sink softly onto the bed and a hand reach out and hover above her arm before being retracted.

'Hey, Lae? I just wanted to say, I don't blame you.'

She heard him suck in a breath and bit her lip to keep from crying.

'My dad, he wasn't well for a long time. You know that. Neither of them has been, really. And you've helped me through all of that. It's not your fault.'

She stayed silent, not knowing what to say.

Jacob's voice wavered. 'I'm sorry for what I did.'

'Jake! You don't have to apologise.' Laela turned over and grabbed him, burying her face into his neck. 'I'm so sorry all of this is happening.'

'It's not your fault,' he said again.

She saw the seriousness in his face, the honesty. That face and its inability to conceal anything from her made him her most trusted friend.

'This is mad,' he began, 'I can barely believe it either, and I have no idea how I can help you, but I will. I'll follow you to the ends of the world if I have to. The Witch can't get away with this.'

Emotions and words surfaced and dragged others down. In the end, Laela nodded and said, 'Thank you,' and hugged him again.

'Good. Now let's work out how we're going to get this witch, *witch*.' Sharp jabs dug into her rib cage, and soon they had fallen from the bed and were fighting to tickle the other amidst breath-snatching laughter. It went on until Jacob begged for her to stop.

'Okay, okay,' she giggled, rolling off him. She rested her head against the mattress, and the smile slipped from her face. 'I'm so tired, Jake.' She knew her eyes were hungry when she looked at him. He crouched next to her, and she huddled under his arm, enjoying the feeling of warmth and the smell of his t-shirt.

'I know.'

'And I don't know what I'm doing at all.'

He gave her shoulder a squeeze. 'Most people don't, Lae. But you have me. And I'll always help you. Any way I can.'

~ XVII ~

CHAPTER SEVENTEEN

> *It was not so much a modification of the darkness, as a sigh of relief, a slight relaxing of tension, so that one felt, rather than saw, that the night had suddenly lost a shade of its density... ah! yes; there! between these two shoulders of the hills she is bleeding to death.*
>
> — Hope Mirrlees, Lud-in-the-Mist

They reverted to the basics. Lorna was reluctant to broach lessons on spatial magic or dimension-shifting after the rift incident, so instead focused on teaching Laela herbal lore and cures and incantations. Laela made poultices to heal her hand and, whilst the damage didn't disappear, the scar flattened and embedded itself smoothly into her palm, leaving only a spiral of swirled plum on its surface.

In moments like those, Laela caught herself feeling pride. And then she'd see her aunt in the corner of her eye tightening her lips, and she'd remember how far she had left to go, and how insignificant and ineffectual a thing a poultice was against the rising surge of evil. She fought hard in those moments not to hate herself.

The foundation of a witch's magic, Lorna said, *was a centre of calm.*

'No matter what the circumstances, while everything else is beyond your control, within you there is always, *always*, a core of silence. You must remember that. You are not the disturbance on the surface – events and emotions are no more than wind on the face of the ocean, there to fuel the waves – but the depths are calm. It is your choice to follow each wave and get swept up, or remind yourself that you are more than that.' She took Laela's repaired hand in hers. 'Should you lose focus, if you allow yourself to be overcome, *this* is just the beginning of the consequences.'

When she wasn't training with Lorna, Laela took to spending quiet hours in the lantern room gazing at the surface of the ocean, listening to the circus of gulls and wind and waves mingling with the sound of her breath. Jacob, as his anger settled to sad acceptance, started to join Laela in these meditations, lying with his back to the faded carpet, staring steadily into the sky. Neither said a word, yet the shared stillness under the glass smoothed the remnants of the rift.

Once Lorna was satisfied that Laela had mastered the basics, she began talking about physics again. She showed her how the trees in the garden were bound within snippets of portals, enveloping them in warmer, more stable climates than the lighthouse on its cliff could offer. Magic like that, said Lorna, came with significant risk, and so they started small, Laela creating invisible bubbles around small objects. Laela knew, reminded by the damage on her palm, that even the smallest magics she made were grave things, that each time a rift or a cut was made, the universe had to compensate; consequences were born.

While the after-effects of performing magic no longer weighed as heavily in her body, these new challenges took their toll and she found she could do no more than force herself to eat before falling asleep afterwards. As her magic progressed, it became a tool for her to wield, a thing she could control. Once she'd proved herself, Laela lit fires using magic and spun shields around them, preventing them from spreading. This was delicate magic. She found that if she closed them in too tight, they'd suffocate, too loose and the shield was prone to letting small flames leap through. But if she held them just right, she could create small orbs of fire around the garden that burned gently in the darkness.

'And soon will you teach me how to kill the Witch?'

At this Lorna smiled sadly. 'My darling, I don't know how to do that. You've been chosen for a task that none of us has managed. By the time this is over, you'll have shown us how it was to be done.'

'Surely there's spells I can cast? Magic to kill or maim or,' Laela threw a frustrated gesture at the orbs, 'what, do I set her on fire? Why can't you teach me how to kill her?'

'Would you want to? Could you? The things I teach you are the foundations. You must decide where you take it from there, and your magic will grow as your heart wishes it to. The Elders bound her, and your mother tried to kill her; neither has brought her violence to an end. It's in your hands now. I can only lead you so far.'

* * *

When darkness had eaten into the last half of the moon, Lorna said that Laela was ready to try doorways again. They left the lighthouse garden and its herbs, Jacob and the cat behind, Lorna making a doorway once more through to the woods behind Laela's house.

'Make a containment around the grove.'

'How big?' she asked.

Lorna smiled, a peaked eyebrow the only sign she had spotted Laela's apprehension. 'Up to the edge of those trees and,' she looked around, and pointed further into the shade of the grove, twenty or so paces from Laela, 'end it before the rocks on the other side of the stream. Give us some leeway.' She stooped, brushing moisture from a rock before sitting down next to the water.

Laela gritted her teeth. The birch grove was silent, cool. Laela sat on a thick, wide tree root, trying not to remember the feeling of shock from the night with the Stranger. She looked up, watching the canopy sway past pale yellow sunlight and brought her focus back to her task.

She had come to think of containment charms as the opposite of doorways. Both relied on an understanding of the world's fabric, but while making a doorway created a tear in its seams, the skill of creating a containment charm lay in snipping gossamers from spatial strands and plastering them over the existing structure, forming a thick, impenetrable web. It took time.

And energy. And an area as large as this worried her, but she persisted.

A couple of times, she wavered, losing hold of the fine threads, and she had to peel them from where they'd tangled themselves amongst the solid structure she'd already made.

Like fucking Clingfilm, she thought, then remembered the Witch and stopped laughing.

Her arms ached, and every quick, light beat of her heart resounded through her bones making the fine mesh tremble. By the time she'd finished, fatigue sucked at her muscles. It felt as though it had taken an age, although she knew it must have lasted only a handful of minutes.

When she turned to the rock where her aunt had sat, she was gone. Laela looked, listened, but couldn't hear footsteps, nor could she see any sign of Lorna through the trees. She closed her eyes and reached out with all her senses, feeling for a shadow or an echo of a closing doorway. Nothing. And then, something vibrated, *no*, sung by her right ear. She thought she felt a breath on her cheek and spun to look but saw only the birch grove, empty and quiet.

Her aunt's voice grazed her face. 'When we walk through the world, we need to be able to hide ourselves in its fabric,' she murmured. 'Sometimes we must pass unnoticed through dark places, lands we might be considered unwelcome. Old women can do this without struggle. They wrap themselves in strands of shadows, cloaking themselves in reality's threads to walk untroubled. Young ones must earn this right. Work at it. It is the only magic you should be able to do anywhere, regardless of territorial boundaries.'

She appeared, gradually, as if shrugging off a shawl, by the straight silvery trunk of a birch. 'Your turn.'

'How do I...?'

'Figure it out.'

'But–'

'You have the tools. It's all the same. Do it.'

Part of Laela wanted to argue, wanted to rage at Lorna to just bloody well *tell* her. But another part was already thinking. She found the world's fabric and teased it out until there were loose threads drifting softly around her, like strands of cobwebs blown by a gentle current. And then instead of spreading them out to form a hidden bubble, she wrapped one, then another, and another around her fingers, hands, cheeks, shoulders, feet, until her whole body was covered in the tiny, delicate fibres.

'Good.'

The praise didn't touch the satisfaction Laela already felt.

'Now try to maintain that while moving.'

'Can you see me?' Laela studied her aunt's face, but while a smile came to her lips, it was directed in Laela's general direction only, fixed on a point beyond her.

'No. Try moving.'

Laela began to slide one foot in front of her, but only got part-way before the delicate fibres snagged. She saw the stick in her aunt's hand, too late, and received a smack to her foot.

'Again.'

She didn't argue. She could do this. Laela allowed the fingers on her right hand to uncurl and flex. She felt the cobwebs strain slightly against her skin but, by shifting her hand and letting the pressure tease out the length of the strands, found she could raise her arm. She allowed it to unfold, stretching her fingertips out to the side, her elbow straightening, and the muscles in her rib cage tensing in support of the motion.

It felt utterly unreal, as though myriad webs of pure electricity hummed over her skin, its sensation all at once charged and soothing. She could feel every living thing connected, abiding in an infinite sea of energy, and she knew that there was nothing else but this, only this; everything existed within *this...*

Laela felt the strands snap seconds before the stick struck her fingertips.

'Again.'

'Wait!'

She'd tumbled from the rabbit hole, from the comfort of eternal calm and the jolt was too much. If she could, she'd float in that sensation forever. The idea of instead returning to it, yet remaining separate, seemed perverse. Overwhelming.

'It takes courage,' her aunt said. 'Now, again.'

Laela closed her eyes. She felt her body, bound up in cob-webbed strands of the universe, the fabric around her swaying as if in some invisible ocean. This time, she did not pull, did not strain to stretch them to give her movement - but nor did she abandon herself to the feeling. This time, she let the strands breathe; sensed them sensing her intention, and how they opened up, loosened in front of her to make space for a limb, her torso, her face.

Her foot touched the coldness of the stream, and she felt the fibrous web snap around her as she flinched. She opened her eyes but Lorna was well behind her, the stick at her side, watching her with amusement, and satisfaction.

'It'll get easier with time. You'll be able to do it without thought. Without effort. *Again.*'

A few more attempts and Laela found that if she kept a slow, steady pace, she could move within the flow of the undercurrent and go unnoticed by Lorna, even when she was within inches.

'Right,' Lorna's eyes looked squinched, angled. 'Let's try this out for real.'

Tiredness had crept up, but the excitement was still fresh enough to override it. 'Sure.'

'Good. There's something I need. Information I need to check.' Laela noticed her aunt's body had tensed, her movements jittery. 'I need ash from your hearth. Make a doorway through to your kitchen and cloak yourself.' She checked her watch. 'Your father should be home now; it's a good opportunity to test your skills.'

'But... wouldn't it mess my dad up if he saw me? 'Cause of the Forget-Me?'

Laela heard a shadow of a growl in Lorna's response. 'Then don't get caught.'

* * *

Oh, if trees could lick their lips! She couldn't see it, but she could sense it, there, tickling at the fronds of the earth, humming. And she couldn't wait, *couldn't wait* to eat it all up.

Eat.
It.
All.
Up.

* * *

The house was quiet. All its creaks and groans were reserved for night-time, Laela knew; but still, the silence unsettled her. The kitchen floor held muddy boot prints, too wet to be anything but fresh, their toes leading to the living room. Laela followed them, taking care to slip through the gaps in the world's woven seams and not break the threads.

Wood croaked against a nail upstairs, its low, rubbed murmur telling her that someone was in her bedroom. She prickled and felt the fibrous shawl stretch taut around her body but immediately found her breathing, slowed it deliberately, and, safely hidden, crept to the fireplace. The grey stone slabs had been swept, but a small dune of ash skulked in the farthest corner.

Laela opened the pouch that Lorna had given her and scooped the ash inside, feeling the powder soften and collapse under her fingertips. She tucked the pouch into her pocket and turned to the kitchen.

Metal and wood grunted again. Laela froze. Lorna had said she had meant her to test her cloaking ability. Surely she should go find whoever was upstairs – her father presumably – and see if she could remain hidden? The pull was too strong.

She dusted the ash from her hands and went upstairs, avoiding the ones that would creak despite her cover. The landing was dark as if light realised that it, too would break the silence if it intruded. The muddy boot prints confirmed Laela's suspicion that the noise had come from her bedroom. She tightened the shrouds of the world around her and looked in, just her upper body sliding past the door frame at first.

Her father stood, hunched over something held in his hand, back to the door. Every few breaths, his back would shudder, and Laela realised that he was crying. She dared another step closer. Her father didn't move, nor did he seem to have heard her, and so she inched forward another few paces. She could now see his face, all caved in and anguished, but not what he held. A slip of yellowed paper was on the bed, and as Laela bent to reach it, she saw her bedside drawer was open. In his hands was the photo Laela had quietly and furtively stolen as a child – a picture of her mother.

She dragged her eyes away. Their grief was shared, or it had been. Now it was a splintered thing, coated in lies and deceit and rank with secrets. She ran. She felt the threads snapping as she reached the bottom step, and heard her father's voice calling out, a half-threat in the tone. Laela bolted out the kitchen door and back to the birch grove where Lorna was waiting.

'What is it? What happened? Did you get the stuff?'

'Yeah, yes. My dad saw me. We need to go.' She tried to find the edges of fabric but fumbled and tangled, and Lorna pinched her, hard and urgent.

'Focus. Laela. *Focus.*'

Laela blotted out the sound of the kitchen door opening, her father coming after them, and somehow her fingers caught on something. The doorway was there.

Lorna grabbed her and pulled her through, and once more, they were in the cavern under the rock.

* * *

Her head spun. She felt wretched.

'Did you get it?'

Laela handed over the small bag of ash and picked herself off the floor. 'I'm sorry, I tried, but he – I got –' But Lorna was already distracted, eyes sliding from Laela to the pouch and her hands fumbling with the drawstring, her jaw clenching and unclenching as she looked inside. Her dismissal was hurried.

'That's great, Laela. You did great. Let's leave it there for today.'

* * *

Laela climbed the stairs to the lantern room, allowing the ache in her calves to walk off the image of her father. She felt exhausted, as though every cell in her body had been burned out, but despite her tiredness, she couldn't resist performing her new skill for Jacob. She hid herself, tiptoeing invisibly to where he lay reading.

'Ooooh,' she moaned and prodded him in the ribs.

'What the-?'

She laughed and shed the layer that had kept her hidden. 'Surprise!'

Jacob fell sideways off the bed, landing with a loud thump and a groan. She flopped onto the covers, dangling an arm down to poke him. 'So it works, then.'

'Well, if you mean, did I see, hear or feel you coming in any way, then no I did not, and yes, it worked. Scared me half to death,' he muttered, slumping back onto the rug. 'Productive day, then?'

'Mmm,' she said, and tried to not think about anything at all.

* * *

Lorna made herself wait through the long stretch of afternoon, a seemingly endless dinnertime, until she'd sent the children to bed. Only then did she make her way to the Elder Lands.

'I know I said I wouldn't do this anymore,' she muttered.

The hearth-tender kept her bland, silent stare.

'Yeah? Well, screw you. You don't know anything.'

Lorna poured out a heap of ash into her palm and threw it into the fire, waiting for the memories to take hold.

* * *

Laela listened to Jacob's soft snores spin around the corners of the lantern room. Her eyes were fixed on the clouds as they went racing against the star-speckled sky, but her mind wandered still farther from her bed. Remote places in her history beckoned. She took the edge of her thumb across the scarred skin of her palm, feeling the healing bundles of cells tug under her touch.

Jacob shifted under his duvet, murmuring sleepily as Midnight curled his body further around himself, gentle snuffled purrs escaping as he breathed at the foot of Jacob's bed.

Laela thought of home. Seeing her dad had only intensified her sense of longing for the familiar, and she wondered what he would be doing now, if he were asleep, or whether he'd be sat at the kitchen window carving shapes from wood. He'd made her a hare once, its ears stuck up to the sky and its muscles knife-smoothed and tense as though it were ready to sprint through autumn air. Jacob had snatched it and fractured its left ear, leaving it lopsided and jagged, but her father had just smiled and made two more, one for each of them.

She sighed, and then made a pact with herself. The days of training had been long, tiring, but her magic felt more under her control than it ever had.

If I can make a doorway, I'll go, just for a little bit.
If I can't, it won't matter, and I'll go back to bed.

The moonlight turned the lantern room's glass to grey steel, skipping over Laela's furtive glances as she slipped from the room. She tiptoed down the stairs and into the quiet of the living room, listening for her aunt's footsteps, or the sound of Jacob creeping downstairs, but nothing stirred.

Laela cleared her mind and let the image of the garden's oak tree sharpen. She watched the details grow, following the lines in the bark as they formed thick ridges that travelled up the trunk and spread into the branches and leaves. She felt the fingers of her damaged hand snag first on the rift's seam and allowed them to catch and pull at the sharpness until the doorway began to peel outward. She smelt the garden's scent of summertime and felt night's currents on her face. As she felt the doorway settle, she opened her eyes. The tall oak smiled down at her as she stepped through.

Just five minutes.

Light spilt out over the grass from the kitchen window. Remembering the lesson with ease, Laela took only a moment to hide. She wrapped a patch of night air around her shoulders, cloaking herself in a swathe of its fabric.

We can walk through this world unnoticed, if we choose…

Her own light buried in the layers of the night-coat, Laela approached the window. A crack let the sound of laughter tumble out, and Laela smiled as she heard her father's deep chuckling muffle into a chipped mug as his companion recited a story.

Laela moved around, leaning lightly on the frame of the window, and saw the broad-shouldered back of Penny-Jane shuddering with a fresh bout of chortling. She stayed, crouched under the windowsill, watching her father for a while, noting the grey in his hair and the extra crease that seemed to fold into his face as he laughed.

Penny-Jane said something which made Laela's father look up at the window and move across the room toward it. Laela held still. As he reached his hand up to unhook the metal arm from the window frame, he paused. Father and daughter stayed motionless, two frozen figures separated by inches of air and a thin sheet of glass, and though his eyes stared past her,

Laela got the feeling that her father could *sense* her. She floated a hand up to trace the outline of his shirt through the glass. She stood on tiptoe, wanting to reach out and break through all the barriers, tangible and intangible, to yell and tell him she loved him and that witches were real, that Mum had been murdered, that Aunt Lorna had drugged him to make him forget and that Laela now had to fight a witch that had killed so many people, including Jacob's dad, and that she had no idea what she was doing and could they please just forget everything about magic and duty and murder, and play cards on the kitchen table instead. But she knew she couldn't.

She gathered the snippets she'd taken of the night around her, tightening their folds, and reached up to kiss his framed face. The glass was cold on her lips, and there was no mark left on the window where she'd pressed them into her father's cheek. And then she realised that he was looking straight at her. Right into her. She gasped and pulled back, but even as he turned his head and walked back to the table, the eyes in the glass stayed where they were, staring.

They were not her father's eyes. They were black, dead eyes that she'd seen before - only this time, instead of being held within a tree, they were in the midst of a most terrible, wretched face that sneered and parted thin, purple lips to reveal pointed teeth in splintered rows. As Laela stumbled back, she heard muffled laughter from inside the house. She hit the hard, dry ground and the face lunged after her, brandishing teeth, coming closer and closer until Laela thought it would bite her face and all she could do was clamp her eyelids shut and...

It's you.

Laela opened her eyes. The face in front of her, the Witch's face, had drawn a flicker of neck and shoulders and arms from dust in the air. It hung above Laela, watching with cold, appraising eyes.

I've been looking forward to meeting you.

Her father was almost crying with laughter now, hitting the table with the flat of his palm.

You brought me back, little one. I should thank you for that.

The Witch smiled.

Penny-Jane's voice had grown louder and louder, the story now coming out in staccato bursts as she tried to contain herself. Laela could see the edge of the open doorway behind her in her peripheral vision. If she could just make it...

Mmm, you taste delicious, so much power.

She could feel the roughness of the door seams...

It gives me such a buzzzz. I'm going to eat you all up-

The Witch struck at the same time that Lorna burst through the doorway.

'Laela! Shield!'

The Witch growled and pitched forward at Lorna.
Laela panicked. In her mind, white cloud obscured everything. She fumbled the shield. Lorna was struck. Laela tried again and this time, a steady veil held and she managed to keep it going as Lorna dragged them both into the living room and sealed the door shut.

'You can drop it.' She was panting, and Laela saw her aunt's arm was bleeding where the Witch had lashed out. Lorna ripped a strip of cloth and bound it.

'I'm sorry Lorna, I- I wanted to see my dad, and I didn't think – I thought I could go there and not be seen.'

'Forget it.'

'No, I'm sorry. I didn't mean to get you hurt.'

'I said stop.' She wheeled around, and Laela saw the blood vessels in her eyes had coloured the whites red. Mean, blood-shot eyes. Her mouth looked hard. 'I don't want to hear it. Your mother *died* for this, for *you*, and you seem to think it's just some game we're all playing for the hell of it.'

'My mum's dead because you didn't bother helping her because you were too wrapped up in your own life!'

'You have absolutely no idea what you're talking ab–'

The air changed. Laela felt the disturbance, and one look at her aunt told her she'd felt it too.

'Get back, Laela.' Her voice was low, quiet.

A bulge swelled in between them, like a distended picture.

'She's trying to get through.'

'What? Who?'

Lorna had planted herself, but Laela could see her hands were unsteady. The bulge in the centre of the room had bloated, and sparks fizzed around a jagged seam in the centre. The coffee table trembled and capsized, giving way to the growing energy.

'She's followed your magic back to us. We need to get you away from where your doorway was. If you're not nearby, the trace will weaken. Here...'

Lorna walked over to the stairs to where the cavern's doorway lay in wait. She brought its opening out of hiding, opened it. Only, it wasn't the doorway to the cavern. Laela knew it must have been a fixed doorway, hidden there all along, its edges worn and frayed even more than that to the cavern, the other side unfamiliar.

She eyed Lorna. 'Where does it go?'

'Laela! Just go!' Lorna's eyes flicked to the bulge of swelling matter behind her. 'God DAMN IT!' She made to close the doorway, but the structure of the living room was disappearing fast, and in its centre, a seam like solid lightning was appearing, ready to rupture at any second. She pushed Laela toward the opening, her eyes wild and desperate and her voice a strung-out screech. 'Christ, Laela! You need to go!'

Over her aunt's shoulder, Laela could see the rift start to open.

'Go!' She shoved Laela into the doorway's open jaws. 'Now!'

The last thing Laela saw of the lighthouse's living room was a burst of static and flung furniture as the rift became unfastened, and Lorna's fraught hands closed the portal between them.

'Lorna! Lorna!'

But Laela's cries only met mute walls. She fumbled at the brick where the doorway had been, but its seams remained hidden.

* * *

Laela looked around. Candles flickered, their wicks nearly down to the stub. Wherever Lorna had sent her was cold. Silent. The magic Laela had used to evade the Witch had depleted her strength and it took everything she had to edge over to the wall and prop herself against it. Gradually, her eyes adjusted to the dim light and shapes began to cut lines in the darkness.

The room was small and barren. Only a low gilded table occupied the room, huge, unlit tapered candles at its sides and a collection of objects on its surface. There was no door.

Laela took one of the candles and lit it with her remaining strength. As it flared it picked out shadows clinging to the walls – hundreds, smattered across the wall like cockroaches, square and oblong and crumpled and ordered into rows. The light simmered to a steady burn and her eyes adjusted. Curling corners and creases of photographs caught the candle's light. She knelt up to look closer.

No.

Her mother's face was everywhere, laughing, caught mid-speech, lips parted...

Laela retreated from the images and turned instead to the low table. At the centre stood a photograph of her mother. A small, glass bowl filled with liquid was placed in front of the photograph, fragments of bone bound tightly with hair and thread floating within it. There was blood smeared on the lip of the bowl, and faint droplets of red stained the table.

Magic.

She stumbled back, forgetting what had led her here, forgetting the candle in her hand and trying only to keep breathing, to keep upright. She fell. The candle slipped from her grasp and its flame leapt from wick to photograph. The room began to fill up with smoke. The air became poison.

Laela felt panic spasm through her heart. She grabbed a photograph from the wall to her chest and tried to weave a containment charm around herself. It flickered, but she gritted her teeth and made sure it held. The flames jumped from image to image, their chemicals dancing blues and greens and purples above her head.

She backed into a corner. Even through the containment, she felt the heat start to prickle and sting, a dry heat threatening to strip her flesh of all moisture. Around her, her mother's face burnt to ashes again and again. And then the walls were as hot as the fire itself, and her head was reeling and her vision distorted with the heat, and it was all she could do to keep the barrier from slipping away, its thin layer of magic the only thing stopping the flames from consuming her. She squeezed her eyes tightly shut and clasped the picture ever closer to her body.

Please help. Please help. Please help.

And then the doorway opened behind her, the fire swelled and vanished, and she was back on the floor of the living room, the door to the secret room sealed shut.

Laela stayed curled up, gripping the edges of the photograph, not noticing the world around her until Lorna's trembling voice cut in.

'What did you do?'

Lorna was sitting awkwardly on the floor of the wrecked living room. The sofa and coffee table looked as though they had imploded, and the floorboards stuck up through the rug like jagged teeth. But amongst all of the chaos, the most devastated-looking thing was Lorna herself.

~ XVIII ~

CHAPTER EIGHTEEN

'Sit.' The word was etched out of stone.

'I think,' Lorna said, unable to meet Laela's gaze. 'I think I've fucked up.' She was quiet, looking at the lines on her hands. 'After your mother died and I bound your magic, I wanted to forget.' She gave a wry smile and threw a gesture towards the doorway from which Laela had just come. 'As you can see, I didn't quite manage that.'

'What was that place? That thing, the bones...'

Lorna shifted on the floor. 'It was a memorial to her. A blood talisman. Each year on the day of her death-'

'My birthday.'

'I perform a remembrance ritual.' She sighed, kneading her brow. 'I can't be sure, but I think in doing so, the intention, the magic, enhances what's already in the village. That, combined with your neglected power, has allowed the Witch to grow stronger.' She paused, eyes flickering over her niece's face. 'Laela, I've fucked up. I know,' her voice softened. 'It wasn't enough for you to gain control of your magic; the Witch is still connected to you. That's how she could follow the residue of your magic to here.'

'She said I brought her back.'

'Your magic, my spell, brought her back; but she can only feed off the lives she takes. I'd guess that she's using what she has with you to maintain a physical presence outside of the Tree. But it's still not a connection you want her to have.'

Laela pushed the knuckles of her fists into her jawbone. She felt sick. 'You said I wasn't strong enough.'

'We don't have a choice. If we wait too long, she'll be too powerful. She'll have... killed more. We have to act as soon as we can.'

'But I might die? I mean, she might overpower me... I could end up a - a *husk* with her inside?'

'Laela! There's no time!' Lorna snapped. '*Fuck*, I'm sorry. We have to do this but... we'll have to wait until the day before the new moon. It'll give us the best chance.'

Laela worried at a hangnail and found her teeth shook against her thumb.

'In theory, she won't have the ability to sustain herself; she'll return all of her energy to the Tree. She'll be trapped. That gives us time to figure out how to get rid of her completely.'

Laela nodded, but she felt a knot worry itself into a ball in her stomach. 'What needs to be done?'

'You'll perform a severing. It'll undo the connection. Only, Laela, the Witch is bound to be aware of what you're doing. You can't mess around with breaking bonds like this and not expect her to feel something. But that won't happen unless you've found the tethering point – where you're connected – and that's halfway to breaking it.'

Laela sat silent, taking it all in.

Lorna, her face showing shame and sadness in its folds, couldn't help herself. 'You have to know. I did what your mother asked because I loved her, and I thought it was the right thing to do. And the remembrance ritual... it was part of what kept her alive to me. It's beyond terrible that all I was doing, all my selfish wish was doing, was feeding the Witch.'

Laela wanted to reassure her, to tell her that it wasn't her fault, but there was too much in her head and instead she offered a half-smile and retreated to the lantern room to fall into sleep.

* * *

Training now centred predominantly on the severing. If Lorna were satisfied, she'd move on to drilling Laela in defensive magic, ensuring the Witch wouldn't be able to draw on any of her magic and making sure Laela didn't let her guard down when challenged. They didn't practise making doorways and stayed far from village.

With days to go until the new moon, Laela and Jacob had one last meal in the lighthouse. Elliott had arrived that afternoon, and the three who were privy to what the future held – what reality really was – looked almost sadly upon his innocence.

Dinner was quieter, more uneasy than it had been that first night, and Elliott, sensing a shift in mood, retired to bed early, the others following.

* * *

Laela crept out that night, slipping from her bed and down the lighthouse stairs to the front door. Lorna stood on the dark edge of the cliff, facing out to sea. The moon had waned to a fragile crescent in her ebony cradle. Tendrils of light cast down upon clouds plucked from the sky and rode their fine cobwebs to the land below. She was so far from her plumpest, and yet, under her, the world lit up like a silver etching of grass and waves and earth.

'Lorna.'

Her aunt turned.

'I'm so sorry about your shrine, the talisman, the photo-graphs.'

Laela could see that tears had trickled down her aunt's cheeks.

She twitched a smile and then spoke, 'It's probably for the best. I got stuck... hadn't moved on. But we have bigger things to worry about. You've released me in a way. Thank you.' She smiled and turned back to the water. Her skin shone, the face of a smaller, terrestrial moon amongst the land.

Laela felt time slipping by, felt the tension of the past days ease, and then the shadows and depth of darkness gave her the courage to ask: 'Will my mum disappear if we kill the Witch? Will she... will my mum die? Again?'

Eyes on the black ink, Lorna spoke softly. 'Once, in the darker realms, the night sky shed us like glittering teardrops, and we fell to earth, burying our atoms deep within her. We formed our-selves, unique as snowflakes, each an intricate array of peculiar-ities, rarities. Some have been here for an eternity. Others are just arriving or recreating themselves as new and bright young shinings. When we shed our shadows and sink into the source, the earth takes our tired, old skins and absorbs them, so that in their absence we may be free. We fall, like snowflakes, into the ocean. We melt into one. And yet still, we exist. No matter how our bodies fade, we all end up here.'

Laela gazed up into the cavernous heavens, imagining all the stories ready to be woven into Time with ink and bright white stardust. She thought of her mother.

Lorna continued, 'I can feel them around me. Your mother was a part of them. She is, still, in those moments between her appearances.' She held Laela's hand and fixed her with sombre eyes. 'You can't be afraid to lose her, Laela. She'll always be here. But un-trapped. Free. As I'm sure you want her to be.'

'And do you? Do you... want her to be free?'

Lorna winced but nodded. Her eyes welled, and their moisture ran down her cheeks to the ground on which they stood. Over time, rainwater would carry her tears to the ocean. Salt to salt. 'I've held on to the past for too long. It's time to let go.'

Something shifted in Laela's chest and she felt a glimmer of what her aunt had harboured for fifteen years. 'Me too,' she said. And then she surprised herself by asking, 'You could heal yourself, couldn't you? But you don't. Why? Is it to, I don't know, remember?'

Lorna raised an eyebrow. 'You think because I use a walking stick, I need fixing? Am I not capable? Fulfilled? Brilliant?' A flash of ire darkened her face but then she sighed. 'There are so many different ways to be, Laela. Society tells you there isn't – that one way is right and that anything outside of that must be pitied, feared or hated. But my body and I have an understanding. We *work*. There are many things I've done to punish myself for your mother's death, but this isn't one of them.'

Laela's cheeks reddened. 'Sorry,' she mumbled. 'I didn't know. I just assumed. When I smoked, it was like I could block out all the feelings of guilt. Like I had a companion, something that I was in control of. And when it hurt my throat, it was like I was paying for losing my mum, for taking her away from my dad. I didn't realise until now, it was a punishment. I shouldn't have assumed that you were doing the same thing with your leg. With your pain.'

Lorna's lips curled into a wry smile. 'They're very different things, but I'm glad you've cut out the smokes. You'll need every ounce of magic you can muster, and smoking isn't going to help that.' Lorna squeezed Laela's arm. 'And nor is guilt.'

Laela whispered. 'Will our plan work?'

Lorna brushed the tears from her cheeks and gazed up into the night sky as though trying to foretell the outcome. 'We have to try,' she said. She turned to Laela. 'You're so brave,' she added. 'We're all so proud.'

* * *

Laela held reality in check until the time came when they were due to head back to the village, and then big gulps of dread rattled through her. Jacob squeezed her hand and tried to keep Elliott from wondering too much about his daughter's mood, or the purple-grey tattoo swirled on the palm of her hand and fingertips.

Bags repacked and van loaded, Lorna saw them off, with tight hugs and a brown-papered parcel of homemade ginger snaps. At the bottom of Laela's satchel was swaddled the potion she would use for the severing.

'You come and see me whenever you want,' Lorna sang. 'Let me know how the severing goes. We're in this together,' she murmured into her hair.

The three piled into the van and, with windows open and arms waving, they rattled off down the track and away from the lighthouse, Afternoon, and Lorna.

* * *

Laela and her father sank into the sofa in the front room, a plate of Lorna's ginger snaps and steaming mugs of tea between them. Elliott had lost the gauntness that had haunted his body before their trip, and his face was ruddy and relaxed. The fervour of the village was locked safely outside their door. To him, everything was forgotten but peace.

Deep in Laela's stomach, however, a wriggle of nerves uncoiled and flexed, squirming through the night. In her dreams, she saw flattened faces, eyes murky and urgent. The blank terror that possessed them laid waste to their pallid skin; it crawled over their features and blanketed them.

* * *

The funeral was held the next day. Jacob's mother, now home, stood tall and gaunt in swathes of silk and veils. Their black rang out in the sun and drank its heat with greedy, unwelcome gulps. Next to her, Jacob was stuffed into a polyester suit, too numb to itch now that the reality of his father's death was before him.

Laela and Elliott wandered over to them. The gathering had stored within itself kind words and pithy social gestures of sympathy, ready in preparation to greet the widow and her son.

Neither received them with grace. However, the broken family met Laela and her father with anaesthetised acceptance.

The villagers were tense, paranoid. The spate of deaths that had haunted the village had taken its toll, and now there was a sort of absence of purity there, in the graveyard. The ground seemed bereft of sanctity, the words of the sermons empty and devoid of meaning. There was no celebration of his life, no mention of his works or loves, beyond that of his family. It seemed now that he only existed in memory, and she only as an unhooked attachment to a man now dead.

* * *

As dawn brightened, the air was so pure it had almost liquid clarity. Birds began their chorus, and the Earth sped toward the sun at terrific velocity.

Laela hesitated in the garden, unsure of which way to go. The sunlight had not yet penetrated the darkness of the grove, and the memories of the Witch's attack so near her house were still unsettlingly fresh; and so, with furtive glances at the blank eyes of the windows of her house, she flung her satchel over the flint wall to Jacob's garden and followed. Her legs coiled as they absorbed the shock of the jump and up she sprang again, bag on her shoulder, ready to walk the road to the ruins.

She flinched as above her, an urgent whisper escaped.

'Pssst!'

Laela looked up to see the torso of Jacob leaning out of the upper window, clad in the superhero shirt he habitually slept in. The dark russet of his hair was thrown into rowdy curls over one of his eyes, giving him the appearance of a small and scruffy dog.

'Jacob, shh! I've got to go!'

He raised an eyebrow and called a little louder, 'Where you off to?' - threatening to expose her truancy.

Legs rubbing against each other in frustrated jitters, Laela rolled her eyes. 'Look, I haven't got time for this,' she groaned.

He flashed a grin and disappeared from view.
Laela's breath steamed in the morning air. Dew from the grass began to bloom on her plimsolls.
He reappeared, his head shoved through a blue shirt with a rip in the shoulder exposing white skin. With balletic grace, he slid through the open window and climbed skilfully down the brickwork below, clinging to its vertical face like a lizard.

'Your mum won't miss you?'

That was the wrong way to try to dissuade him; she should have known.

Jacob looked back at the window of his parents' bedroom. Snores and stale smoke greeted him. He shook his head. 'She's back, but she's still not exactly keeping tabs on me. I just can't believe you were going to sneak off without me!' He jabbed her in the ribs. 'You're going to do the severing, aren't you?'

'Um, yeah.'

'Well, then you need me! Come on.'

Laela tried to protest, but Jacob took off in the direction of the road, crouching low to avoid detection. She followed. Once they were out of view of his house, Laela relaxed. She let out a sigh that dropped the weight from her chest into her stomach, but a little tension still remained.

'Jake, are you sure?'

'I overheard most of it. About what you have to do.' He looked slyly at Laela. 'I can help, Lae.'

'Thanks, Jake, but–'

'When you go inside yourself, for this severing, you might not be able to come back. That's right, isn't it?'

'Yeah, but–' Laela shifted the bag on her shoulder awkwardly.

'Well, wouldn't it make more sense if I were there? You know, just in case?'

Laela had thought the same thing, yet guilt had held her back from involving her friend. She couldn't be the source of more pain. 'My mum will be there. I should be okay.'

'It's okay, Laela,' he said. 'If anything happens to me, I won't blame you. Let me help.' He gave a lopsided grin. 'I know everything anyway.'

'Jake, if anything happens to you...'

'I'll kick your arse afterwards. Now come on.'

Relief burst through guilt. She gave him a fierce hug. 'Thank you,' she whispered. The truth was, performing the severing while the Witch had power was dangerous. But they hadn't been able to find a way around it, and so the comfort of Jacob's company gave Laela a much-needed confidence boost.

They passed the silent graveyard and its neat rows of dead, including the graves of Jacob's dad and Sam. The cool morning breeze followed them over the wall and across the field to the ruins, catching the hairs on their skin as they sat on the rock.

She handed him her watch. 'My mum should appear once these bells strike six. She'll only be here for a few minutes, and then you'll hear the others chime from the church.'

Jacob squinted up at the old tower, devoid of bells and dripping with shade.

'By then, I should be ready to come back, if I haven't already. Before my mum disappears, she'll take care of it...' Her voice quavered. 'She'll know how to get me back... if she can. Jake, if I come back and I don't look like me... If I'm acting odd...'

'You'll do great, Lae.' He biffed her on the arm. 'And if you come back all possessed, I'll kick you in the shins and run. How's that?'

She tried a smile. 'Perfect,' she said.

'But when you *do* make it back and the Witch is dead, you have to ask magical Mira on a date.'

'Jake, for the love of-'

'Lae. If you can take on and defeat an ancient evil, I think you can ask your crush to go see a movie with you.'

His face was almost comical with its earnestness, but under Jacob's fierce gaze, Laela nodded.

'Not a movie though.' She couldn't stop the smile creeping onto her face, nor flutter in her chest. 'I'd take her for a picnic up where the riverbank looks out over the valley. Near that wild garlic patch. Maybe the book shop, too...' After all, what was one more epically terrifying thing?

Jacob grinned and squeezed her arm. 'Good.'

Laela took a deep breath. She shrugged down onto the grass until she was leaning her back against the rock. She drew the bottle from her bag and unwrapped it, carefully removing the stopper with a smile that was mostly bared and gritted teeth. 'Here goes,' she said, bringing the bottle to her lips.

'Of course, your aunt could have just put lemonade in there or something... looks a bit like it, doesn't it?'

But Laela couldn't answer. The concoction fizzed across her tongue, like electricity. It crackled down her gullet, fast, faster than ordinary liquid. And then she could feel it clipping sharp jagged lines as it rebounded around her insides.

In the distance, she could hear Jacob's voice wobbling in his throat. 'Laela? Laela…?'

And then it began.

~ XIX ~

CHAPTER NINETEEN

The trees are falling away and showing their true colors.
— Charmaine J Forde

Laela slipped under quickly, quietly, as though there were no transition at all. The sounds and sights of the world dissolved, and her awareness was thrust into the web of energies that made her. She could still feel her outer body, could still feel the sensation of her whole body being inside herself as a tickling, prickle of motion, as though she were a matryoshka doll. Each inner sensation ricocheted off the outer and back again, throwing her balance. Mirrors in mirrors.

And then that's all there was: mirrors in mirrors in mirrors and she was an image shuttered back and forth, repeated, miniaturised, distorted, with kaleidoscopic intensity.

She stumbled backwards, trying to escape the infinite reflections. They were all around, above, below, and new facets were emerging, mirrors turned fractal, new Russian dolls splintering outward in a prismatic horror until Laela cowed in the midst of concentric madness. She shut her eyes and tried to calm her breath. She could feel her heart beating in her chest, her heart beating all around, somewhere, above her, around her, in her body, in the body that sat against the rock watched over by Jacob...

And yourself? You will need to know who you are...

'I'm Laela. I'm Laela.'

You are not your name. It's deeper than that.

Laela pressed her knees against her forearms. 'Am I this? Am I flesh?' But as she said it, she knew that wasn't it. She forced herself to open her eyes.

The growth of mirrors slowed. Towers of Laelas and questions retracted back until there was only one mirror in front of her. The paint melted and left her reflection hers, skin and eye human, unadulterated.

And if this face were gone, what then? Would you still be you?

'Yes,' she said aloud. 'Yes, I – I would.'

Deeper. Go deeper.

As Laela peered into the mirror, she realised that the answers weren't in its cool reflections, but inside her, somewhere amongst her mind and actions. *This is me,* she thought. *And this is not,*

The final mirror melted away, leaving an empty calm.

She could see herself clearly, sense herself. Everything was sharp, vivid, pure. But... there was something. A niggling, shadow creeping around the edges: a speck of dust in the corner of her eye, vanishing from vision every time she tried to turn to look.

The Witch.

It scuttled in the periphery. Laela got to her feet and rallied her courage. A blink of darkness slinked past, a deliberate slowness to its pace, as though it wanted her to follow, and, even knowing it would be a trap, she did.

Shards of jagged mirrors leapt up, showing Laela the fear on her own face.

YES, CHILD. WOULD YOU STILL BE YOU IF WE SLICED OFF YOUR FACE? CHOPPED YOU LIMB FROM LIMB?

The Witch's voice was louder now that she was in her head... in the space that they both occupied. Now that Laela was aware of what was her and what was not. She swallowed the fear and summoned all the authority she could.

'I'm not afraid of you. I need you out of me. You don't get to use my magic anymore.'

Fractured fragments of laughter sliced around the mirror edges, followed by a darkness that left trails of shapes and glittering malice. Laela hounded it, never letting it escape her vision until the fading trails caught up with their owner, and Laela stood face to face with the Witch. At least, it was a foul, malignant force, twisting, its form ever-shifting, changing – building up and breaking down to make a new figure but the same, wicked entity driving its movement.

'I need you gone,' she said.

Cruel lips wrangled a rictus. 'You have less manners than your mother. And no less temper, I see. Do you know who you are?' the Witch said, her face temporarily sharpening into solid skin, stretched over cheekbones. She almost looked human, Laela thought.

'Who you were when we walked this land centuries upon ago?'

She drew nearer, and Laela felt her legs tremble.

'Are you one of the ones who stuck me in that tree? Who cut my tongue out? Drained me of life? Or before that, are you one of those who cast me out? Left me to die?'

The Witch's words pounded through Laela's head. She tried to summon her strength, 'I don't know!' she cried.

The Witch stepped forward, bones like knives and eyes like daggers, and a face of shredded skin and rivulets of blood. 'How easily you forget your own violence, and condemn me for mine. I am merely repaying the Elders for what you did to me.'

'What am I supposed to have done? You killed my friend and Jacob's dad. And...' Laela stood her ground, but she could not say the words.

The Witch withdrew a pace. 'And I killed your mother,' she said softly, with no hint of cruelty. The knives retreated, and the head bowed, almost sorrowfully. Child's eyes peered out from the shifting shadows. 'I am sorry, Laela. But the Elders must pay. And they have left me no choice! How else can I gain enough energy to return? Just as you have your duty, I have mine. I hope, soon, you remember.' The Witch's form began to melt, returning to the shapeless mist.

'Remember what? What am I supposed to know? I- I can't let you carry on,' Laela whispered.

The mist glittered a placid smile and then began to dissipate, a cloud of glinting motes, sweeping away from Laela. The mirrors were gone, the corners liquefied, any sense of bearing evaporated and Laela felt the inner landscape start to crumble.

Laela gritted her teeth. 'I won't.'

'So be it,' the Witch growled.

Laela followed the whirlings of light and glittering wisps in a haze of a crimson sea, solid yet undulant. She half swam, half stretched and glided, the Witch always just beyond her fingertips, not knowing what she'd do if she managed to catch up. Lorna had said that magic during a severing was a fickle thing, unpredictable. Would it drown her? Could she die here, inside herself? Would her body be taken over by the Witch and Laela be left in this ever-shifting landscape?

She came to where the Witch had woven her magic. She knew it was the core of the attachment, even before her eyes could fully take it in. Its blackness was unlike any other she had seen – it seemed to radiate and exhale decay. It was the absence of light. It stretched from where it latched onto Laela's heart like one long, thick vein into distant nothingness.

She waded closer. Suddenly the red seemed to darken and suffocate, closing its walls over her. She felt light-headed. Something was weighing her down, making her heavy, threatening to drag her beneath the surface of herself. Breath came in ragged drags; the air seemed to scratch and catch at her lungs and throat.

Somewhere outside and above her, she felt her heart expand, and hang in free-fall. It dropped a beat.

With bolting intensity, it burst back into life. Wild things leapt at her. Flitting shadows danced and snatched. Vision spun. Her hands slipped. Laela saw flashes of teeth like rows of razorblades, snicking and slashing, clattering closer, hissing their hungry metal mouths into her ear. She fought up and raked her nails through the dark that was consuming her and howled yowls of pain and savage grit into their faceless mouths. She flung herself onto the tethering cord and began to tear and rend and slash. She gouged and dug, scratching at layers, tissue like, with her fingernails, until strands of shredded bloody crepe hung like disintegrated cobwebs from the frayed cord.

It dawned late that her flesh was burning, the Witch's link preserving itself. Those strands, ripped from their mesh, now wound around her wrists and neck, blistering her skin, choking her. Red smudges of mass and magic began to tumble down. Black whippings bit at their forms, dissolving the soft fibrous tissues with their acidic, flicking tongues.

Laela felt her hands as they began to decompose. Fingers no longer responded. They twitched and jerked as nerves and tendons snapped and fried until only bone remained. Sharp and white and gleaming. Useless. She tried to summon a shield, but found her magic unresponsive.

That was when the blows hit. They pelted from all sides like an unseen torrent of hailstones. Her skull cracked and fractured, her ribs snapped. The blistering choke around her neck sluiced through another layer of skin. Claws reached out from the dark and slashed. The world had turned to tar and was filling her eyes and mouth and nose with its foul stench.

Laela sank into her darkness, feeling the inevitability of death.

She was blind, tumbling through an abyss of nothing but despair. She felt the core of her erode and knew how easy it would be to slip into the void of defeat.

Then, as the last shard of her heart looked to be consumed, instinct fired and kindled resolve. She remembered her aunt's advice: *She will come for you, but only when you're close.*

Laela clawed her way back from the depths and braced herself. She found the cord, now hardly more than a thumb width.

She bit.

One by one the wiry sinews rent and shrivelled as she gnawed. Electric charges flickered up and down its length, sparking and hissing. The acid burnt her mouth. Still, she pinned it between her teeth, scraping them back and forth through its layers of tissue. As she ground her teeth she pictured in her mind the severing of the connection, her energy complete and whole and contained.

It tore. She felt its severed end flailing in the inside of her mouth against her cheek, choking her. As muscle and tendon dissolved, Laela coiled the cord around her wrists and wrenched it out, feeling its electric tail as it flicked off into the darkness.

And then the red and black world disappeared.

* * *

When she came to, coarse hands were shaking her shoulders. A voice was grating in the air and vomit was jerking from her mouth. Her eyes made a long, shaking journey up from the sick-covered grass.

'Oh my God, Laela!'

Laela looked up at her father's face, ragged and pinched.

'Bloody hell. What were you thinking?' His voice was ratchet-strap rough. He hauled her up by the collar of her shirt and began dragging her back to the road. She thought she could hear another voice, a woman's...

Laela reached up to her mouth, fingertips meeting smooth skin and a trail of bile. Her hands were whole. She examined their flesh, the criss-cross of lines on her palms, her fingers eager to bend and flex and grip.

'Dad...' she began.

He stopped, released her collar. 'I mean, what the *hell* did you think you were doing?'

'Dad, I...'

He rounded on her, pulled her up to his face, her feet dangling above the ground.

'You're an idiot. A bloody idiot. And as for your mother, well she, she...'

His eyes glazed over. They landed about a foot away from Laela, somewhere in the air, and stayed there, unblinking. He looked drunk. Bells were chiming.

'Dad!' Laela whispered. *Oh, no.* Spittle was dripping from his lower lip, his upper snarled.

'Dad! *Dad!*' She yelled, but no response.

She kicked her legs and struggled to free herself. The fabric around her neck was making it hard to breathe.

'DAD!'

He was motionless. *Where the fuck was Jacob?*

The statue of her father gripped her with unfeeling fingers. She pried them from her shirt and fell to the ground. His figure loomed above, like a sick marble monument of violence. Laela stood, her head barely at the height of his still outstretched arms. She pushed at his face, trying to get it to turn to her, to change, anything, but he remained frozen.

Laela looked around, hysterical. They were alone. She began to run, tripping over her feet, unable to focus on the world in front of her. Her eyes fixed on the spire, and her feet followed. She hammered her fists into the closest door and screamed for help.

* * *

The vicar took Laela inside. He left her with his wife, who ushered her onto the sofa with cooed words, whilst he went to investigate.

By the time he found Elliott, he had moved. He now lay, cradling his head on the grey tarmac of the road in the clear daylight of the morning. He stared at the vicar with mournful eyes.

'What's real?' he asked on a softly uttered loop.

The vicar placed a threadbare blanket over his folded form and tentatively whispered words of reassurance. He turned to stare at his beloved church, until now only a symbol and an income, and wondered for the first time if there was a God, or if prayers weren't just cold, unanswered beggings, destined to be scattered to the wind.

* * *

The ambulance arrived under a blanket of silence, lumbering through the village like a voiceless beast. The vicar's wife called out, pleading, but Laela watched, transfixed, from the window as they gently ushered Elliott in through its gaping doors and onto the gurney inside.

Laela felt numb.

She picked up the house phone and shut herself in the downstairs bathroom, clutching the handset in fingers she could hardly feel, the ringlets of its long cord stretched taut under the door. She tried to focus on the shrill of the ringing, but instead sounds and images of her dad's anger bled into her eyes and ears, his hands hauling her up, the fabric nearly choking her. Gradually the voice on the other end came through.

'I said, who is this?'

'Mattie...' She barely had the breath to speak. 'I need you to come get me.'

Laela didn't trust herself to create a doorway – she could barely make a phone call – and so after she'd told Mattie where she was, she phoned Lorna.

'Jacob was with me! I... I'm not sure what happened to him.'

'I'll find him.' She'd meet Laela at the cottage, she said.

Some minutes later, Laela was staring at crustless sandwiches in the living room when the doorbell rang. The room sighed relief and, as the vicar opened the door, the palpable tension wavered and spilt out onto the doorstep.

'She's had quite a shock,' the vicar said, his head cocked to one side.

Mattie barged past. 'I haven't got all day,' she retorted. 'Come on.'

The vicar nodded and mumbled, and his wife's eyebrows rose and knitted, but before either of them could speak Mattie had thanked them both for their kindness, and bundled Laela up and out of the door and down the street. As they walked, all Laela could see was the swaying grey of the pavement. At each step, images of her dad and the Witch rose up and threatened to blot out the rest of the world. Mattie's voice and the grip from her arthritic fingers kept Laela from disintegrating entirely.

'You don't have to say anything now,' she said, 'but when you're ready, you can tell me what happened.'

* * *

The door to Laela's kitchen was open. Mattie and Laela hesitated in the doorway.

'Lorna...'

There was a loud clang as something was dropped in a hurry, and then Laela was enveloped in an embrace filled with both relief and fear.

'Where's my dad?'

'He's in quite a way. His mind isn't sure what's real right now. But he'll be fine. The doctors will discharge him soon, and then we can take a proper look at him.'

'And Jacob?'

Jacob was not fine. His eyes were red and raw, and a seeping gash ran the length of his cheek. The cuticles on both of his hands were lined with dirt, and the usual dirt-grained white under each fingernail was the rusted colour of dried blood. There was no smirk on his face, and his eyes were devoid of emotion as he spoke. He turned to Laela as she walked in.

'I'm sorry,' he whispered.

'Jacob! What happened?'

'My *god*,' Mattie whispered, a hand fluttering to her mouth. She cleared her throat and rearranged her face back to its regular impassive state, but something behind her eye could not be quelled, and a nerve quivered the lid intermittently.

Jacob shrugged off Laela's attempt to put her arms around him, and while he turned to look at her, his eyes slid to the floor.

'She was there,' he intoned. 'The Witch. I tried to pull you out of there but I couldn't... You wouldn't move. There was a cloud, a mist. It hung over everything. It was thick, with these bits of floating silver.' He frowned, rubbing the torn side of his face, puckering the skin. 'It sort of hummed. It turned into this shape... into *her*. And it started lashing at you. Pummelling. I didn't know what to do. The buzzing, it was... *loud*. I tried to punch it. Kick it, I dunno, just anything to get it off you. Then it started to come for me and... I'm so sorry, Lae.' He began to heave huge sobbing tears. 'I ran. I kept running, and I don't know what happened after that. I was stumbling through the woods, and I ran into something hard. And then I knew it... It had the same eyes as *her*. It was the Tree, Lae. *Her* tree. It felt like it was staring at me.'

He stopped, touching his finger to the lump of ripped flesh on his face. 'She made me... I thought I had something in my face. I started scratching and scratching and then...' His face gave way to brackish tears. 'I don't remember. I'm sorry, Lae. I'm so sorry. I was so scared.'

Lorna walked over to them and put her hand on his arm. 'It's alright,' she told him, gently easing his hand away.

She turned to Laela. 'I found him by the Tree. It's not clear if the Witch survived past the severing. It's very likely she didn't. Perhaps what she did to Jacob was her final stand.'

Laela looked to the wreck of Jacob and his nail-trenched face. Her jaw clenched. 'How would we know for sure?'

Lorna placed her tea deliberately on the mat, lining up the handle with the corner with careful precision. 'We go to the Tree.'

~ XX ~

CHAPTER TWENTY

'I can go alone.' She eyed Laela. 'But it'd be easier with two of us.'

Laela exhaled and straightened her back resolutely. 'I'll come,' she said, managing an anaemic smile. 'Besides, I'm the one with the power here.'

Jacob's hand darted out and caught Laela's wrist as she tried to leave.

'Be careful,' he warned, his gaze as intense and vice-like as his grip.

'We will,' she said, although she wasn't sure what that meant.

* * *

They left Jacob with Mattie and headed off through the grove and its darkening recesses, the shadows whispering as they passed. The Tree lay at the farthest boundary of the land, past the open clearing where Laela's father had often chased away teenagers with cans of budget-brand cider and pungent-smelling joints. In the centre of the clearing, a charred circle still blackened the earth where they'd lit a fire only weeks ago.

A little way beyond the clearing, the grass gave way to pale chalk and then, abruptly, a ditch. Its bank struck steeply downward, almost vertical in some parts. Its sides were tangled with dead roots and loose rounds of chalk. The smell began there. It lingered in the low parts, snaking its way into nostrils and lungs with putrefied stench.

'It's the rot of undead,' said Lorna, as Laela retched and coughed. 'It's always smelt like this here; there's no getting used to it.'

'But I've never smelt it...or seen this part of the woods. How can this have been here all this time and I've never noticed any of it before, not even the ditch?'

'It's protected. There are charms surrounding it. The Elders couldn't risk village folk wandering around here and disturbing the Witch. I don't know how Jacob saw it... he shouldn't have been able to.'

She placed her hand over her nose and tried to climb up the furthest side of the trench. A root snapped off under the weight of her hand. She emitted a low snarl of annoyance. The going was hard.

The depth was less than seven feet, and yet, when at last they summited the top and hauled their way out, they were exhausted. Their fingers, which had dug, clawed and gripped were cramping and bleeding. They lay on their bellies, fighting the body's urge to pant and suck in air lest they should taste the reek and retch.

Laela rolled her eyeballs up to her brow. A few hundred paces over barren, stinking earth reared the Tree. Nothing grew in the no-man's land between. The thought came unbidden: *It's watching me.*

They staggered to their feet. In the distant space at their backs, birds still cawed and the occasional rumble of tyres over tarmac marked the road. But here was dead. Heel first, then toes flattened down; hand in hand they silently paced over the ground.

Toward the Tree.

The stench worsened. It became an all-pervasive fug that stripped the bones and lurked around the senses. The Tree was not the same as it had been in Laela's dream, but Laela felt the same oozing dread throb inside her as she approached.

The trunk was well-rooted and solid, as though it had sucked itself back into the ground. It stood insolent and strong. Thick lines like water-run rivulets scored its length and spread up into its head. The branches that extended from its central trunk were few and stumped, like amputated limbs. Beneath it, the small carcasses of animals and their inedible components adorned the blank earth.

They walked around its breadth, eyeing it for signs of life or movement. It remained silent.

The air was yellow and cold. They waited for hours, crouched away from its brutal shape. Laela tried not to think of the conversation she had had with the Witch.

Do you know who you are?
Who you were when we walked this land centuries upon ago?
I hope, soon, you remember.

Laela tried to put it out of her mind, but she'd felt it. She'd walked amongst the dead in the village, performing rites, lighting pyres. She'd been with the Elders as they hunted the Witch. She looked sideways at Lorna and wondered if she'd been there too.

'We look different, do we? Each time we're reborn?'

Lorna turned to her, brow creased. She glanced back at the Tree. 'Yes, I suppose. I mean, I've never recognised faces in my memories of past lives.' She returned her gaze to Laela, the furrow in her brow deeper, her mouth pinched. 'What's this about?'

Laela knew she couldn't tell her aunt. She was one of them – she'd been there as they cut out the Witch's tongue, and yet... Instinct said to keep quiet. She shrugged and stared pointedly at the Tree. 'Just wondering.'

They stayed in silence after that. Eventually, as dusk grew heavy, Lorna spoke. 'I think she's gone,' she whispered.

Laela peered around at the landscape as if expecting retribution from those words, but nothing stirred. The two gingerly unfolded and stood, taking in the view.

'It'll be a while before the land recovers, but it will. Nature has a way of doing that,' said Lorna.

Laela looked unsure. She could not imagine a place so inherently filled with malevolence becoming lush with blossoms and children and picnic blankets. They turned away and moved in the direction of home.

They relayed the good news to Jacob. His face had already gone a long way towards being healed, courtesy of Lorna and her herbs.

He, too, had news. 'The hospital called. Your dad should be ready to come home tomorrow.' One side of him grinned at Laela. 'They said he's to be booked in for tests, but they're happy to discharge him if there's someone at home to look after him.'

Lorna gave a fragile smile and turned to Laela. 'I'd be more than happy to stay for a while, if it gets him home.'

* * *

The next day, although her body felt exhausted, Laela was awake with the dawn chorus and preparing for her father's return. A sense of unease prickled at her stomach and made it impossible for her to concentrate on her tasks. She sought refuge in the familiar arms of the oak. Its old limbs swayed as she climbed its height and it felt to her as though it groaned through its trunk and sorrow flowed through its leaves. She clung to her perch and watched.

A skylark fell from flight and dropped the edges of its song. The vast blue before her was blank. The waters of the stream no longer chortled but seemed choked by their passageway, and no one paddled in its cool shallows as they once had; and where blankets and picnics had once strewn the green under the feet of children and families, there were only stacks of flowers wrapped in their cellophane sheaths, wilting in the sun – a reminder of death. The rhythm of the village had changed.

The village hum was strange. Strained. The tin-sounds of machinery clanged erratically. Neighbours' voices pitched and fell in tense discourse, but there was no chatter. The villagers were far from laughter. And when the church bells rang, they only seemed to intensify the gap between peace and terror, and show the village to be so deep in the grip of melancholy that even their god-construct stood empty and useless. The reverberations swilled darkness around the woods. From their depths, Laela heard the movements of creatures untouched by daylight, and for once, in the sunshine, she shivered at the thought of their prowling.

The house beneath had yawned itself awake, and Jacob and Lorna had begun skulking their way around its limits, making coffee and nibbling burnt toast. The smell wafted up into the branches of the oak and reminded Laela that food was a necessity. She trailed the scent back to the house and joined the others in the kitchen for breakfast.

When they'd had picked their way through their plates, Laela walked Jacob back to his front door, opting to use the road rather than scale the wall. The street was quiet, as though news of the village's plight had staved off the rest of the world from even using the village as a thoroughfare.

'I'm glad you're okay, Lae, and I'm really sorry ab–'

'Hey, it's fine. I understand. If it weren't for you, I'd be a total mess right now. Thanks, Jacob.' They hugged goodbye, and each returned to their home.

Lorna was waiting, one leg suspended in the air and the other in the footwell of the van. She jerked her head toward the passenger side. 'Wanna come?'

Laela's face creased into a grin. She ran around the van and hopped in, her heart skipping. Here she was, everything back to normal; just a girl on her way to see her dad.

* * *

The hospital lay about an hour's drive from home, and with every turn of the wheels, Laela felt her excitement wane. Her thumbnail picked at her bottom lip for the whole journey, peeling away thin layers of white skin, mile by mile.

'What if the Witch isn't dead?'

'Don't worry, love; he'll be fine.'

Laela's gaze remained fixed on the passing carousel of colours and signs. 'He was horrible.'

'He wasn't himself.'

Black letters on yellowing-white boards led them through unfamiliar, grey territory to the hospital.

'Look, he's sustained a lot of damage, but he's still your dad. Once we get him home and sort him out, he'll be right as anything. But he needs you, okay?'

Laela looked into her aunt's determined face and felt her worries subside – the love for her father sliced through the niggling shrouds of doubt. 'Okay,' she said.

The ward that held her father was at the end of a myriad of white corridors and bleach-stinking floors striped with coloured lines. Laela saw a collection of shoes – rubber squeaking trainers and clip-clopping heels – passing by as they traversed its disinfected labyrinth. Some travelled by wheels: self-propelled or pushed, broken-limbed or invisibly disabled. Others shuffled by, painstakingly covering floor space.

The nurse at the reception ignored them. A stacked barrier of folders and reports crowned the desk. Along the walls, the human contents of the waiting room sat on murky coloured plastic chairs and coughed and raved and shook and picked. Some chattered cheerfully, reassuring whoever had brought them in. Others whistled or sang low sweet songs. Occasionally, a door would open and their heads would sway to its sound, like the heads of wheat turning in the wind.

Elliott's room was small. In fact, it wasn't his at all, but a shared blank space divided by a pleated blue plastic curtain. His roommate wasn't in. He sat, on the edge of his bed, staring into a place no one else would ever see. Lorna listened and nodded respectfully to the advice the doctor gave, reassuring her that she'd ensure Elliott would take the prescribed medication and attend the follow-up appointments.

Laela stood behind her aunt, taking it all in whilst at the same time, remaining trapped in a sort of muzzy haze. Her father didn't look at her. Every so often, the doctor would smile down, showing pearly white teeth.

They walked back along the corridors and into the car park. Laela thought the sunshine made her dad look more bewildered, the hollows in his cheeks more pronounced, but perhaps it was a trick of the light.

Once more the van rumbled over the chewing gum-mottled tarmac. Laela was pressed uncomfortably between her dad and the gear stick. Lorna patted her leg and gave a small sideways smile, but the journey was silent.

Curtains twitched as they drove through the village, and heads pressed together with whispered words and gossip-hungry, gleeful mouths. The more bitter and painful for the victim, the juicier the rumour was, and with greater relish devoured. Scandal was a great alleviator of the tragic.

Jacob was standing with his hands in his pockets, scuffing his boots on the gravel of their drive. His face was a black cloud in which darkened eyes and troubled, gnawing mouth lurked.

Elliott stepped out of the van, almost as reflex. He approached Jacob, but only because he stood in between the van and the back door. He stared blankly through the boy as though wondering why the door was not open.

Jacob opened his mouth to speak, 'There's b–'

'We can discuss that later, Jacob,' cut in Lorna. She beamed for all the world like there was a party inside for them to get to. 'Let's just head into the kitchen and put that kettle on, hmm?'

Jacob tried again, but Laela caught on and swiftly kicked him in the shin. She nodded at her dad, still baffled by the door. He turned at the jangle of keys and shuffled his body aside when prompted.

Whilst Elliott was manoeuvred into a chair, Jacob pulled Laela into the living room. His voice grated with urgency under its hushed husk.

'The Witch isn't dead.'

'What?' Laela felt her stomach plunge into ice. Lorna came in. 'But–'

'Someone else has been found. This morning. There's something else too...'

The kettle began its arcing shriek with a low whistle.

'The bodies, it's pretty clear they'd done it to themselves. All of them. They'd hung themselves.'

Laela felt sick.

'They found them in the park – lines thrown over the swing set. The mother was still kicking when they got to her, but her kids, they were... well, she'd helped them... then hung herself.'

Laela felt herself take a sharp intake of breath. Lorna swore under her breath, and any pretence of happiness vanished. The kettle reached its peak and sent its screech through the house.

Lorna turned to the doorway and found Elliott blocking it, his body awkwardly straight and rigid.

Knife.

She flinched. 'Elliott, I was just coming to–'

Not Elliott.

'I was coming to get you too, Lorna.' He flicked and twisted the silver gleam through the air beside him. His lips were tight and blue, peeled back over a sick grin on his face. 'Pretty little picture they made, on their family outing.'

Lorna took a step backwards, her arms out in front of Laela and Jacob while Elliott's eyes, like beetles red with fire licking across their shining backs, flickered over them. They didn't move. Couldn't.

'Yessss, oh so pretty with their tongues poking out and their eyes all a-bulging. Beautiful. So full of *life.*' The knife jerked in emphasis of each word.

'Get *out* of him!'

The Witch moved Elliott's body forward. Lorna retreated, pushing the children back as she went. He bent down and cocked his head to stare at Laela. 'You weren't very nice at all, sweetheart. You tried to get rid of me. Naughty, naughty.' His smile was placid. Mechanical. 'Naughty girls don't get to play with Daddy.'

The blade was a glint of silver. Blood appeared. Elliott's hand gripped the enamel handle of the knife as he see-sawed it down over his ear. Chunks of flesh dropped to the ground. His laugh pierced the air in high manic bullets. The knife was moved to his throat.

'*Dad!* Lorna, do something!'

Lorna snapped back into movement. She grabbed the lamp from the nearby table, kicked his knee – a sick crack clapped – and smashed the heavy base over his skull. He dropped to the floor, the knife inert and mundane.

'Jesus…' Lorna managed. 'Get some rope. Tie him up. Laela, *Laela!* Make a shield around him and a doorway through to the lighthouse.'

* * *

They had been in the dim shadows of the lighthouse for hours. Lorna had taken Elliott into the safety of the hidden cavern, woven a containment charm, and tipped a sleeping draught past his unconscious lips.

When they'd realised the implications of what had happened, Laela called Mattie. 'I can open a portal for you. You can come straight here; we'll keep you safe.'

There was silence and then, 'I'll stay.'

'But–'

'You'll need someone to fix an eye on what's happening here. I'll stay,' she repeated. 'I'll keep tabs on the Witch, give you updates. I can't do much,' she sighed, and Laela could picture her massaging the crease in her forehead as she spoke, 'but I know better than most what this witch is capable of, and any way I can help, I will.'

Laela couldn't speak. The lump in her throat threatened to explode into an endless course of tears. As though she could sense it, Mattie's voice softened. 'You do what you have to do, Laela, and so will I.'

Laela placed the receiver down after their goodbye, the gravity of the situation hitting her harder at that moment than it had before. She returned to the others, a sense of hopelessness creeping at her edges.

'Mattie?'

Laela shook her head. 'She's staying. Says she'll give us updates on what's happening in the village.'

Lorna paused to fix Laela with a sympathetic look, nodded, and then returned to analysing Elliott.

Despite the precautions of the charms and sleeping draught, the feeling of unease had yet to dissipate, but it took only minutes before Lorna broke the quiet melancholy. 'I think I've got it.'

Laela and Jacob stirred, but held their distance, reluctant to approach.

'The Witch controls her victims by sending out part of her consciousness in dust particles from the Tree. It's similar to how she took energy from you, Laela, sort of. Only, once infected, the particles enable her to influence the victims' movements. When she's finished with them, the particles return to the Tree, transferring the energy from the victims to her, and their deaths cultivate a sense of panic amongst the survivors, leaving her with more potential victims. It's a perfect blend of magic and biology.'

'So, my dad...' Laela slowly began.

'He'll be fine. All we have to do is find a way to starve them without killing the host, and,' she said hurriedly, seeing the panic on Laela's face, 'that should be easy, now that I have them in front of me, and I can probably find a way to treat whoever else she tries to infect... provided we know who they are, and can get to them in time.'

Laela nodded and shuffled upwards against the wall until she was standing again. 'How come she didn't infect us, then?' she asked.

'The lessons that we've done together,' Lorna paused, and when she was sure he was staring into the space that Elliott occupied, gave a quick nod toward Jacob. 'They set up your body and your mind so that you're not receptive to control like that. It rejects anything that comes close to trying. In short: the spores can't latch on to you, because of your strength of mind.'

The words were received with silence, knocking around the cavern until they'd been absorbed, really absorbed by the occupants.

Finally, Jacob said, 'So what about me?'

Laela spied him from between the triangle of the corner of her eye. He'd kept staring at Elliott, transfixed and pale.

'Jacob,' began Lorna, softly. 'There's no way anything can get to you with your resolve to be so bloody difficult.' She managed an awkward laugh, but it was a laugh that Laela had head from her aunt before, its texture brittle, the tone tinny. 'The Witch goes for the weak, or fearful. Besides, we're not going to let anything happen to you. You'll be here, and she's not.'

'My dad was weak? *Sam* was weak?'

Laela saw the spark of anger flare in his eyes, and she silently begged Lorna to rephrase the facts into something less blunt.

'No! I meant... We all have our insecurities. Anxieties. Everyone struggles, but,' Lorna spread her hands, reaching for words. 'The Witch preys – in the early days of her return at least – on those who feel isolated, hopeless. It's easy for her to walk in to someone's mind when that person believes they have no one to turn to. When they feel alone. As she gets stronger, she'll be able to take energy from anyone – we all have cracks in our armour. We all have doubt and sadness and guilt and grief. We're human. Look,' she put her hand on Jacob's shoulder. 'I shouldn't have said what I did. It was wrong. Someone who struggles through each day isn't weak. In some ways, they're the strongest of us all. I just meant, you'll be fine.'

A corner of Jacob's mouth twitched, but in the darkness of his heart, he felt unsure.

* * *

'Now, I just need to collect a few more things, and then I'll be ready to begin.' Lorna grabbed the bag that had been used for their picnic just days before.

'Wait!' cried Laela. She clasped her aunt's hand, desperate to drag her back into the house. 'What about Jacob? Are you sure he's okay? What if...' her words died out, but the sentiment behind them echoed frantic in her eyes. Her shallow, jittering breath galloped away from her.

'Laela, he's fine. And if he's not, you know *you* are. If anything were to happen, you run and come find me. He can't get to your dad or the Witch's spores; he's safely sealed in. But I doubt Jacob will go that way, love. He's too far from the Witch for her to have a great effect, and those spores start dying out if they don't get fed.' She gave Laela a quick kiss on the cheek. 'I'll be back in a flash. Hang tight, sweetheart.'

Lorna walked off down the path, leaving Laela at the intersection of the cultivated garden and the wilds that surrounded it. Laela felt the jagged edges of panic grate and nick at her insides. She felt so alone. Her dad was unconscious, Jacob needed her – the village needed her, and her aunt's speech to Jacob had probably done more harm than good. But what could she do? She barely understood anything herself.

* * *

Inside, something was brewing.

Fear need only get a minor foothold before it spreads like a cancer - as Jacob was about to discover.

~ XXI ~

CHAPTER TWENTY-ONE

There must have been a moment, at the beginning, where we could have said -- no. But somehow we missed it.

— Tom Stoppard, *Rosencrantz and Guildenstern Are Dead*

Jacob had waited several minutes before descending the stairs to the hidden cavern. A vague fugging of his mind had drawn him over the edge. He'd even felt a little apprehension as he'd trod those last steps. But not enough to dissuade his curiosity, or whatever it was that pulled him there.

His throat had begun to itch. He raked his fingers over it, feeling the lump of his Adam's apple slide beneath the pressure. He approached the cavern with magnetic trepidation. Elliott was still subdued; unconscious but breathing. Jacob padded forward, his feet quiet on the stone floor. He stood over his friend's father, peering down into his crinkled face.

He looks feeble, he thought.

Not like Elliott at all.

He leaned closer, examining the twitching eyelids and the blue veins that twined across their surface. New lines had formed – deep fissures of wrinkles that dug their way and sawed their paths across his face.

The sudden 'thwuck' of a door slamming made him jump.

Elliott slept on, the sleep of the dead.

The boy looked up, inspecting the shadows, reassuring himself that on this not-particularly windy day it was normal for doors to slam of their own accord. He called out hesitantly, 'Laela?' and found his voice had a high, cracking tweak to it, like a bow being dragged over the strings of an untuned violin.

Something was creeping. His feet had instinctively shuffled backwards, and now, behind him, rough wall met his back.

'Laela, c'mon, it's not funny. Say something!'

Outside in the garden, Laela said nothing.

Laela's doorway, left open and forgotten amidst the panic, felt nothing as the mist drifted in from the village, almost as though it were invited. It couldn't alert or warn, or wail, as Jacob was now doing.

He whimpered as loose threads of sparkling greys seethed through the room, their tendrils curling, filling the space. It crawled over the walls and past the hanging strips of rock up to the high ceiling, and wreathed along the floor, silver shreds of smoke silently stifling his shrieks.

* * *

The mist reached the table where Elliott lay. Wisps of turning, glinting metal stroked the containment that surrounded him. He coughed, wet and grating. Jacob watched as a spiral of flecked mist escaped Elliott's lips and caressed at the barrier. They remained, twisting toward one another, two metal wraiths unable to connect.

Jacob felt his lungs retch. He wondered if they could vomit. Sharp scratches of tingling spores rose up his throat and sought to join the mist. It hung low. It billowed from the ceiling. It shrouded everything. Jacob's palms were flat against the wall, pressing himself into it, trying to find a way out.

It crept forward.

He clamped his lips together and felt the razor blade particles shred at the inside of his mouth. And then, the mist was there; softly, gently, it cut at his skin and eyes and mouth and ears and nose until it got in. A blinding scream of pain ripped through his mind, and then he was trapped inside his own skin, feeling, seeing, tasting, but inert in his own fleshy prison.

So much sadness in here, eh, Jacob? We'll be such good friends...

* * *

Outside, the sky was bright, but the world had already begun to turn her back on the sun. Butterflies with white wings flitted and bit at the leaves of the garden and seemed such pretty, fragile monsters.

Laela inhaled the sweet air, trying to settle the pit of her stomach as it pitched and rolled.

She should probably go and check on Jacob.

But she didn't want to.

She was scared.

Terrified.

Something was happening, and she knew it somewhere inside her, a part that she couldn't break open and show you if you'd asked where it lived.

But she knew.

She closed her eyes and breathed in the day as it died. Then she turned away from the sunlight and walked back into the house.

~ XXII ~

CHAPTER TWENTY-TWO

*The moon was absent, a circle of darkness denoting the
possibility of presence, the inevitability of return.*
— Naomi Alderman, Disobedience

Laela moved through the kitchen, past the cold hearth and
down the stairs, treading softly. The lighthouse spoke no secrets.
The hidden room, like the rest of them, was silent.

She stepped through to the cavern, sealed the doorway to the
lighthouse closed behind her, and peered around the corner.

Be brave.

Jacob stood with his back to her, unmoving. At his waist,
partially hidden by Jacob's body, her father seemed to sleep.

'Jacob?' she called out, her voice a steady whisper. He remained rigid.

The tone was flat, dead. 'Laela, thank god you're here. I think something's wrong with your dad. He was struggling to breathe, can you get him out of this containment?'

Quick steps took her forward. She faltered. 'You know I can't. We need Lorna. Jacob, is he... will you turn around?'

He didn't move.

'Open it, Lae.'

She stepped closer. 'Jacob, what's wrong with you? I can't.'

'Ah, yesss, that's right.' The words were like a knife tearing through metal. 'You have no power here.'

'What?'

Jacob turned, blooded tears crusted on his face. 'You're helpless,' he said; she said. 'And I am here. And you're here. And I warned you. Now, let's play.'

Run.

But she didn't. She rooted her feet to the spot and waited, braced. She had no magic, but she wouldn't run this time. The body of her friend lunged toward her, grappling for her face. She brought her foot between his legs. He grunted and fell forward. She struck against him – not the wild blows of their childhood fights, but deliberate, de-mobilising strikes. She made a knuckle-ridged fist of her hand and swung it against his jaw. She battered. She kicked, belted and beat him until she was gasping for air and he was on his knees.

A sick, jerking puppet, he reared up, blood bubbling from his mouth as the Witch laughed through his lips.

Then she ran. Down the passageway she fled, and dived through the open doorway to the village, into her father's cottage. Her last glimpse into the cavern was the twisted grin of Jacob's stolen leering face. Blisters formed as she tried to scrub the passage shut. She scratched it from the air and pushed herself to her feet. Her insides were shaking. She turned, thinking to run to the graveyard to wait for her mother, but bumped into the solid body of Penny-Jane. Her face wasn't hers either.

'Oh, ssssweetheart, don't be like that, come back here.'

Penny-Jane's clumsy, rigid arms grabbed at Laela. She managed to duck and run out of the door.

The village was steeped in dense fog. Mist. It seemed to falter several feet from where she stood. There, as if braced by an invisible barrier, it recoiled and eddied.

Laela could hear voices in the murky white. The vicar and his wife started to stroll haltingly up her drive; Jacob's mother was climbing over the wall – all their faces nothing but different masks on the Witch.

She ran.

The field was less than a mile away, yet beneath Laela's running feet, the land seemed to drag and cling. Blind in the clouded land, she took wrong turns, stumbled in ditches, slid and slipped in mud; brambles ripped and tore at her flesh. Her knees began to give way.

The ground came up hard.

* * *

When she woke, darkness had resumed its control. Inky black spotlights rose in the grey behind dim silhouettes of trees and lingered in shadows, and in the foreground, paper-skinned fingers snapped inches from her nose.

'You have to get up.' The fingers seized Laela's collar and pulled her upright.

Her head pulsed and she tried to push the hands away, to say that she just needed to sleep a little longer, but they didn't yield. She followed the arm up to the face of Mattie.

'Laela, they're everywhere, *she's* everywhere.'

Laela snapped awake then and became aware of the sharp edges of flint that dug into her hip. She pushed herself upright and looked at Mattie, whose face was more drawn and paler than usual. She was clutching at something under her cardigan, and when she saw Laela looking down, she gave a wan smile and lifted the fabric. 'I came to find you. I didn't realise how... *it* would look. I thought I'd be able to tell who she'd taken, but instead,' the laugh she gave was broken by wet coughing, 'it could be anyone.'

A blade had darted in and created a wide-stretched mouth that oozed. In the darkness, the blood looked black.

'Mattie...'

'I'll be fine.' More coughing. 'Make sure you stop her.'

A rustling, approaching through the darkness stopped Laela short.

'Go. I'll deal with this.' Mattie slipped a wrench, rusted and bloody, from the ground and coughed out another wet laugh. 'This is the best I could do, under the circumstances. I wasn't prepared for this... I guess no-one was.'

Laela thought about making a portal through to somewhere safe for Mattie, but the rustling neared, and soon the source of the shuffling, awkward gait would be upon them. And then she heard bells. '*Fuck.* Mattie. I have to go. I'll be back. This should hold them off.'

She summoned a crackle and then a spark to the air between her fingertips and spread it in a wall between Mattie and the on-coming noise. The fire blistered, but held the greater evil at bay.

There was no time to weave a containment. There was no time for anything. She found the place in her head, made it real, spread it out in front of her. The doorway opened. Through it, in the darkness, sight gave no information, but she could hear breathing. Cautiously, she climbed through the hole in the world.

'Laela!'

'Mum!'

The second bells began to chime.

'I've got seconds. You have to stop her!' Her eyes were wild and desperate and she reached out to Laela, held her as she faded. 'I love you, sweetheart, don't be afraid to lose me.'

Laela wanted to stay wrapped in her mother's arms, but she was gone, and there were others who needed her. By the time Laela came back to rescue Mattie, she'd propped herself against the trunk of a tree, the firelight lending an exuberance to her face that almost covered the pallor of blood loss.

'She wants us to lose hope. But we mustn't.'

'Mattie, don't talk, please, I need to get you somewhere safe.'

'You need to take this bitch down,' Mattie forced through gritted teeth. And Laela saw the extent of her injuries, knew the wounds wouldn't heal.

'You didn't succumb to her, even after you'd lost everything.' Laela grasped her hand. 'You're a hero.'

Mattie laughed, a sputtering, wretched sound, and shifted her weight, leaning on the wrench to push herself up. 'We each play our part. We are only ourselves, and can be no more or less.' Her fingers found her handkerchief and brought it to her brow, which she mopped, carefully, pointedly. 'I'd like to die with some dignity,' she said. And then her eyes popped wide over the cotton and Laela reached to catch her, thinking she was falling. But Mattie wasn't falling.

Before Laela could understand what was happening, Mattie had gripped Laela's shoulder and hauled herself upright. She stood, unsteady, levering her weight against Laela for support, and swung.

The wrench *thwucked* through the air and hit something, hard.

Laela remained frozen as the sounds of impact morphed from loud *cracks* to quieter, sloppy thuds as metal broke through skin to skull to grey matter; and then a dull crumple of staggered weight landed behind Laela.

Mattie let the wrench clang to the ground beside the body and laughed again, looking at Laela with a victorious black glint in her eye. But her laughter was wet, cold, somehow. 'Hero!' she cawed, a wry smile on her lips. And then she stopped breathing. Her hands still clung to Laela, her eyes half closed, her head lolled slightly to one side as though she were contemplating the firelight.

'Mattie?'

But Laela knew she was dead.

She lowered the body until it sat, resting again against the tree. By the flickers of flames, Laela laid the wrench in Mattie's lap and straightened her cardigan. At last, she mopped the sweat from Mattie's brow and pocketed her handkerchief.

'All the dignity, Mattie. You deserve it all.'

No tears came. Instead, something iron appeared: something that made Laela resolve that this was the last friend she'd lose to the Witch.

She tried to avoid looking at Mattie's final triumph, now a mess of wrench-dented blood and bone, and opened a portal to confront Jacob.

* * *

Laela gave a harried glance around the lighthouse kitchen before entering, but all was quiet. Arms drew her into an embrace and then Lorna pulled back, scrutinising Laela from top to toe. 'Are you alright?'

It took Laela a few seconds to adjust. She wasn't in danger. Despite everything, she nodded grimly. 'Mattie's dead,' she said, and waved away Lorna's attempt to console. 'Jacob? I didn't close the doorway... I let the mist in. Where is he?'

Lorna stepped back and stripped the conversation to the essentials.

'I've figured out a way to reverse the effects of the Witch's spores. Jacob's fine, he's upstairs resting. Your dad, too. And,' she continued, lowering her voice, 'your dad's memory is back.'

Laela felt the shock churn through her body. 'I thought he wouldn't cope?'

'We didn't have a choice. The Witch's magic had consumed too much of his mind, and the rest was addled from seeing your mother during the severing. The effects of the original Forget-Me became intensified – that's why the Witch was able to infect him so easily.' She shrugged. 'He was defenceless.'

Her father's gruff voice interjected, 'Your mother didn't want me to remember what happened. She felt that, were I to forget the reasons behind her death – as well as a great part of her life and yours – I'd be protected from the full extent of my grief and guilt and be able to raise you without that burden hanging over either of us. And you wouldn't have to grow up a guardian. She wanted a fresh start for us both. She wanted us happy.'

He reached out a hand to Laela. 'But that came at a cost. It left your lineage hidden and your magic unguided. I forgot who your mother truly was... who you are.' He found her eyes. 'I'm so sorry. We wanted what was best for you.' He tried to quash the shame in his chest as it rose. 'Please forgive us.'

Laela took a breath, and used it to quell her flickers of anger. 'I understand why she did it. It can't have been easy for either of you.'

She broke away and eyed both of them with intense determination. 'But look. I have a plan,' she said quietly. 'And you both need to listen.'

* * *

She began, and at first, they did listen. Then came protestations from Elliott.

'And how does that get rid of the Witch? Surely that accomplishes nothing but hurting your mother?' His protectiveness twitched like a tail.

Lorna soothed, explained, 'The Witch will be trapped. And Vie can only appear in the ruins, between the bells…'

'How does–'

'Sometimes divides smudge, become indistinct, and dead things lurk and mingle with the living. If the Witch is trapped there, we have an advantage.'

Laela took a deep breath and addressed Lorna. 'We don't know who the Witch has taken over. It could be anyone. It's likely that with all the chaos and fear she's causing, more people could become vulnerable to her as time passes, so we can't assume that anyone that's fine now will stay that way. We need a way to lure them to one spot so that you can cure them.'

'The only thing the Witch wants is you.'

'Can we make it look like I'm somewhere I'm not? Throw her off for long enough for me to get where I need to be?'

Lorna considered this. 'You should be able to leave a trace of your magic where she can sense it. It'd take big magic though, Laela; it'd leave you vulnerable afterwards.'

'Fine, I'll do that. And then while you're curing her victims, I'll get her to follow me.'

Elliott's eyes rounded into saucers of alarm. 'How?'

Laela checked the shadows above and continued in hushed urgency. 'The spores from the possessed villagers will look for a new host once they're released: without one, they'll die. If Lorna saves some after curing the villagers with the draught, we can re-infect Jacob.' She allowed a moment to pass for this to sink in. 'I'll head for the graveyard. By then, as all that's left of the Witch will be contained in Jacob, he'll follow me. But we need to time it so that we arrive just before the bells. When Mum appears, I'll use the potion on Jacob, freeing him and at the same time, Mum's going to let down her protections and allow the Witch to infect her. There's nowhere else for the Witch to go, so even if she does see through our plan, by that point, she'll have no choice. To make sure, I'll cast a containment charm around her.'

The room was silent, taking in the information and its every drop of its madness. From the centre of the floor, Laela looked up with serene eyes and a resolute chin. 'Before the second bells ring, you open the doorway under them. They – she'll fall through into your territory. That should remove any magic taken from my mother or me.'

'It should kill the Witch –'

'And your mother.'

Elliott left the room.

Lorna hesitated, and lowered her voice to a hush. 'You've only done the containment charm in practice, and your doorways are still unreliable...'

'I'll be fine.' Laela was unshakeable. 'We haven't got a choice.'

Lorna looked back at Laela. 'It's a fine plan.' She said slowly. Gravely. 'I'll talk to your dad. You get ready.'

'Lorna…'

The aunt stopped and peered into Laela's face, seeing the flickers of the trembling child underneath.

'I want her to be free.'

Lorna inclined her head and smiled, then walked off to find Elliott.

*　*　*

Few words can help the pain of a heart. Elliott's was heavy with the burden that soon, again, his wife would be gone.
Lorna found him, gazing out at the sea from the lantern room. He stared into the grey distance and its all-consuming depths. Lorna opened the doorway to the lonely field and its ruins, and brushed his shoulder.

'Come and see her.'

'How?'

He looked at her with blank desolation, saw the open doorway, and took her hand. 'Don't you want –'

Lorna shook her head. 'I've said my goodbyes. It should be about time for you to be able to do the same.'

The sound of the bells and their distant chime drifted faintly into the lighthouse. Elliott stepped through. He stared in wonder at his wife.

'I got to meet our daughter, after all.' She smiled.

He studied her face, tried to burn it into his eyes. 'She reminds me of you,' he said.

'Able to keep you in line?'

'Stubborn.' He grinned. He wished he could absorb her into his own skin. 'I love you, Vie,' he managed, but it didn't sound enough.

She stepped forward and threw herself against his body, buried her face in his neck. 'I love you both so much. Tell Laela.' She pulled away and looked into his face, her expression urgent. 'This isn't the end, Elliott. I'm always around. You'll see.'

Elliott wrapped his arms tighter around her, tracing the shape of her shoulder blades with his thumbs. As the final bells rang out, he breathed her in, as though he could keep her scent of jasmine in his lungs forever. And then the press of her weight against him slipped away until he was left holding nothing but his own arms.

Afterwards, Lorna was waiting for him back in the lighthouse.

'Are you ready?'

Elliott nodded and gave a smile. He felt a spark of something rekindled in his eye, and a looseness in his muscles he hadn't enjoyed for a long time.

'Good,' she said. 'We need to prepare.'

Lorna sealed the doorway shut and swept down the stairs as she briefed him. 'Whilst I'm getting everyone out, we need you to go to the Tree. Remember where it is?'

'I do now. Everything's worn off...'

'Good. Destroy it, totally.'

'Chop it down?'

'Blow it up, more like. Remember those 'fireworks' you used to make?' She snorted, 'More like bombs. Arrange a few of those, and that should do the trick. Burn anything that's left. We need every twig in cinders.'

Elliott grinned, 'I'm sure I can manage that. As long as she doesn't come for me.'

'She won't. The draught I gave you not only eradicates the possession, but should also make it harder for her to possess you again. Besides, we're hoping her attention will be on Laela. When you're done, soak the area in this,' she handed him a dilution of the pale concoction. 'That'll ensure her energy can't thrive on the land afterwards. The last thing we need is for her to come back unexpectedly again.'

~ XXIII ~

CHAPTER TWENTY-THREE

*For the earth is filled with violence, and every living thing
has lost its way.*

— Naomi Alderman, The Power

At last, as the summer's evening drew to a close, they were ready. They stood in the sealed chamber of the cavern, now a warren of containment charms and restraining spells. Large pewter jars of the cure waited for their moment on trembling shelves.

Lorna made a doorway. She looked exhausted. Thick swirls of mist obscured the village and streamed in smoky spirals through the gateway. Elliott clambered through first, his pockets and hands and bulging bags laden with the labours of skills honed in his misspent youth. He headed out onto the road behind the woods, now black as the descended night, lit beams of grey occasionally flashing white before him. They watched as his torch went swinging off through the trees and disappeared into the impenetrable clouds.

Lorna checked her pocket watch and handed Laela the draught. 'You've got forty minutes until your mother appears; that gives you a long time to evade Jacob and the Witch. Once you're in the village, make something, anything, to attract her attention and draw her to you. Then cloak yourself and get as far as you can toward the ruins without her suspecting what you're doing. I'll have hopefully gathered the possessed villagers into the cavern and cured them by then. When he catches up with you, make sure you get this in Jacob's face – he has to breathe it in. Good luck.'

Laela hugged her aunt and climbed through to the village. She acted quickly, not knowing how many villagers to expect, or from what direction, and so she summoned fire, cast a containment around it, opened a doorway, everything she could think of to make an energy signal the Witch would pick up on to attract the possessed villagers, and then extinguished, flattened, closed.

She picked the threads loose and wrapped them around herself, creating a cloak, and got herself as far as she could toward the ruins, travelling cautiously to avoid detection, and then in the dim of the treeline, she waited.

* * *

Lorna wove deflection after deflection into the fabric of the cavern. She'd have to time it just right so that each villager was trapped at the same time, or risk rousing the Witch's suspicion.

The walls shuddered as a storm raged above her, and brute waves shook the depths of the rock. Lorna shivered in the half-light and blamed the damp of the air for the chill in her bones.

When they came, she would be glad of the distraction.

* * *

Jacob flinched and pushed himself along the table until he was scrunched against the wall. He eyed Lorna and the vial of the glittering, noxious mist. She'd done her hard part, now it was his turn.

'How will it feel?' he asked. 'Will it be the same as last time?'

He watched her as her lips gathered around a lie, and then the lines on her face softened. 'I don't know, Jacob. I...' He heard her search for a kindness. 'You may not feel anything, or be aware of what's happening; the next time you wake up, it could all be over.'

'Or I could be awake for the whole thing.'

'Yes.' Her eyebrows knitted. 'I'm so sorry; I wish there were another way.'

Jacob set his shoulders back and jutted out his jaw. 'It's fine,' he said. But he licked around his lips, noticing how dry his mouth felt, and how his tongue stuck to the roof of his mouth as he tried to speak. 'Just promise me we'll win.'

Lorna smiled and ploughed through the doubt. 'We'll get it. It'll be thanks to you, and we'll get it.'

Jacob closed his eyes and nodded. He heard the containment close around him and the gentle *pop* as Lorna removed the cork from the lid of the vial. He squeezed his lids shut in case any of his fear came out, took a deep breath and waited.

It trickled in through his nose. He felt its scratch, sharp as before. He opened his eyes and saw Lorna, pale and concerned, and then the world went black.

* * *

Jacob awoke as the mist took hold. It was a violent awakening. Lorna watched from behind the safety of the containment charm as his body trembled and jerked, convulsing as though something was shrugging itself into his shape. She cast the containment charm aside and watched as he tasted the air, searching; hunting.

He found the trace of Laela on the air and pushed his way out into the night, following his prey.

* * *

Laela pushed her back into the rough bark of a tree. Her breath steamed clouds into the night. She checked her watch.
Not long.
Jacob would soon be near.
She looked up to the stars, for comfort, or blessing. The refracted light twinkled back blankly. The world over which they glinted was absorbed in silence, so still, so quiet.
And then the night cracked open.
The explosion broke the air in two, splitting across the woods and fields in deafening fury. Shadows ignited. Light hung in suspended shattered brilliance.

Under the yellowed grey of the fading flare, Jacob's face flickered, ghoulish and terrible.

Laela's stomach pitched as the scream rose. She staunched its ascent, flattened it; turned it into something she could use. She slugged off the threads wrapped about her, left the refuge of the tree and sprang out into the night, away from the noise, away from the doorway and toward the lonely field, in which Death lay waiting.

* * *

The explosion injured Elliott badly.

He'd crouched behind the remnants of a decapitated trunk, well outside the expected blast radius. Perhaps the Witch had known. Perhaps the potion had added an extra potency to Elliott's arsenal. Perhaps the Tree was implementing its death throes. Whatever, it hurt like hell.

Elliott had cringed as his creations had detonated. But he had not considered their quarry, nor the violence of the reaction between them that might ensue – and did. The force penetrated the flimsy protection of the tree trunk. Tinnitus rang. The skin of his right side had peeled back. Charring and bleeding discoloured his face, and his right ear was no more than a shredded stub, thick with blood and hair. Fabric and flesh melded along his arm. He reached to touch it with the fingertips of the other hand, but instead felt the wood of a tree trunk.

Suddenly it wasn't night-time, and he wasn't by the dead tree. He was in the field behind the carnival, and in his hand was a rope.

'Please...' A plea rasped from the ground by his feet. 'Please, I have children, I–'

The rope tightened around her neck. She brought her hands up and tried to find a gap. But there was none. Elliott watched in horror as he looped the coiled end of rope over a branch.

'No!' he was saying, 'No, no, no...' but nevertheless, he continued, feeling the weight of her lighten and wrench at his hands as she kicked and jerked. He pulled her higher. She ceased to beg. Something in him grinned.

It was you.

'No–'

You did this.

He watched her clawing fingers still fighting at the ligature around her neck. She stared down at him, her eyes beginning to bulge as she tore at the skin under the rope.

He wanted to save her.

He fumbled with the rope, trying to ease her down – to fight whatever had control of him. But instead, his arms heaved on the line, drawing her up, up toward the limb of the tree over which the rope had been slung until her feet thrashed metres above the ground, and her tongue protruded from her gaping mouth.

You did this. You're a killer...

And then she was gone. And three different bodies hung from a swing set. His hand toyed with one of the children's shoes as he strolled past.

All of this.

He was on a bridge, standing behind a man...

And then he was back. He was in amongst the aftermath of the explosion, his face burning and his arm throbbing where his jacket had melted into his skin. He retched.

As he wiped the spittle from his mouth, he looked down. He saw his reflection in the stream: no charring, not even a smudge of dirt. And then he noticed his hand wasn't at his mouth anymore. He turned and saw the terrified face of Sam Matthews.

All of this is your doing...

Elliott felt the thing in his head writhe with glee. It had already been decided; it was already done.

The pale boy was crying, 'Please, I'd like to go home.' And Elliott's own voice was choking through tears, begging the thing in his head to stop. But it wouldn't.

He felt his hand propel the boy toward the water, felt it push him down and force his face into the stream. He turned his own head away as the boy's thin arms flailed and scratched at what he could, trying to save himself. It could have been over in moments, but the Witch wrenched Elliott's head back to the boy, and he watched helplessly, as his own arm drew the boy out from the water and allowed him the smallest of breaths before plunging him back into the icy depths.

Watch my game. Watch how the life slips away...

The boy's struggles grew weaker. Elliott felt the warm glow of the boy's life join his own – *her* own – and the thing inside him beamed.

He dropped to the ground. Back in semi-darkness, he painstakingly groped in the last bag for the remaining bottles Lorna had given him. He stumbled to his feet. His left eye scanned the ground for what he needed. With the last of his strength, Elliott scattered the draught over the roots and tatters of tree. There were no impressive flashes or flames, just a quiet, hissing sound, and the work was done. The Tree that had held the Witch its captor for centuries was gone. It lay now in the midst of a crater, greedy flames licking odd bits of branches and debris.

There was nothing left here, not really. Elliott sank down into the steaming mud and allowed his eyes to close. He wondered idly if he'd see home again, then fell into the deepest of sleeps, haunted by the things he'd done, and the things he hadn't.

* * *

The long hand of the church clock raced to meet its shorter counterpart at the zenith. Laela glanced at their progress across the gilded face as she ran, panting, along the graveyard path. Time continued its steady arc. Laela felt the breath of seconds on her neck and the jaws of minutes snapping at her legs as she ran. She thought of her father's face as he changed into something less than nothing, and of the people she had known in the village who were now dead by their own hand – or the Witch's hand – and of her mother; her mother who had died for this and would, *if all went well,* die again. She stumbled. How could this be her hope?

Her legs felt her doubt and slowed. They seemed to lose their coordination and running became a task she needed her mind to process muscle by muscle. *But if not this way, then how?*

She heard a stone skip, flint on tombstone, and threw a glance over her shoulder. Graveyards are silvery places – all grey stone and shadows and shifting phantasms of chrome, and yet the place of the dead seemed to throb with life in contrast to the hollowed puppet of Jacob's body. He was a void in the world, threatening to suck everything around him into that same blank place.

Run, Laela told her legs.

Run.

* * *

Laela was already over the wall at its farthest end when Jacob came stumbling past the spire. He watched her swing her leg over and disappear into the blackness beyond, then followed. Inside, he was screaming.

Part of him shouted for Laela to run, whilst he struggled to prevent his own legs from running after her. But he was caught. The Witch had staggered in his body as the Tree had fallen. He had felt her anger surge into terrible gusts of violence. They had felt, together, every person under her spell as they were cleansed and the particles of her destroyed.

But then he felt every atom as it returned to her and strengthened her. And now he felt how much she wanted to obliterate Laela's bloodline; how that rage and loathing seethed and seared inside and consumed them both.

They were close now.

Laela stood, facing them, defiant and serene on the edge of the rock. The wind blew her hair and scattered her words to the earth. He felt the Witch's heart beat faster in his chest. He ran at Laela, headlong and mad, wanting to stop, but driven by a part of something that wouldn't let him go. The vacant tower's bells rang out their cry and then, suddenly, he wasn't hurtling toward Laela anymore, but away. He stopped. Turned around.

She was standing there, perfect and lunatic and pale under the moon's caress. Her mother stood by her, staring into her face and smiling in blissful peace. In Laela's left hand shone an empty vial. He looked down and saw, as though through the bottom of a glass that he was wet with its contents.

He walked toward her, tried to reach out to her, to say he was sorry, but his hand made contact with an unseen shield. A containment. As he watched, it glimmered under the moon's soft light, and he noticed that within his body, he was alone. He looked at the mother and daughter trapped in the transparent dome. Then the third entity began to emerge.

Laela's mother began to turn. Her face twisted in rigid contortion and her mouth became a grim gape. She lunged forward and dug her nails into Laela's arms. With that sick mouth, she bit at Laela's cheeks and forehead and chin. Blood spurted and trickled and ran, cascading black down Laela's exposed flesh.

Jacob hammered at the protective surface of the bubble, scraping and scratching and begging to be let in. The Witch turned to him and grinned. In her arms, Laela flopped like a rag doll. But when the bells began to chime, panic set in. The Witch could feel her form slipping away. She clawed at the inner sides of the bubble. She mirrored Jacob's terror and desperation. Yet neither gained passage. Both entry and escape were denied.

When midnight's final note reverberated in the night air, all went quiet, and the field was left with a bloodied rock, a mangled girl and a quietly sobbing boy.

~ XXIV ~

CHAPTER TWENTY-FOUR

He turned away, and suddenly she thought about the old children's story, where the stupid girl opens the box that God gave her, and all the evils of the world fly out, except Hope, which stays at the bottom; and she wondered what Hope was doing in there in the first place, in with all the bad things. Then the answer came to her, and she wondered how she could've been so stupid. Hope was in there because it was evil too, probably the worst of them all, so heavy with malice and pain that it couldn't drag itself out of the opened box.

—K.J. Parker, Sharps

The body in the containment twitched, then lay still. Tears rolled down Jacob's cheeks, though he was barely aware of them.

Somewhere amidst the blood and chaos of her face, Laela's lips moved, and fingers jerked, and the barrier which supported Jacob's pounding fists disappeared, tumbling him onto the grass beside Laela.

'Lae?'

A faint and pained sigh rattled from her rib cage.

'Laela? God... I...' he fumbled for words, for something to do. He'd tried so fiercely to be able to get in and hold her, protect her, and now he didn't know what to do.

'Please...' he breathed.

Other voices drifted in.

'Jacob, love. Come on.'

'Mum,' he looked around, bewildered, shocked. 'I... don't know what to do, I...'

'I know, love.' His mother took him gently into her arms and led him away. Lorna began to manoeuvre Laela's body into the open doorway.

The rock and the ruin above were left quietly to their own devices in the dark, silent field.

*　*　*

Piles of flowers, cards, gifts and foodstuffs blocked the door-way. Inside, the kitchen was strewn once again with scraped-clean baking trays and half-eaten dishes. The house suffered in its neglect, but its inhabitants were at no risk of going hungry.

After they had returned to their respective homes, the villagers had whispered and wept and huddled together to offer thanks to the fifteen-year-old girl who lived on the outskirts of the village and had saved their lives - though no one quite knew how, or from what.

When no one answered the cottage door, they left their parcels and gratitude on the step and went back to their jobs and families and televisions and transient desires; they forgot.

* * *

Having done what she could to heal Laela, Lorna had returned to the ruins and stood alone, a silent sentry. For two days, she had monitored the containment charm surrounding the rock and ensured it held, returning every third hour to do her duty.

She took her role as atonement – guarding the Witch and Violet, who were locked in each other and trapped in their half-life – silently. Sometimes, the Witch spoke softly to Lorna and pleaded with her, begged to make a deal, offered Lorna her sister back, alive. But Lorna never wavered – confronted with her greatest desire, she found it had been false, and that what she really wanted was her sister's peace. Then the Witch cursed and stamped and yowled and threatened to break her sister's body into miserable ragged pieces. Lorna bit her lip and felt the pain, and tasted the blood as it spooled in her mouth, but it covered the sting of her sister's limbs dancing in obedience to the Witch.

As soon as Laela was able to walk again, she met her at the rock.

'It's the last night of the new moon. Your mother–'

'I know. It needs to be tonight.'

'You should say goodbye.'

Laela nodded and then said, 'I– I think we need to talk. All of us.'

* * *

The group gathered in the dwindling sunlight in the living room of Laela's cottage. Elliott was propped up on the sofa, a scaffolding of poultices and splints supporting his injuries. They listened to Laela, but what they heard took them far from their instincts.

'Our ancestors couldn't kill the Witch because of the darkness that lay in their own hearts; they harboured and nurtured their own violence and fear, and by doing so, they kept her alive. Don't you see? She thrives on it. She'll never be gone until we've found a better way. We need to deprive her of what she craves, what she survives on. It doesn't always have to be a battle. It doesn't always have to be done with violence.'

The room held silent in front of her. Jacob pushed himself away from where he had been leaning against the fireplace. He opened his mouth to speak, closed it, snorted and walked out of the door to the kitchen. Lorna looked after him, but bit her tongue.

Laela crossed the floor and lowered her weight onto the floor next to her father. 'We can–'

But before anything else could be said, Jacob stormed back into the room.

'My dad is dead. This isn't some fairy tale, where wishing on some magic star is going to help you, Laela. This *thing* isn't going to roll over because you ask it nicely. I *felt* it inside me. I know what she thinks. How she works. We need to kill it. And that takes violence. It just does. Because if we're not brave enough to do that, then how many more people are going to die, huh? You'd be okay with that would you?' His rage came out raw. 'You need to grow up, Laela. This is how the world works, this is–'

Elliott raised his head and spoke, his voice hoarse from his scarred lungs. 'She's right.'

'What? Wait, are you seriously going to listen to this? I've got possessed *twice* because of you. My dad is dead–'

'And so are a lot of people, Jacob. Including Laela's mother.' Elliott's voice was soft, low. 'This needs to end. Destroying her body won't end it. Laela's right – history's proven that. The Witch is in pain. We need to change her, make her something that doesn't feel threatened and isn't a threat. Remember,' he took a juddering breath, 'I've felt her too. I know what it's like.'

'And just how do we do that?'

Laela inhaled and, readied, let her idea slip from her mouth. 'I want to take her to the Ancient Hearth. I want to listen to what she has to say.'

~ XXV ~

CHAPTER TWENTY-FIVE

I awoke one night to find the Sage's son within my bed. I reached for curses but my tongue was bound, his hands so pale in the night, trapping my words. I felt him through every move but could not grasp his hair and wrench it from his head, nor tear the flesh from his pinning-me bones. So, I cast my eyes aside and slipped into a twilight land. That night I broke in two.

— The Tree, the Witch, the Outcast. The Girl.

They gathered at the rock that night. Laela kindled the flames and stepped into the isolation of the space where Violet and the Witch were held. Her mother's wretched face sneered up at her from where she sat.

'What now, child?'

Laela ignored her and spread the charm to encompass the fire. She knelt at its edge and blew softly into its heart, allowing the flames to rise and broaden their grasp.

'We're going to take a journey to the Elder Lands, where we're equal. I want to talk.'

The Witch spat into Laela's face. 'You still don't know who you are, do you?'

Laela tried not to falter. She steadied her hands and grew the flame.

'I won't go back to that place. They exiled me. They left me in the wilds, alone. I shall not return to their lands!' The Witch flew at Laela, using Laela's own mother's arms to lash out at her. But Laela carried on. She drew the fire outward until it filled the dome, consuming the figures within it.

Laela heard her father's shouts, and then fell through the fire into something like sleep.

* * *

The touch of cold woke her in the Elder Lands. The pine forest was dark, lit only by twilight on snow. Footsteps led away from where she lay, toward the darkness of the trees, to a point beyond which Laela could see. There was no light burning where the stone entrance of the roundhouse should be, but Laela thought she could make out its rough silhouette in the dim undertones of night.

Cutting through the scent of wood smoke was the clarity of cold and pine. And something else. It clung to the air as though shredded bits of it hung like drapes from the branches and starlight.

A black void in the sky rushed toward her. Instinct brought her arms up to cover her face, but the expected blow didn't come. The crow landed on the snow beyond Laela's feet but remained silent. Laela knelt and returned the crow's steel gaze. It seemed to survey her, taking time to cock its head and peer at her angles, as though examining her. Satisfied, it flew toward the pines, signalling without sound for Laela to follow. She got to her feet and followed into the dark the fluttering of wings and the hollows in the snow left by the Witch's feet, though she knew nothing of what awaited her there.

As she walked amongst the trees, the darkness grew. It seemed to cloak the forest in thick, black ink and stifle the air into noxious clouds. The mist drew in close around her.

'I could kill you here, little one.' The voice came from every-where at once. 'My power is strong here. I could burn you where you stand.'

'But you won't.'

The silence spread, uneasy.

'I warned you.'

'I want to give you freedom, help you find rest,' Laela said. 'The Elders will help you–'

'The Elders are responsible for the violence spun upon the world. They *did this*. They *made* me. They *must* suffer. I did this for us! You must know who you are!' The words amplified until Laela felt her eardrums would burst. 'It's time for you to remember.'

Laela tried to stopper the sound with her hands clasped over her ears, burying her head into her body, but the roar bled through. The world began to shake. Heavy slides of snow crashed down from trees, and dead boughs creaked and snapped. The earth thundered beneath her, and vast pines toppled and smacked to the ground. Laela screamed into her arms.

Silence's reign returned abruptly.

Then footsteps. The smell of dirt. The sound of breath. Laela looked down at her toes. They were no longer dug into snow but rather, buried into brown earth. She looked up and saw flickerings of posts and thatch and curved walls. This was not the roundhouse; it seemed older, different.

Firelight from the hearth caught the rough shape of a sleeping figure amidst a mass of straw. The footsteps hesitated. A shadow crept in. It stole over to the bed and pressed a hand to the mouth of the sleeper.

Laela watched as the Girl woke and her eyes flashed terrified at the intruder. She appeared younger than Laela, although the man's hand was large and covered such a vast portion of her face that Laela could not make out her features. The fire flickered light onto small shoulders and a slender neck as the shadow gave a low laugh and pressed the Girl back onto the mattress.

'My tribe is grateful for the hospitality your people have shown us. But I might press for one last act of kinship...'

Laela watched as he reached under the blanket that covered the Girl. She shrank back and her hands grasped and scrabbled at his arm. The muscles flexed and twitched under her desperation, but he did not let go. He rumbled that low laugh again and, with his free hand began to uncover himself.

Laela tried to stop him. She tried to scream. But she found that her body had no impact on that world. Her voice made no sound. All she could do was watch.

He did not rush.

The Girl's eyes slid away and into the fire. Laela couldn't watch, but this was what she was there for – to witness. To see the pain that the Witch needed her to know.

Once he'd finished, the man left the hut. The Girl lay quiet as the embers died.

Earth and rafter wheeled, and when Laela could focus again, the Girl stood before the Elders of the clan.

'A great misdeed was done. The man who took so much from you was filled with pain and ruled by fear. That same fear has corrupted you. This clan cannot be home to anything that harbours such pain. For aeons, we have valued peace above all else. You are invited to step out across the plains, that you may shed your fear for the peace of death. Should you refuse, you will be exiled from our lands. We are assured that you will make the right choice.'

The Elder turned away, and the tribe parted, a sea of fabric and colour and home lining the first steps on the path toward the bleakness of the barren tundra.

'Mother?'

The Girl reached out to clasp the cloak of her mother. The woman snatched the fabric away and kept her face absent from view. The Girl wobbled slightly on her feet, and Laela heard her breath catch in her throat.

Laela scanned the faces in the crowd, impassive, stony, and not one was recognisable. Had she been here? Had this been her doing?

The Girl drew herself up to full height and straightened her head. Her feet trod firm along the line of clansmen. Once she had passed their limits the Girl turned, her chin stuck out and proud. Her voice was as hard as her gaze.

'If hurt is what I am, and corrupted is what I am, and pain is what I am, then may it be so! Let me be nothing but the embodiment of these things that have entered and defiled my body. I will seek those corrupted, those hurt and in pain, those embraced by fear, and I will do your bidding. If you say that I shall spread nothing but fear, then so be it. Know: *I am made by your hands.*'

It seemed in that moment as though something separated itself from the Girl. Something small. A spark. No-one else it seemed could see it, but the Girl did. And Laela did.

As Laela tried to make sense of what she was seeing, the Girl plucked the firefly-like light from the air and smothered it in her pocket.

The Girl left the lands of her clan, and Laela followed, half-running to keep up. Ice caught in her lungs and shredded the soles of her feet. She felt herself staggering, although the Girl didn't waver as she walked on through the snow, across the icy tundra, leaving red footprints in an ocean of white.

The world flew away around her. Snow and ice and rock tumbled into forest, and the frozen earth was hard when it stopped her fall. Images drained from one realm into the other, as though reality were broken down into grains of sand then built up again, the picture altered.

It happened faster now, as though the screen of a film were flickering all around her, speeding through the life of the Girl, the Outcast. She could *feel* through the Outcast's senses.

Laela watched.

The Outcast found a new people, with a new tongue. Some took pity on the unkempt girl and bade her come with them into their homes. They gave her food to nourish and a place to rest, and yet a part of her could never rest and was never nourished. And a part of her was separate. A dancing golden spark of light. Waiting to be reborn.

The Outcast began to watch. On the periphery of towns and villages, she slipped into obscurity, cloaking herself with shadows. She spun murmurings of tales that left enquiring townsfolk little reason to remember her. She found it was easy, to move through the world like that. And as a stranger and outcast in violent men's lands, hiding herself in her coat was her freedom – and her safety. She learnt to walk unnoticed, except by those whose souls she saw were harmless. She learnt to judge a man's heart by his hands and the shadows in his eyes, and to tell gluttons from the thieves who needed bread for hungry mouths. And in this way, she could almost live.

Eventually, she found her head rested in one place for more than one moon cycle, for her heart felt settled there, and her bones ached for a place to rest. And so, she stayed. She found work in exchange for food and shelter, and took in the goodness and kindness of her new companions. But in the shadows, the rumours stirred. Travellers told of a young girl banished from her tribe because she had suffered shame. They sneered and laughed as they shared how the Outcast had lost her family and her tribe and her honour and now, alone and on the run, would be seeking a new place to stay and a new life to live, away from her past. *How dare she?*

Women began to spit at the Outcast's clothes as she walked past, suspecting as they did her origin and the disgrace she brought with her. The men leered and suggested they would take their comforts from her as had been taken before.

The townspeople hounded her and ran her out of their precious streets and once more she found the loneliness of the road the safest comfort. She knew the berries and barks and brooks, and the cries of beast and bird. She knew the scents and sounds of hunters and men and which to avoid and how to cover her tracks. And when she came to the next village, she did not give in to the cravings of her stomach and her aching heart, but instead clung to the shadows and veiled herself in the night and the whisperings of passing storms.

It was there she saw the reflections of her own life in a young girl. She watched as a man, drunk-pink and sweating, fumbled around his crotch, eager to make use of finding the girl child alone in a quiet space. The Outcast saw it all so clearly now; how the feebleness and flaws of men would always be excused; that it would always be for the others to bear the anguish of the world's persistent violence... unless revolution came.

The Outcast felt something rock in her belly and twist and burn and then realised that she was not in her own body. She looked down at the young girl – face pressed into the wall by the man's grotesque hand - and she found that she smiled through his teeth. She flexed his fingers, wearing his body like a glove. She released the girl.

The Outcast found the knife at the man's belt and made quick work of ensuring he could never allow his lusts to overpower again. As the girl ran from the alley, the Outcast felt her terror and relief.

The Outcast walked the man's bones, with their bloody mess laid bare, to the town square where bodies pressed and thrummed. She proclaimed with his mouth and in his skin what it was that he had done, and how he had been punished, and how all with evil hearts would be exposed for what they were; their very nature revealed and exhibited, and their weaknesses no longer to be borne by their victims.

The Outcast watched the world of men.

And her power grew.

She stayed in the shadows and cured the world of the weak – the ones to whom vices would crawl and sweet-talk in sunless moments, bidding them to defile and deface and destroy – and she would rid the streets of their filth. And move on to the next town.

Across seas and high mountain passes she journeyed. She settled, and built with her own hands a shack of wood and stone and shadow amongst the wooded fringes of a strange town. The people there knew her for the incantations and curses she sold for bread and grain. They came to her with their violence, which she spun out in swift and supple rays of blood and misfortune. The leaders there, both afraid of and in need of her magic, let her be.

And then she grew so tired.

The Outcast came to rest in familiar arms in a strange place. She was weary, and the palms of her hands and the soles of her feet and the chambers of her heart were stained dark with the deep red of blood. She longed to rest.

'I missed you.'

The woman stroked the Outcast's hair and face and hummed softly as she did so. 'I know you did, sweetheart. And my heart is filled with joy that you are here.'

The Outcast smiled a tired smile to herself, and sank further into the Elder's lap, allowing her warmth and the scent of her hair to soothe and comfort her. By now the spark of life that had separated itself from her was dim, and carried reverently in an amber locket around the Outcast's neck.

'And your mother sent you all this way by yourself, hmm?'

The Outcast tried to smile and hide the sharp pang that stung her when she thought of her mother, so far away in the lands of the tribe.

'She said it was time for me to find my path. I always felt such peace when you used to visit that I thought I would like to come to find you.'

'Mmm.'

The Outcast sat up and looked at the Elder with wide, bright eyes. 'I thought perhaps I could stay with you for a while, learn from you how to use the sacred power and be a travelling healer, like you...'

The woman smiled and gathered the Outcast to her breast and murmured into her hair only practicalities. 'The day is nearly out and night draws in fast here. Would you gather wood for the fire?'

The Outcast nodded and left the hut and entered the dusk that had begun to settle around them. Dull orange glows from far away hearths glimmered through the dense wood of the forest and punctuated the black of the shadows. She turned from the path and picked her careful way through the trees on the other side of the hut.

A sound snapped. Her ears pricked. She held the breath in her lungs the way she had when tracking creatures of forest and mountain as a child.

Nothing.

But the fear stayed with her. She tried to tell herself that she could take on any enemy, that she was the beast with the most vicious teeth and the sharpest of talons and that the forest could hold nothing as powerful as she was.

Yet, the fear remained.

Still, she gathered wood that was damp from the day's rain and asked herself why her friend would ask her to bring in soaked wood for a fire when she knew dried logs lay bundled under the raised floor of the hut. But she was desperate to rest, to trust.

She carried the logs back in her arms and placed them at her friend's feet in the entranceway. She looked up at her friend. 'I love you,' she said.

'I know, darling.' The Elder walked into her hut and left the Outcast facing the forest.

From among the trees stepped members of their tribe. Her mother stood in front of them and called to her. 'My beautiful blood!' She ran forward and fell at the Outcast's feet. 'Forgive me, my daughter. How I have missed you!'

Tears rolled down the Outcast's cheeks, but she stayed silent.

'I tried for months to leave, to come to find you and bring you home, but I would have been shunned, dismissed from the tribe, you must understand. And now, to see you only when the tribe has had to hunt you down, it breaks me inside.' Her mother wept and kissed her feet, begging forgiveness.

The Outcast shook her off. 'And now, you have found me again. Am I now once again a part of the tribe?'

Her mother fell silent.

Another Elder stepped forward from the trees. 'You must pay for your deeds. It is the tribe's duty to answer for the troubles that stem from its source.' As he spoke, more members of the tribe surfaced from the shadows around, all grim-faced with rope and chain and daggers and magic burning in their hands.

The Outcast laughed. It was high and manic.

Her mother pleaded with her. 'I beg you, do not fight them, go willingly. You cannot continue this pain. Let it be ended.' She kissed her daughter's face and walked back to her place in the crowd.

The Outcast allowed the men to bind her with chain, and whilst they busied themselves with their study of knots and fettles, she sought out their weaknesses.

'Daughter of our beloved tribe, you have threatened the peace of our world and the mortal earth. For this, we must carry out our sacred duty and put you to death. Please submit to us your final words.'

The Outcast let the little particles of her magic hunt out those weak places. She allowed her eyes to grow hard and fierce and her voice to sink low into her bound throat so that all around her had to strain their ears to hear her.

She faced her friend, her betrayer. 'This tribe values peace above all else. Above the worth of the individual. Above the needs of the individual. For that, they shall never have peace.' She faced her mother. 'I have fought my way here and saved the lives of many – many women; many children, many who were left to fend for themselves – and they will never suffer what I have suffered. The world has not had to bear their hurt and the sins of men who would have hurt them.' Her mother's eyes shifted down to the dirt.

The Outcast turned once more to the Elders, 'I came here and sought rest: a new future of my own, with this pain behind me, and peace ahead. And I am sorry.' She took a deep breath and wriggled her shoulders against her chains. 'But now, I see I cannot have rest. Elder Law says that I must be punished for the things that I have done, and for the things that have been done to me.'

The men around began to feel an itch in their throats, just enough to scratch, to grate, but nothing more. Some coughed, but the itch remained.

'I have been labelled 'defiled' and been shamed and cast out and hounded and judged and abandoned.'

The itching was painful now, like tiny daggers cutting from their mouths to their lungs.

'I have been labelled 'bad' and now,' she said, raising her chin in triumph. 'Now,' she said through the voices of many and with the mouths of each man about the shadows.

'Now, I *will* be bad.'

Each man's guts burst, shards of bone pierced through their eyes and flesh. The Elder male and her betrayer and her mother screamed, but the Outcast entered them in dust and air and played their bodies like no more than strung-up dolls.

When she was done, the Outcast stood tall in her garment of chains by the hut in the clearing of the woods. Then she shook the metal from her bones like it was drops of rain and painted her face with the blood of the fallen. With the dagger they had meant for her, she sliced the heart from the Elder male's chest. She asked it carefully where she might find the son of the strange clan's leader, the one who had hurt her on the other side of the tundra, on the other side of her life, and she followed its dwindling beats into the forest and across the world toward her vengeance, high on somebody else's life.

* * *

The images blurred.

The Girl turned to Laela in the pine forest of the Elder Lands. Laela looked into the haunted, hunted eyes of the Witch, the Outcast. The Girl.

'Do you take delight in what you see? Is this the past I deserve?'

'No. Nobody deserves this. You should have been cared for.' She felt the hatred slip away. Of course, she killed those who attacked her; in another life, perhaps Laela would have done the same. 'Let me talk to the Elders... They'll realise what they did. They'll listen.'

'They won't.'

'They've changed. Everything's changed. So much has happened in the world since you were... What happened to you was–'

It looked – for a moment – as though the Witch was going to attack. There was a flash of the old viciousness that hummed through her. Laela stood her ground. Then something softened between them, and in that snippet of time, they were just two people looking at each other across the abyss of fear.

'I don't want your pity.'

'And I wouldn't give it.' Laela stepped forward in the snow. 'Give me a chance. Let me try. Please. What's your name?'

The Outcast smiled. It was not unkind. 'Who are you, Laela? Did you figure it out yet?'

'I– I wasn't there... I would recognise myself, wouldn't I? I'm sorry if–' Threads began to weave together in Laela's mind. Her heart plummeted, and she staggered backward on the snow as the shock reeled through her body.

The night sky shed us like glittering teardrops. A portion of us are reborn to protect the world.

She looked at the Witch. 'What happened to that bit of you that broke away? Where'd it go?'

The Witch's eyes stayed fixed on Laela's. 'I protected that part of me as long as I could. It hurt too much to keep it inside. I thought, perhaps, if I made the world safe, that I could return it...' Her gaze shifted to somewhere between past and present, and she worried at her lower lip before returning her eyes to Laela. 'But it always felt like there would be something out there to hurt you. To attack us. And at some point, we just... drifted apart.' The Witch's gaze held Laela's steadily. 'Do you remember, yet?' she whispered.

'No,' Laela said. She'd known, on some level she'd known, but she couldn't accept it. 'No, no,' she said again, hoping that by repeating the word like a mantra, she could push the truth away.

The Witch stepped forward, imploring. 'I did the ugly things I did to protect us. To make a world where you wouldn't have to be scared. Where you wouldn't feel what I felt.'

The Witch edged forwards again, her face scrunched, pleading. Gone was the rage that Laela had seen before. Gone was the menace. Laela could see now that she was just a terrified girl, lashing out in fear. Her goodness and softness and morals had been carved out and boxed away to be protected and kept from harm. And that protected jumble of hope was *who Laela was.*

'After you left me. All I wanted was for you to come back. I didn't know if we could be whole again, but I *need* you. I- I've done all this for you. For us.'

The Witch's face crumpled as she saw Laela's fearful retreat. 'I've had centuries bound within that tree to think about what I've done. I- I've forgotten the other way. I've forgotten how not to kill, and... this is why I *need you.* I need to have that part of me back to heal. I need you back, please!'

The Witch clutched Laela's arm and it all flashed into Laela's mind. She felt everything, remembered everything. It toppled her, took her breath away and she gasped, trying to find her feet and her own body, trying to remember who she was. Who she is?

Laela swallowed. She looked at the Witch. Her monster self. This was the part of her that had split itself off and used itself as a shield when it had felt like there was no other way out. When it had felt like the world was ending. It had protected her and planted her like a seed to be nurtured, even as it had wrought havoc on those she loved most.

'You've endured so much pain,' she whispered.

The Girl sat abruptly in the snow, and her heart cracked open. Tears poured down her face. 'I don't want to be this anymore. I want more. Help me!'

Sobs wracked her body, and Laela felt the urge to reach out and soothe her. But how could she find compassion for the thing that had killed those she loved? Even if it was, somehow, her. She thought again of her mother, Sam, Jacob...

'I'm sorry... I can't–'

The Girl looked up at Laela, disbelief and pain twisting her features. She scrubbed the tears from her face, and it hardened. The Witch let out an agonised shriek, but it was more reminiscent of a child's tantrum than evil. A blizzard leapt up around her, obscuring Laela's vision with a tumultuous wall of impenetrable snow. Then, as suddenly as it had started, the blizzard stopped and Laela was standing alone once more.

There were no footsteps to trace, but a lone wail rang through the pines. The crow returned and harried Laela through the trees. Unthinking, she ran, following its path. When Laela could run no more, it swooped and dropped from the air and scratched at the stone entrance of the roundhouse, but it would not enter. Laela heard the sounds of struggle from within. She hesitated, her breath uncontrolled and desperate, but she knew, deep in her heart, what she had to do.

She stepped into the shadows.

* * *

'How long will it take?'

Elliott was pacing back and forth across the grass in the twilight. The fire still burned and lit the crooks of the rock with ochre. Jacob had curled up next to its shelter and fallen into a sleep punctuated by nightmares, which made him twitch every so often, and in turn, made the others jump.

Lorna walked over to Elliott. 'I don't know. They may be some time. If you want to head back, I'm happy to–'

'No. I'd rather wait. Thanks, Lor. Will Violet come back?'

Lorna eyed Elliott with steady and uncompromising compassion. 'It's hard to say. She might. The Witch won't live in her anymore. But she will be in great pain... All that's happened to her won't be healed. She won't be the same.'

Elliott studied the contours of Lorna's face; saw the shadows nesting there. 'What needs to be done?'

Lorna's speech was slow, kindly. 'We lay her to rest. Bury her in the ocean. With the Witch gone and Laela's magic controlled, there won't be enough energy for her to come back from that. She'll be free.'

Elliott nodded.

'And what about Laela?'

Lorna laid a hand on Elliott's, and they stood staring at one another in the field. Elliott looked away. 'We just have to wait. There's nothing more we can do.'

He thought and spoke as though trying to reach out from a no-man's-land the world never knew existed. 'I saw some things, Lor. At the Tree. Things I'd done. I... I don't know that I can forgive myself.' There was no trace of self-pity in his voice, only steady recognition.

'The deaths in the village...?'

Elliott nodded.

Lorna took a moment before she spoke, 'That wasn't you. All those things you saw – terrible things – you didn't *do* them, Elliott. She might have made you think you did, but it was her. *She* killed them.'

He shook his head. 'I killed someone... lots of people. I killed the woman at the carnival, and I killed Sam, and I would have killed you and Laela and Jacob, too if–'

'You killed Sam?'

They looked around. Jacob was on his feet and staring straight at Elliott.

'Jacob, I–'

'You killed Sam? And I'm out here helping you, why? So, you can kill more of us? I can't believe this.'

Jacob picked up his jacket and began to walk back to the village.

'Jacob! Wait! He didn't know; the Witch had him, he didn't have a choice-'

'Yeah. I know. I've been there too, remember? It doesn't mean I'm going to stick around and play nice.'

'Jacob, wait!'

Jacob's jacket fell to the floor. His hand found a rock, smooth and weighty in his palm. 'I've had enough. I'm going home. Leave me alone.'

'Jacob, I...'

'Don't do that. Don't give excuses. Don't *apologise.*' He took a step forward and raised his arm, rock held high, ready. Then let his arm fall, and the rock dropped from his hand into the dirt. 'I'm going home,' he repeated. 'I can't help how I feel. Just... Leave me alone.'

* * *

The Hearth's fire was left untended. Billows of smoke curled around and obscured the thatch and stone of the ancient round-house. Laela crept in, listening.

At first, the sounds weren't clear: they seemed to come from every direction, whispers of echoes rebounding in the gloom. She pressed her face into the nook of her arm and stepped further into the suffocating clouds. Scuffling sounded from beyond the fire.

Laela summoned to mind all the teachings and charms and incantations her aunt had taught her over the span of summer, but nothing seemed right. Not knowing what else to do, she sealed the roundhouse around them and brought all the courage she had into that place, and with the pads of her fingers followed the curve of the wall around to the source of the disquiet.

Grey shapes danced. Fought. Laela heard the screams of the Witch and the cries from the hearth-tender and rushed forward into the chaos. The hearth-tender had a sputtering ball of lightning in her hands. The Witch, now behind Laela, had conjured flames to her fingertips.

'Move aside, child!'

Rough hands pushed her to the ground, but before she could pull herself up, her ears filled with a sound abysmal and raking, as though a mountain was screaming.

Light filled every crack and shadow, and the hearth fire swelled outward, its blazing flare eradicating all darkness and air within its grasp. At the centre of it stood the Witch, flames crawling up her arms. She was drinking it in, absorbing it into her.

She meant to consume the hearth fire.

'Wait!' Laela cried. She could see the Witch's face now; despite the heat from the fire, tears ran down her cheeks. Torment contorted her features, making her look once more like the monster so many had seen her as before. 'Stop! I'll take you back!'

The hearth-tender's eyes grew wide. 'What are you doing?'

Laela dragged herself to her feet and found the edges of the fabric of the world. She dragged them outward, made a shield, and stepped forward into the inferno.

'I'm ready,' she yelled over the roar.

The Witch, the Girl, the Outcast looked at her with solemn eyes. Her breath was ragged, her face pained and desperate. 'You think I'm a monster!'

'Child,' growled the hearth-tender. 'Our sister tried to destroy us! Destroy humanity! She intended to reduce the Hearth to the coldest ash. Instead, we can use her spirit to rekindle its flames. She will remain there under our care until she finds atonement.' The hearth-tender took a step forward. 'So, move aside or I'll kill you both.'

The hearth-tender's magic broiled and Laela felt the Witch's instinct to retaliate stir.

'No,' she said, and to the hearth-tender, 'She's mine. She is who I am. I take responsibility for her. Leave us alone and I promise, neither one of us will feel the need to defend our-selves.'

Her jaw clenched. She'd never felt more certain of who she was than in that moment.

'I– she will be loved and cared for; tended to. She wanted understanding,' Laela said, her voice hitching. 'She needed love and comfort. Not exile. She shouldn't be kept on the edge of death in perpetual torment because you're afraid of something *you* created.'

With the last of her energy, Laela extended the shield to cover the Witch within its safety, staring at the hearth-tender defiantly. Breath by breath, her doubt diminished.

The hearth-tender paused, and seemed to consider Laela's words. Eventually, she spoke. 'If you are prepared to take this part of you back into yourself and heal it, we shall allow you to do so.' She lowered her hands, the lightning diffusing into the smoky air. Her brow creased and then softened. 'The *wise* Elders of the tribe were once not so wise, and while we cannot take back what we have done, we can and must ensure that no further harm is caused.'

Laela nodded and bit her lip. She tried not to think about what would come next. She turned to the Witch. 'You're right. I did think you were a monster... You did terrible things,' she said. '*We* did terrible things.' Laela stared into her protector's eyes, the hearth fire still raging all around them, the things she'd done – they'd done – already weaving themselves into Laela's memory as having been done by her own hand. The pain of absorbing these memories felt like knives in her chest.

As though she knew, the Witch bent down in the midst of the fire and held out her hand. The torrent of flames quieted. 'I didn't want you to have these in your head,' the Witch said. 'Or any of it. To be a part of any of it. I wanted you to live. Free.'

'I know,' Laela said. The hearth fire now quiet, Laela lowered her shield. She reached out an uncertain hand. 'Thank you for protecting me.'

The Girl shook, her tears flowed freely down her cheeks. 'I lost my way. I've killed so many,' she breathed.

'I know. But you don't need to be that way anymore. We can deal with whatever comes next together.'

'You have to invite me in,' she said, and Laela heard the desperation of her hope.

Laela took the Witch's hands in her own, pulled her toward her, cradled the Girl's head to her chest, and welcomed the Outcast home.

~ XXVI ~

CHAPTER TWENTY-SIX

*We're each of us alone, to be sure. What can you do but hold
your hand out in the dark?*

— Ursula K. Le Guin, The Wind's Twelve Quarters

Laela was weak.

Lorna had healed what she could and the rest, she said, was down to time. No magic could touch her hurt.

Elliott's marred face had pinched and puckered as he'd tried to shed a tear for his daughter, but nothing had come out. His very soul hurt. He'd taken the night watch at her bedside, and now sat on the chair they'd moved into Laela's room. He shifted whenever his legs lost circulation, but upon attempting to stand, found that they were still largely unstable. He pulled himself over to the wood of the windowsill and found it warm as he leant on it, staring out into the morning light.

The normality out there confused him; he had expected that the world would look and behave differently than it had the week before. A slight breeze stirred the branches of the oak tree. *Normal.*

The fragrance of dewy air danced into the room and Elliott stooped to inhale its freshness. When he opened his eyes, a figure stood in the shadows of the treeline at the garden's end. It looked up at him and then began to walk toward the house. It had a face Elliott recognised, although it had looked different when he'd last seen it. He brought himself to the foot of the stairs; she was waiting.

Her pale, grey eyes fixed his; her voice a guttural mesh.

'I've come for Laela.'

Elliott began to protest, wanted to say something about her last visit, about what she'd done, but saw the quiet urgency in the Stranger's face, and gestured for her to follow him up the stairs.

She stood over the bed in which Laela lay unconscious. Elliott saw how fragile his daughter looked, her face a papery white crumple amidst the sheets.

'My little girl...'

'She's gone,' growled the woman.

Elliott sank onto the bed. He stroked his daughter's hair back from her scarred cheek.

'And you must accept it.'

Elliott started, grief-worn and anguished; yet when he faced the Stranger, he was met with a calm that spread through his entire body. He dropped back from the bed. As he watched,

Laela's eyelids fluttered open. Her gaze was unwavering, fixed on the Stranger.

The woman bowed. 'The duty of protecting this land goes to you, Laela. You have healed her well. May you continue to do so until you pass this honour to another.'

Laela pushed herself upright.

'Do you accept?'

Laela's voice came out steady. 'Yes. I accept.'

The Stranger plucked a smudge of ash from her palm and shaded the hoods of Laela's eyes, her mouth and tips of her ears with black. She knelt in front of Laela and bowed her head. When her face turned upwards again, it was shining. 'We'll be sending you a guide. Someone to make sure you're... adjusting.'

'Thank you.'

'This land thanks you for her freedom.'

The Stranger turned and walked away, each footstep shrinking into silence until there was nothing left.

Elliott grasped his daughter's hand in his and they sat in silence. He thought of Vie; of the Witch; and of his daughter's duty, and in a daze, retraced his steps downstairs, mumbling about making tea, leaving Laela alone on the bed in her childhood room.

* * *

Jacob felt the sorrow build. And it wasn't some implanted melancholy, nor did it stem from dark and potent magic. Instead, it came from deep within and felt to him as though a vortex were sucking him into its whirling madness, stomach first.

He heard the clink of bottle on glass echo up the empty stairs, and the scrape of the rounded feet of a kitchen stool as his mum dragged its steady frame under her diminishing weight. He pushed his bedroom door closed until it clicked but left it unlocked; there was no need to prevent anyone from coming in – his mother wouldn't try – and he didn't expect anyone else to come to their house either.

The hatred he'd had for Laela and Elliott had grown until it weighed even his smallest of movements so that he could scarce take a step without his anger threatening to blaze a hole through his chest. But now he felt weak. Exhausted. Tears caught inside but wouldn't flow. It left his grief inescapable. Unremitting.

When the pain got too much, he'd thought again about killing himself, that perhaps it was the only way to stop the hurt, the grief he felt consuming him. He'd snuck downstairs, past the slumped shoulders of his mother, drunk and with her head snoring on the table, and stolen the sharpest knife from the kitchen drawer. And then he'd sat upon his bed and cried, hot splashes of that sorrow finally able to come out and cleanse a little of his pain. And then he'd gone to sleep, and woken up feeling the same, blank hatred and desolation the next day.

Now, he brought himself onto the bed and sat, staring out of the window at the trees as they bowed gently in the breeze. Dusk was coming, and bats had begun to flit around the shadowed treeline of the woods bordering Laela's garden.

A figure stirred in the gloom. Jacob recognised the lithe-limbed frame of Elliott. Only, he didn't look strong anymore.

Where he usually held himself upright and steady, now he walked with a certain moroseness, which collapsed his frame inward toward his chest and hunched his shoulders around his own pain, nursing it, protecting it. Jacob watched as he headed into the treeline and disappeared amongst the shadows that played there.

He turned his back on the window and stared at the knife, still there from the night previous. He picked it up and played with its edges, testing its sharpness, and headed downstairs.

His mum was still in the kitchen, awake this time but gauze-eyed and wet-mouthed. He hid the knife in the fold of his jumper and slipped it back into the drawer without noise.

'And how's my lovely son, huh? Jakey? Aren't you gorgeous? Come here, sweetie, Mummy could use a hug.'

Jacob slid into his mother's embrace and allowed her to squeeze her arms around his ribs. 'I'm going to pop next-door. Check on Laela,' he lied.

His mother's kiss halted on the top of his head, and he wriggled free. Her eyes were mean. 'I don't want you hanging around with that family no more. They've caused enough trouble. You better say your goodbyes then come straight home.' But her eyes had receded even further from their glossy surface, and each word was said with painstaking trouble.

'Sure, Mum.'

He put on his shoes and clicked the latch on the back door before closing it behind him. It took him quick moments to scale the wall and slip down over into Laela's garden, and from there, only a few light footsteps over the grass to find Elliott in the birch grove.

He was sat on a rock, face in hands and fingers pulling at ends of hair when Jacob approached him. He seemed lost in thought and didn't lift his head until Jacob's shadow met his feet, and when he didn't look up, such a display of sadness was on his face that Jacob had to turn away.

'Jacob, I'm so sorry –'

'It's fine. It wasn't your fault. I know you didn't kill my dad. And the rest, it wasn't you, not really.'

There was a pause, strange and seemingly unending until Jacob prised apart the sheltered fear and spoke. 'Do you see them too?'

Elliott nodded. 'Every time I shut my eyes and more.'

'It's like, when I get distracted, or tired, I can see what happened. Like it's a movie playing over the world.'

'And it can be anywhere, anytime, but you're back there, with the smells and the sounds and the look of fear in their eyes as you come toward them... all layered over reality.' Elliott forced his stare to find Jacob's face. 'Like you're back there again.'

Jacob dumbly nodded. 'It wasn't us. I know it wasn't.' He squinted at Elliott. 'When I was chasing Laela, it was as though my legs were taken over by something else, and I couldn't stop them.'

'I know,' Elliott said. But the words were almost empty beside his misery. 'I fought it hard,' he said.

'I know.' Jacob took Elliott's hand and squeezed it. 'But it wasn't something that we could fight. Not that way.'

Elliott squeezed back and a little of the hate he had for himself dissolved. 'Laela doesn't blame you, Jacob. She's grateful you played your part. It was a lot to have asked of you – of anyone – and you did her proud. You did your dad proud, too. You saved all of us.'

'I'm sorry I was so angry. I shouldn't have said those things... I don't *miss* him. But I can't get over the fact he's dead. Even if he was a total arsehole.'

Elliott managed a chuckle. 'I know, Jacob. And a pain like that will never truly disappear. But we're all here for you. In whatever way you need us to be.'

Jacob nodded and looked at the ground. He dug the toe of his trainer into a patch of grass.

'What's going to happen to Laela?'

Elliott gazed up at the old oak, its limbs caught in the afternoon breeze. He sighed. 'I don't know, Jacob. She's bound to undertake her duty. There sending her a guide. But she'll still need a friend–'

'And her father, too.'

Elliott felt something settle in his stomach. He allowed his face to break into an easy smile and he put an arm around Jacob's shoulders.

'Laela's lucky to have a friend like you. You're a wise one, Jacob.'

The pair sat and looked out from the darkness of the grove toward the house and felt their breathing ease, their guilt melt.

'It's worth the sacrifice.'

* * *

Only the white-eyed crow and a warm wind accompanied Laela to the rock on the outskirts of the village. As she had to the severing, she walked, feeling the sun-warmed earth under her feet, the scents of summer in the air offering her comfort. Dusk had already begun to shift the colours of the tall grasses and the hummocks of the field, and it felt as though once shadow struck their forms they'd be forever altered, a fundamental change that, come morning when the sun slid onto their blades and leaves once more, would not be undone.

She hadn't told the others what had happened. They assumed the Witch was dead, and in a way, she was. The Stranger, to Laela's relief, had said nothing. Perhaps she'd tell them one day, but for now, her mother needed her.

She'd rehearsed what she wanted to say, going over it until she was sure she'd found the right words to convey a lifetime of emotion, but as the bells rang, she realised it was her heart that needed to speak, and avidly-planned words would lead only to a performance, and not a conversation. She threw her preparations to the wind and watched for the last time as her mother gained form in front of her.

As she appeared, Violet sank to meet the sunset-steeped grass, too feeble to stand.

'Mum.'

Violet looked up at Laela, proud, exhausted, beaming. 'Tell me what you need to say,' she said. 'I know what's coming.'

Laela's stomach flipped and she could barely meet her mother's eye.

Violet gave a weak laugh. 'In the next pocket between the bells you'll free me, and I thank you for that, and with my last moments I want nothing more than to listen to my daughter.'

Laela knelt on the grass beside her mother, the sounds of the village suddenly rushing into her ears. She tried not to think of the minutes ticking by, the cruelty of time, the inescapability of loss. To steady herself in the moment, she stretched out her hand and grasped her mother's, revelling in its warmth, its comfort.

'My whole life,' her voice shook, but she had to say it; there wouldn't be another time. 'I've wanted to know you. To understand who you were, who I was. Finding out what you did... How you meddled with Dad's mind, changed my entire life, caused all this... I hated you. But,' she hesitated, knowing the selfishness of her desire, and yet was unable to feel differently. 'I wish I didn't have to lose you again.'

Violet gathered Laela to her. 'Oh, Laela. You've done more than any of us could do and forgiven more than most of us could forgive.' She pulled away to stroke a tear from Laela's cheek. 'And it's true, without me, without the Witch, with your magic under control, the land here will rest; there'll be no shadowland between the living and the dead. No ghostly echo of bells,' she laughed. 'But I'm never gone.'

'Mum.' She couldn't have her mother love her and not know who she was. She had to tell her. She knew that if she didn't, she'd regret it. 'I'm the Witch,' she whispered.

Her mother pulled back but Laela held on, and let the words pour out without stopping.

'She was hurt. Long ago, and abandoned by her family, by the Elders, everyone. I was the bit of her that broke off. The bit that she thought was *good* and needed protecting. And then she got lost... So lost.' As she spoke, Laela could feel the hurt that had brewed centuries of vengeance, how each pain and wrong done had fuelled her bloody legacy. But she could also feel the Witch's relief at the long-awaited acceptance. 'I told the others I defeated the Witch, and I did because... I've taken her back. That part of me is back, inside.' She looked up at her mother. 'We can heal now, together.'

She kept her eyes on her mother's face, hoping for acceptance, expecting horror, rejection. But her mother looked at her with sadness in her eyes, and understanding.

'I know,' she said. 'I knew.'

As she held Laela close once more, the scent of jasmine enveloped them. 'A witch is never separate from any aspect of the universe, neither in this world nor the realms beyond.' She fixed Laela with piercing eyes, the only remnant of strength within her. 'You and I will always be together, our magic forever entwined. You have only to reach out to know I'm there. I'm so proud of you,' she murmured. 'It's an honour to call you my daughter.'

As the sun dipped further toward the woods, Laela allowed herself to be held. 'I love you,' she whispered.

'I love you,' said Violet.

And the bells rang.

* * *

Later that evening, Laela knocked on Jacob's door.

'It's time to put her to rest. Would you come?'

Her friend smiled out from under his tousled hair and picked up his coat.

~ XXVII ~

CHAPTER TWENTY-SEVEN

Sister Moon comes but unseen, time dissolving through her eyes,
lonely witness to what has been as the circle road moves on...
— Carolyn Hillyer

The evening colours were blossoming. The sun had sunk into the dent of the horizon and showered its red fire over the water. Above, velvet purple spread into great smears of indigo. The first twinklings of stars could be seen.

They stood upon the crag, holding open-faced wildflowers in the dying light. Laela clasped Jacob's hand in hers, and her father squeezed her shoulder. She felt a tremble in his hand and thought how old he looked, and how much older she felt. The wind whipped her hair around her face and mingled her tears with the ocean's spray. Time flowed over them.

Laela created a doorway above the water. Her hands sketched it with rough and halting strokes. Through it, they could see the violet-shaded evening of the village. It looked like someone had darned the sky: a patchwork dusk.

The first bell tolled.

Effortless with gravity, the body fell through the air.

Laela watched her father's face change as he caught a glimpse of his wife's tattered body – all rags and torn skin – before it plunged through the white foam beneath.

She remembered her mother's body in the moonlight: whole and beautiful and *hers*, and wondered if her father was remembering the same image. The memory faded as the ripples smoothed.

The world was still.

Silently, the flotsam re-covered the broken surface, sheathing the body from the living. They let their offerings flutter down to the resting place, adorning the water with petals and silent tears.

Nothing emerged from the ocean.

Her depths remained full and secret.

~ XXVIII ~

EPILOGUE

I whisper to my past,
do I have another choice

— Tracey Emin

Laela eased her feet into the waters, letting its flood of cold soothe the pain and wash the blood away. She waited. It didn't take long. Beyond her toes, a small whirlpool gathered pace, expanding as it spun faster and faster, until the Guardian of the Truth stood waist-high in the river, their gaze steady, a slight curl upwards on their lips.

'You have returned,' they said, their voice like rough desert wind through pillars of stone.

'I know who I am.'

Laela stood, allowing the Guardian to survey her, and wondered if they could see behind the veil into the other part of her – the part she had pushed away for so long, and now kept secret, terrified she'd lose her friends and family. Terrified of who she was.

'I see it all,' they said gently, taking a step forward. 'Do you understand now why the pages were torn from the book? Why you didn't want yourself to remember? Why you couldn't even trust yourself with the knowledge?'

'I do.' Laela's heart was thumping in her chest. She felt sick. She wanted to cradle the hurt inside of her. Make it so that none of it had happened. But she couldn't go back.

'You cannot undo what you have done,' said the Guardian, their body now close to the bank on which Laela stood. 'Just the same as those from your clan cannot take back their actions.'

They rose above the waters and onto the rock, the river clinging to their skin, then receding as they stood, leaving a cloak of vapours which moved ceaselessly around them. They took Laela's face in their hand, and she was reminded of salted sea spray caught on a gust of wind kissing her face.

'Your heart is in pain,' they said.

Laela nodded, and tears began to fall down her cheeks, melting into the Guardian's fingers.

'Your journey doesn't end but begins here, Laela. This is the start of your healing. Embrace the wholeness of your truth, no matter its darkness. From there, I know, you will do even greater things... And for what is to come, the world will need you – *all* of you.'

A NOTE

This book was made thanks to those who gather to tell stories and share wisdom and remember their connection with the land. It draws a lot on mythology, folklore, and wisdom nurtured and passed down through generations.

Whether around the fire in a Dartmoor roundhouse, nestled under tents scattered across the moors, squatted on a grimy city kerb, perched on shingle a stone's throw from the waves, typed in a well-thumbed yoga philosophy book, or half-yelled down a phone from across the globe, I've encountered many tales from around the world, including an abundance of stories from our own little island, which sadly seem to be sliding from our collective memory.

One of the stories I was introduced to on my journey was Clarissa Pinkola Estes' version of the Inuit tale, *The Skeleton Woman*. I instantly fell in love with it. Here, I've used the bones of that story to explore my understanding of trauma, social constraints surrounding gender and sexuality, and that glorious feeling of rebirth when you're able to live authentically and create freely.

It is the origin story for the Guardian of the Truth.

It is also, in many ways, my origin tale.

THE MAKING OF NA'GATHAMUIR

Ka'ael burrowed their face in their wolfskin, trying to keep the bitter wind and salted spray from their face. Three moons they'd been gone, tracking the sea-demon of which their people spoke. Night gathered as their boat swayed in the relative shelter of the cove. They carefully unwrapped a portion of salted fish, remembering their mother's hawkish eyes as she'd pressed the parcel into their hands, her reedy voice telling Ka'ael that *Ego drives many men to the frost-death of mountains and the dark air-hunger of the ocean's depths.*

Ka'ael had been temped then, to stay in their village. But they longed for their father's pride, for the acceptance of the men of the tribe. To wipe the derision from the faces of boys who thought them weak. And what better way to prove themself than to kill that which had the tribe's fishermen trembling and pale as they recounted tales of its horrors? Stories so potent with terror, they dared not spill their twists and turns unless nestled in the sanctuary of firelight. Their voices quelled when others came too near, lest fear spread from tongue to heart to tribe. But Ka'ael had crouched, predator-still on their haunches outside the folds of tents and the doors of huts and the light of the fires and edge of the circles and listened. Always, listened. And they knew: the men's fearful reverence of this monster would buy Ka'ael a place around those fires.

Now, Ka'ael's teeth ached with cold as they bit into the salted fish. They cleaned each bone to gleaming before throwing them into the moon-silvered waves, hunger woefully unsated. Weeks kneeling in their boat, body braced against wind, hunting shadows beneath the waves, saw fatigue leech at their bones. Every fibre craved nourishment. Rest. Yet Ka'ael could not.

Far beneath the shadow of Ka'ael's boat, in the ink-black depths, shingle glanced off elbow and jaw as the sea-demon's bones rolled with the tide.

Unfolding their legs, Ka'ael eased themself down into the cradle of the hull's curve until they could see nothing but the fathomless night sky. Three lunar cycles they'd been gone. They'd counted out their waning supplies as they'd watched the moon grow from fingernail to fat, fingernail to fat, and back. Now, with a once more near-absent moon and the sea-demon's head not yet claimed, they were low on food, their hope dwindling.

A weary sigh passed their lips as they shifted into a low crouch and threaded the last of the fish onto their hook, fumbling as a sudden gust propelled their boat sideways. The hook slipped, its sharpened edges slicing into their thumb. Instinctively, they sucked at the wound, re-threaded the hook, tried to calm their heartbeat. With a near-silent *splosh*, they cast the line into the waters.

Hungry, Ka'ael waited. Clouds gathered. In their marrow, they felt impending storms, and in the barely-there moonlight, they wondered if the sea-demon could smell their blood.

Starlight followed shadow and bone, chased glinting scales of fish through the water's depths. Down, down, travelled Ka'ael's hook until, by fate or chance, it caught around the rib cage of the sea-demon.

Ka'ael, thinking this was some great fish, tugged their catch upward.

The sea-demon struggled, writhing to disentangle itself from the line which pulled it up, up, toward the surface. The waters roiled; the boat rocked. It was not ready for its carcass to be exposed to even the pale light of stars, for eyes to gaze upon the decayed revulsion of its body, for the sins of its past – which had seen it cast from the cliffs into the ocean – to be laid bare for all to see.

It pulled. *She* pulled. But the sea-demon's muscles, broken down by tide's rough touch, were nothing but memory. She could not prevent herself being drawn from her grave.

Sweat pooled in the small of Ka'ael's back as they hauled on their line. Feeling the mark on the rope indicating their catch would soon break the surface, they twisted around to rummage for their net. For an instant, the scudding clouds cleared, and as Ka'ael turned back to their catch, they let out a cry, for now moonlight shrieked across the shining skull and smoothed sockets of the sea-demon.

Ka'ael stumbled back, the movement jerking the boat off kilter. Waves sloshed over the gunwales, soaking their boots. They wanted to cut the line, to loose the monster back into the depths, to turn and paddle for shore. Instead, their hands clamped the rod in place. Their thighs steadied the swaying boat. They shouldered their fear aside. This was what they'd come for. This was their salvation.

Bit by bit, they drew the sea-demon into their boat. Bit by bit, silvered beams revealed the horror: absent flesh, pitted frame, bones crustacean-encrusted. Coral grew from hollowed eyes and gaping mouth. Ka'ael was afraid.

Nevertheless, they seized the skeletal mass and yanked it forward until they could lash it to the bow, thinking only that this would be a trophy better than any beast their brothers had brought home. As they paddled furiously to the shore, they kept one eye fixed on its hideous form.

The sea-demon could not see who had captured her. She could not move. She could only lay, exposed and vulnerable and afraid on the floor of the boat, imagining eyes roving over her body's secrets. Were her sins manifest in the bones of her hands? Or face? She hoped whatever wrong that resided within her and had inspired her being left to drown beneath the waves was not obvious to whoever beheld her now. The boat rocked slightly as her captor propelled them away from her cove, from where her bones had remained for so long. Where restless nights she'd swum, searching the crags for a way up, for a way back home, finding only dread. The movement rolled her head from grain of wood to night sky. It had been so long since she'd thought to look at the stars.

Ka'ael lugged the boat from the water. As they made camp further up the shore, the sea-demon, still bound on the floor of the boat, spied a fish that was snared in the net with her. At once, hunger overtook her. She seized it, gobbling flesh and skin and insides down until the juice ran from her chin and, with a pang, she remembered real hunger – and how it felt to be alive.

By firelight, Ka'ael oiled their fishing rod. They thought of the proud faces to which they'd return, how they'd never again be left with the women to tend the hearth. How someone might finally see Ka'ael for who they were.

As they worked, carefully smoothing oil into grain, they studied the sea-demon, still lashed to the gunwales. Orange flames glanced off curve and crevice, casting strange impressions across its body, telling stories truer than what Ka'ael's eyes told them, imparting flashes of wild and prophetic dreams which made no sense... until Ka'ael saw the tangled heap of bones was not some monstrous demon, but a woman. Yes, there – a jawbone! Her features, thrown into disarray by tide, were adorned with curious ornaments from that oceanic underworld. In place of fingernails, small sea creatures clung. Instead of hair, glistening seaweed wrapped around her face and throat. Fish-eaten eyes held bright coral in their sockets. Barnacles clung to her skull. All of her had been hollowed out, devoured, repurposed. Contorted with new life.

Ka'ael lay down their rod and took in this new reality. Perhaps the flickering fire tricked their tired eyes, but it seemed to them the ragged figure held reverberations of shame. Imagined or not, Ka'ael would be right to find a semblance of order to this heap of bones, and to lay them to rest in the earth with dignity.

Forgetting the trophy with which they'd hoped to return, Ka'ael began to unpick the jumbled knot of woman. Ankle bone here. Collar bone there. Skull, ribs, fingers, shin... Until before them lay a complete and properly ordered skeleton. She looked cold, Ka'ael thought, and unfastened furs from their pack to wrap around her.

Within the furs, the skeleton woman held perfectly still; she did not want to startle the hunter, to once more have her bones vengefully dashed against the rocks.

After an hour, she watched the fire-lulled hunter drift into the realm of dreaming. Perhaps the truth of the sea-demon filled Ka'ael with sorrow. Perhaps Ka'ael pictured returning to their tribe heavy with the truth – that their monster was but a discarded woman, spirit restless amongst the waves – and that brought them grief. Whatever the cause, a tear fell from Ka'ael's eye. The skeleton woman saw this tear and suddenly felt the thirst of all the years fill her. Inch by inch, she dragged her body across the shingle to where Ka'ael slept. Thirst-crazed, she slurped eagerly from the tear. As she drank, it became a river, flowing from Ka'ael's eye, slaking the skeleton woman's thirst and plumping her spirit like she was a raindrop, fat and heavy. But her form was still so feeble. She needed more.

Laying her bones beside Ka'ael, she plunged her skeleton fist into Ka'ael's chest and withdrew the hunter's heart. With that sacred drum secured between her fingers, she beat the song of her own creation. She drummed herself a tongue with which to sing of strong hands – and sang them into being. She used these fine new hands to beat the drum ever-louder, conjuring atoms from the air. She drummed and hollered and weaved a wadge of flesh to sit atop her bones. She hummed of glossy locks of raven-feather black and eyes of gleaming copper. She thrummed rhythms of the fig-sweet chasm between her legs, crooned of silken thighs, bellowed of dancing feet, roared into life breasts plump with sweet milk. When she was done, she slid from the furs and wrapped her naked body around the hunter's. Then, tenderly, she returned the life-drum to Ka'ael's chest, and together they slept, bodies entwined.

When Ka'ael woke, their limbs were tangled around one another's like the lines of a net. Only, this knot felt unbreakable... eternal. Beyond untangling. Ka'ael saw at that moment a return to their tribe with a beast's head of any size, a monster's cadaver – no matter how ferocious-looking –, would be an artificial victory compared to exploring the beauty of what was right here, pressed against their skin.

The skeleton woman, now so full of life, stirred and tilted her chin to kiss Ka'ael.

Ka'ael shifted under the furs, pulled back. 'Whatever I look like, I am not what my tribe think I am,' they said. 'I am not a woman, I don't think. I am... different.'

The skeleton woman laughed. 'And I am not, as your tribe think, a sea-demon.' She cupped Ka'ael's face in her hand. 'But I think we both see each other for who we are.'

Perhaps the skeleton woman's bright copper eyes ignited something in Ka'ael. Perhaps it was the touch of her skin, or that her hand had been wrapped around Ka'ael's heart only hours ago, but with one breath, Ka'ael shed the expectations of their tribe, abandoned the binding notion of *woman* and the path carved out for them, and for the first time, felt the full joyous splendour of living in their own skin.

They rolled over under their furs and kissed the skeleton woman.

Together, hand in hand, they travelled the world – tundra, forest, desert – nurturing and feasting on each other and all of the world's goodness until eventually, Ka'ael's bones crumbled inside their flesh. The skeleton woman lay Ka'ael down in the shelter of the crags.

Ka'ael thought of the crustaceans that had once decorated the skeleton woman's bones, the remnants of invertebrates discarded and tide-raked on the shore, the stars and their atoms, and the rocks and winds that echoed through them. 'We are part of it all. We are it all,' they murmured.

The skeleton woman lay beside them and wrapped around them both the furs Ka'ael had used to keep her skeleton body warm that first night. She used Ka'ael's fishing hook that had once snared her ribs to sew her flesh to theirs and into the sediments of the earth. She cried tears into rivers, used their conjoined bones for mountains, freed Ka'ael's breath with hers and set it upon mistral winds. When there was little more than the idea of their bodies left, she cocooned them both in the memory of the starlight at which she'd gazed from the cradle of Ka'ael's boat, and sang their bodies' dust into vast constellations – strung out across the cosmos – until all that remained of them was everything ever created.

When the cliffs that once overlooked the skeleton woman's grave had crumbled, and Ka'ael's tribe was no more, the Elders came across the bound-together essence of the skeleton woman and Ka'ael.

Seeing their love and the truth which permeated it, they returned to them an ember of life. They shaped for them a paradise so that, should they ever wish to return to human form, they could tread the moss-banked shores of the rivers of Na'gathamuir. In return, the Elders asked only one thing: that they guard the truths forgotten or left behind by the world, and guide those who seek to retrieve them.

Ka'ael and their love, the skeleton woman, agreed. Often though, even when abiding in Na'gathamuir, the two lovers choose to remain in the form in which they died: as one, knitted together by the skeleton woman with Ka'ael's fishing hook, knowing each other and themselves for exactly who they are.

Flint for skin, supple and black,
Maelstrom eyes, to find the heart of the world,
Hair of smoke and shadow and a winter's haar,
That is what the guardian of truth is made of.
And love.

ACKNOWLEDGEMENTS

People often think trauma comes from the event itself, but in my experience, it's what comes afterward – the reactions of those around us – that dictates how ingrained our trauma response is. I didn't set out to write a gory little fantasy novel about trauma and the bloody business of healing, but I suppose that particular part of my story was near the surface of my creative compost heap when I began digging for inspiration.

Many of us suppress the too-large horrors we encounter in life, but they seem to have a tendency to emerge just when you think things might be ok. They start to lurk in corners, skitter fear around your brain. Stalk you in every shadow. I'm thankful I had the opportunity to stop the mind-bastards by pinning them to the page. Only then could I stare them squarely in the eye and start to unpick the twisted little mechanisms they'd triggered in me. Hopefully this book also serves as a map out of the dark woods for others who may need it.

I'd finished at least one draft of *Twisted Roots* before I'd realised I was creatively processing my trauma. I'd spent years dwelling in shame and anger, and it was only through reading the story of the Witch that I began to love her, and with it, that wonderful instinctive protective part of myself that lashed out when life got uncertain. It was, understandably, trying to protect me. I also realised I'd got to a place where I could reconcile *that* self with the other – the one the monster inside you is seeking to protect. I wouldn't have been able to write this – or, indeed, have reconnected the two selves – if it hadn't been for those around me cultivating a sense of safety.

My thanks then to Phil, for patiently dealing with the sudden deluge of grief and PTSD, and for always holding space for me to be exactly who I am. Mad, disabled, queer, weird, a *creative*... you embrace all of it and never shy away from loving me. I know not everyone is lucky enough to have a Phil, and I won't ever take that privilege for granted. It's thanks to you I've been able to move from surviving to (sorry, it's cheesy) thriving.

Huge thanks also to my sister, Ellen, for reminding me of our connection with the land, and earth magic – it's influenced my creativity massively, and keeps me sane – and to her and my mum for reading and re-reading drafts of this book without complaint. Dad, thanks for showing me where the magic in the world is. You made me believe I could do it.

Thanks also to my poet-sister, Jessy James LaFleur. Your ferocious cheerleading upon my finishing a draft in your cramped kitchen in Berlin contributed to the wonderful tapestry of love and support I've had, without which I might've given up. And to Josie, for also being a moon-gazing hearth witch whose friendship keeps me the right side of feral (just), and made the audiobook a reality. And (almost) lastly to Paul, for being such a brilliant and wonderful friend. Thanks for not taking any shit. I'm truly blessed.

And of course, love and thanks to Reconnecting Rainbows Press. Your work tirelessly platforming queer writers is something the world desperately needs. I'm honoured to add my name to your creative family. Kestral and Ash, you light the way for so many.

OTHER TITLES FROM RECONNECTING RAINBOWS PRESS

Twenty-Eight: Stories from the Section 28 Generation
Edited by Kestral Gaian, 2023

TransVerse, We Won't Be Erased!
Poems and Song Lyrics by Transgender and Non-Binary Writers
Edited by Ash Brockwell, 2019

TransVerse II, No Time For Silence:
Words of Survival, Resilience and Hope
Edited by Ash Brockwell, 2021

The Boy Behind The Wall: Poems of Imprisonment and Freedom
Dalton Harrison, 2022

Counterweights - a poetry collection
Kestral Gaian, 2022

Hidden Lives - a young adult novel
Kestral Gaian, 2022

Emotional Literacy: Collected Poems and Song Lyrics
Ash Brockwell, 2022

Forthcoming:

TransVerse III, Transcendence:
Words of Faith, Love and Authenticity
Edited by Ash Brockwell

TransVerse IV, The Wait Is Killing Us:
Trans and Non-Binary People Demand Healthcare Justice!
Edited by Ash Brockwell

Diana: Her Untold and Untrue Story - a playscript
Linus Karp

Potry: A Collection of Stoned Poems
Jenet La Lecheur

Songs of Remembering - a young adult novel
Ash Brockwell